The Girl Who Couldn't Read

John Harding was born near Ely. He is the author of the bestselling *What We Did On Our Holiday*, *While the Sun Shines*, *One Big Damn Puzzler* and *Florence & Giles*. He lives with his family in London.

www.john-harding.co.uk

Also by John Harding

What We Did on Our Holiday
While the Sun Shines
One Big Damn Puzzler
Florence & Giles

Praise for John Harding:

'A tight gothic thriller . . . unbearably tense' *Financial Times*

'Genuinely exciting and shocking' *Independent*

'*The Girl Who Couldn't Read* will prove to be a delight for anyone with a love of Victorian fiction, the work of Sarah Waters or who takes pleasure in a bloody good story well told. Harding is a master story-teller and has produced another classic' *Me And My Big Mouth*

'Brilliantly creepy' *Daily Mirror*

'Hugely gripping . . . the most perfect ending in fiction, I swear' *Heartsong*

'A tour de force' *Daily Mail*

'Full of disturbing atmosphere, mysterious characters, and a page-turning plot. I flew through it' *A Literary Mind*

'Thoroughly ingenious and captivating . . . a scarily good story' *The Oxford Times*

'Nothing prepares you for the chillingly ruthless finale' *The Times*

'The tension is palpable. Leaves the reader gasping' *We Love This Book*

'A fantastic gothic horror story set in an asylum for women in 1890's New England. It will grab you, excite you and leave you eager for more' *The Moustachioed Reader*

'Harding winds things nice and tight . . . brilliant tension . . . The eeriness pervades like a dank fog' *New Zealand Herald*

The Girl Who Couldn't Read

JOHN HARDING

THE BOROUGH PRESS

The Borough Press
An imprint of HarperCollins*Publishers*
1 London Bridge Street
London SE1 9GF

This paperback edition 2015
1

First published in Great Britain by The Borough Press 2014

A catalogue record for this book is
available from the British Library

ISBN: 978-0-00-732425-5

Set in Minion by Palimpsest Book Production Limited,
Falkirk, Stirlingshire

Printed and bound in Great Britain by
Clays Ltd, St Ives plc

MIX
Paper from
responsible sources
FSC **FSC· C007454**
www.fsc.org

FSC™ is a non-profit international organisation established to promote
the responsible management of the world's forests. Products carrying the
FSC label are independently certified to assure consumers that they come
from forests that are managed to meet the social, economic and
ecological needs of present and future generations,
and other controlled sources.

Find out more about HarperCollins and the environment at
www.harpercollins.co.uk/green

For the booklovers of Brazil

1

'Dr Morgan expects you in his office in ten minutes. I will come and fetch you, sir.'

I thanked her, but she stood in the doorway, holding the door handle, regarding me as though expecting something more.

'Ten minutes, mind, sir. Dr Morgan doesn't like to be kept waiting. He's a real stickler for time.'

'Very well. I'll be ready.'

She gave me a last suspicious look, top to toe, and I could not help wondering what it was she saw. Maybe the suit did not fit me so well as I had thought; I found myself curling my fingers over the cuffs of my jacket sleeves and tugging them down, conscious they might be too short, until I realised she was now staring at this and so I desisted.

'Thank you,' I said, injecting what I hoped was a note of finality into it. I had played the master often enough to know how it goes, but then again I had been a servant more than once too. She turned, but with her nose in the air, and not at all with the humility of a lackey who has been dismissed, and left, closing the door behind her with a peremptory click.

I gave the room a cursory glance. A bed, with a nightstand, a closet in which to hang clothes, a battered armchair that looked as if it had been in one fight too many, a well-worn writing desk and chair, and a chest of drawers on which stood a water jug and bowl, with a mirror hanging on the wall above it. All had seen better days. Still, it was luxury compared with what I had been used to lately. I went over to the single window, raised the blind fully and looked out. Pleasant lawned grounds beneath and a distant view of the river. I looked straight down. Two floors up and a sheer drop. No way out there, should a person need to leave in a hurry.

I shook off my jacket, glad to be relieved of it for a while, realising now I was free of it that it was a tad too tight and pulled under the arms, where my shirt was soaked with sweat. I sniffed and decided I really should change it before meeting Morgan. I took out and read again the letter with his offer of employment. Then I lifted the valise from the floor, where the maid had left it, onto the bed and tried the locks again, but they would not budge. I looked around for some implement, a pair of scissors or a penknife perhaps, although why I should expect to find either in a bedroom I couldn't have said, especially not here of all places, where it would surely be policy not to leave such things lying about. Finding nothing, I decided it was no use; my shirt would have to do.

I went over to the chest of drawers, poured some water into the bowl and splashed it over my face. It was icy cold and I held my wrists in it to cool my blood. I looked at myself in the mirror and at once easily understood the serving woman's attitude toward me. The man staring back at me had a wild, haunted expression, a certain air of desperation. I tried to arrange my hair over my forehead with my fingers and wished it were longer, for it didn't answer to purpose.

2

There was a rapping on the door. 'One moment,' I called out. I looked at myself again, shook my head at the hopelessness of it all and heartily wished I had never come here. Of course I could always bolt, but even that would not be straightforward. An island, for Christ's sake, what had I been thinking of? Sanctuary, I suppose, somewhere out of the way and safe, but also – I saw now – somewhere from which it would be difficult to make a quick exit.

More rapping at the door, fast and impatient this time. 'Coming!' I shouted, in what I hoped was a light-hearted tone. I opened the door and found the same woman as before. She stared at me with a look that suggested surprise that I had spent so long to accomplish so little.

I found Morgan in his office, seated at his desk, which faced a large window giving onto the spacious front lawns of the hospital. I could well understand how someone might like to look up from his work at such a capital view, but it struck me as odd that a man who must have many visitors should choose to have his back to them when they entered.

I stood just inside the door, looking at that back, ill at ease. He had heard the maid introduce me; he knew I was there. It occurred to me that this might be the purpose of the desk's position, to establish some feeling of superiority over any new arrival; the man was a psychiatrist, after all.

A good minute elapsed and I thought of clearing my throat to remind him of my presence, although I know a dramatic pause when I come across one, and to wait for my cue before speaking out of turn, so I held my position, all the while conscious of the sweat leaking from my armpits and worrying that it must eventually penetrate my jacket. I did not know if I had another. There was complete silence except for the occasional echo of a distant door banging its

3

neglect and the leisurely scratch of the doctor's pen as he carried on writing. I decided I would count to a hundred and then, if he still hadn't spoken, break the silence myself.

I had reached eighty-four when he threw the pen aside, twirled around in his swivel chair and propelled himself from it in almost the same movement. 'Ah, Dr Shepherd, I presume!' He strode over to me, grabbed my right hand and shook it with surprising vigour for a man who I saw now was dapper, by which I mean both short in stature and fussily turned out; he had a thin, ornamental little moustache, like a dandified Frenchman, and every hair on his salt-and-pepper head seemed to have been arranged individually with great care. He had spent a good deal more time on his toilette than I had had means or opportunity to do on mine and I felt embarrassed at the contrast.

'Yes, sir.'

I found myself smiling in spite of my trepidation at the coming audition, my sodden armpits and the state of my face. It was impossible not to, since he was grinning broadly. His cheerful demeanour lifted my spirits a little; it was so greatly at odds with the gloominess of the building.

Finally releasing my hand, which I was glad of, as his firm grip had made me realise it must have been badly bruised in the accident, he stretched out his arms in an expansive gesture. 'Well, what do you think, eh?'

I assumed he was referring to the vista outside, so, casting an appraising eye out the window, said, 'It's certainly a most pleasant view, sir.'

'View?' He dropped his arms and the way they hung limp at his sides seemed to express disappointment. He followed my gaze as if he had only just realised the window was there and then turned back to me. 'View? Why, it's nothing to the

4

views we had back in Connecticut, and we never even looked at them.'

I did not know what to make of this except that I had come to a madhouse and that if the inmates should prove insane in any degree relative to the doctors, or at least the head doctor, then they would be lunatics indeed.

'Wasn't talking about the view, man,' he went on. 'You're not here to look at views. I mean the whole place. Is it not magnificent?'

I winced at my own stupidity and found myself mumbling in a way that served only to confirm this lack of intelligence. 'Well, to be honest, sir, I'm but newly arrived and haven't had an opportunity to look about the place yet.'

He wasn't listening but instead had extracted a watch from his vest pocket and was staring at it, shaking his head and tutting impatiently. He replaced the watch and looked up at me. 'What's that? Not looked round? Let me tell you you'll find it first class when you do. Adapted to purpose, sir, every modern facility for treating the mentally ill a doctor could wish for. Couldn't ask for a better place for your practical training, sir. Medical school is all very well but it's in the field you learn your trade. And believe me, it's a good trade for a young man to be starting out in. Psychiatry is the coming thing, it is the way—' He stopped abruptly and stared at me. 'Good God, man, what on earth has happened to your head?'

I reached a hand up to my temple, my natural inclination being to cover it. I had my story ready. I have always found that the extraordinary lie is the one that is most likely to be believed. 'It was an accident in the city on my way here, sir. I had an unfortunate encounter with a cabriolet.'

He continued to stare at the bump and I could not help arranging my hair in an attempt to conceal it. Sensing my embarrassment, he dropped his eyes. 'Well, lucky to get away with just a mild contusion, if you ask me. Might have fractured your cranium.' He chuckled. 'Let's hope it hasn't damaged your brain. Enough damaged brains around here already.'

He walked back to his desk and picked up a piece of paper. 'Anyway, looking at your application, I see you have an exceptional degree from the medical school in Columbus. And this is just the place to pick up the clinical experience to go with it. Hmm . . .' He looked up from the paper and stared at me quizzically. 'Twenty-five years old, I see. Would have thought you were much older.'

I felt a sudden panic. Why had I not thought about my age? What a stupid thing to overlook! But at least twenty-five was within the realms of possibility. What if it had been forty-five? Or sixty-five? I would have been finished before I started. I improvised a thin chuckle of my own. It's a useful skill being able to laugh on demand even when up against it.

'Ha, well, my mother used to say I was born looking like an old man, and I guess I've never had the knack of appearing young. My late father was the same way. Everyone always took him for ten years older than he was.'

He raised an eyebrow and peered again at the paper he was holding. 'I see too you have some –ah – interesting views on the treatment of mental illness.' He looked up and stared expectantly at me, a provocative hint of a smile on his lips.

I felt the blood rush to my cheeks. The bruise on my forehead began to throb and I imagined it looking horribly livid, like a piece of raw meat. I began to mumble but the words died on my lips. Fool! Why had I not anticipated some sort of cross-examination?

'Well?'

I pulled myself upright and puffed out my chest. 'I'm glad you find them so, sir,' I replied.

'I was being ironic. I didn't intend it as a compliment, man!' He tossed the paper onto the desk. 'But it doesn't signify a thing. Forgive me saying so, but your ideas are very out of date. We'll soon knock them out of you. We do things the modern way here, the scientific way.'

'I assure you I'm ready to learn,' I replied and we stood regarding each other a moment, and then, as though suddenly remembering something, he pulled out the watch again.

'My goodness, is that the time? Come, man, we can't stand around here gassing all day like a pair of old women; we're wanted in the treatment area.'

At which he strode past me, opened the door and was through it before I realised what was happening. He moved fast for a small man, bowling along the long corridor like a little terrier in pursuit of a rat.

'Well, come along, man, get a move on!' he flung over his shoulder. 'No time to waste!'

I trotted along after him, finding it difficult to keep up without breaking into a run. 'May I ask where we're going, sir?'

He stopped and turned. 'Didn't I tell you? No? Hydro-therapy, man, hydrotherapy!'

The word meant nothing to me. All I could think of was hydrophobia, no doubt making an association between the two words because of the place we were in. I followed him through a veritable maze of corridors and passageways, all of them dark and depressing, the walls painted a dull reddish brown, the colour of blood when it has dried on your clothes, and down a flight of stairs that meant we were below ground level, then along a dimly lit passage that finally ended at a metal door upon which he rapped sharply, his fingers ringing against the steel.

'O'Reilly!' he yelled. 'Come along, open up, we don't have all day.'

As we stood waiting, I was caught sharp by a low moaning sound, like some animal in pain perhaps. It seemed to come from a very long way off.

There was the rasp of a bolt being drawn and we stepped into an immense whiteness that quite dazzled me after the dimness outside. I blinked and saw we were in a huge bathroom. The walls were all white tiles, from which the light from lamps on the walls was reflected and multiplied in strength. Along one wall were a dozen bathtubs, in a row, like beds in a dormitory. A woman in a striped uniform, obviously an attendant, who had opened the door for us and stood holding it, now closed and locked it behind us, using a key on a chain attached to her belt. I realised the moaning noise I had heard was coming from the far end of the room, where two more female attendants, similarly attired to the first, stood over the figure of a woman sitting huddled on the floor between them.

Dr Morgan walked briskly over to the wall at the opposite end of the room, where there was a row of hooks. He removed his jacket and hung it up. 'Well, come on, man. Take your jacket off,' he snapped. 'You don't want to get it soaked, do you?'

I thought instantly that the armpits were already drenched, but there was nothing for it but to remove it. Luckily Morgan didn't look at me, although as he turned toward the three figures at the far end of the room, he sniffed the air and

8

pulled a face. I felt my own redden with shame, until I saw he wasn't even looking at me and probably assumed the stench originated from something in the room.

Rolling up his sleeves, he strode over to the two attendants and their charge, his small feet clicking on the tiled floor. I followed him. The attendants were struggling to make the woman stand up, each tugging at one of her arms. At first I could not see the sitter's face. Her chin was on her chest and her long dirty blonde hair had tumbled forward, shrouding her features completely.

'Come on, come on!' chided Morgan. 'D'you think I have all day for this? This is Dr Shepherd, my new assistant. He's here for a demonstration of the hydrotherapy. Get her up now and let's get started.'

The sound of his voice seemed to have some magical effect upon the crouching creature, who stopped resisting the attendants and allowed herself to be pulled to her feet. She threw back her head, tossing her hair from her face. I saw she was middle-aged, her face well marked from an encounter with the smallpox at some stage of her life. She was a big woman, large boned, and towered over Morgan. Her cheeks were sunken and her eye sockets dark hollow sepulchres. She looked down at Morgan for a moment or so with a suggestion of fear in her expression, but perhaps respect too, and then lifted her eyes to me. It made me uncomfortable, this uninhibited regard. It was not like the look of a human being, but rather some creature, some trapped wild animal. It had in it defiance and the threat of violence and somehow at the same time something that tore at my heart, an appeal for help or mercy perhaps. I well knew what it meant to need both and be denied.

I stared back at her a long moment. I was all atremble

and in the end I could not hold her gaze. As I looked away she spoke. 'You do not appear much of a doctor to me. I shall get no help from you.' And then, so suddenly she took them by surprise, she wrenched herself free from her keepers and hurled herself at me, her nails reaching for my face. It was fortunate for my already battered looks that O'Reilly, the woman who had let us in and had now come to help us, reacted quickly. Her hands whipped out and grabbed both the woman's wrists at once in a tight grip. There was a brief struggle but then the other attendants joined in and the patient – for such this wretched being obviously was – was soon under control again. At which point she began once more to wail, making the pitiful sound I'd heard from outside, twisting her body this way and that, tugging her arms, trying to free herself but to no avail, for the two junior attendants who had her each by an arm were themselves well built and evidently strong. Having failed to free herself, the woman began to kick out at them, at which they moved apart, stretching her arms out, one either side of her, so that she was in a crucifixion pose.

'Stop that now, missy,' said O'Reilly. Her voice was as cold as the tiles, and it was obvious this flame-haired woman was as hard as nails; the words were spat out in an Irish accent harsh enough to break glass. 'Stop it or you'll find yourself getting another slap for your trouble.'

Morgan frowned, then looked at me and raised an eyebrow, a semaphore that I immediately read as meaning that it wasn't easy to get staff for such employment and that you had to make the best of what was available. He glared at the attendant. 'None of that, please, O'Reilly. She's under restraint; no need to threaten the poor soul.' He turned to me again.

'Firmness but not cruelty, that's the motto here.' Then he told the attendants, 'Get her in the bath.'

I expected the woman to object to this, but at the mention of the word 'bath' her struggling ceased and she allowed herself to be guided over to the nearest one. 'Raise your arms,' said O'Reilly, and the woman meekly obeyed. The other women lifted the hem of her dress, a coarse white calico thing, the pattern so faded from frequent washing that it was almost invisible, rolled it upwards and pulled it over her head and arms, with O'Reilly cooing, 'There's a good girl now,' as if she were talking to a newly broken-in horse or a dog she was trying to coax back into its kennel. The woman was left shivering in a thin, knee-length chemise, for the room was not warm, as I could tell from the dank feel of my damp shirt against my back.

O'Reilly put a hand on the woman's arm, guided her over to the bath and ordered her to get in. The woman looked quizzically at Morgan, who smiled benignly and nodded, and she turned back to the bath, even allowing a certain eagerness into her expression.

'She is looking forward to a bath,' Morgan whispered to me out of the corner of his mouth. 'She hasn't been here long. She's never had the treatment before and doesn't have any inkling of what's coming.'

I saw that the bath was full of water. The woman lifted a leg over the edge and put her foot into it and instantly let out a gasp and tried to pull it out again, but the attendants immediately seized hold of her and pushed together so that the woman's foot plunged to the bottom of the bath, where-upon she slipped and as she struggled to regain her balance the attendants lifted the rest of her and thrust her in, virtually face down, with an almighty splash that sent water shooting into the air, with more than a little of it raining down on Morgan and me. The woman's screams ricocheted off the tiles from wall to wall around the room.

Morgan turned to me with a grin and a lift of the eyebrows, by which I understood him to mean that now I saw the necessity of removing my jacket.

The woman in the bath twisted around to get onto her back and lifted her head spluttering from the water. She tried to get up, but O'Reilly had a hand on her chest holding her down.

'Get the cover!' she said to the other women.

They reached under the bath and pulled out a rolled-up length of canvas. The patient tried to scream again but it came out as a wounded-animal whimper that pierced both my ears and my heart.

'Let me up, for the love of God,' she begged. 'The water is freezing. I cannot take a bath in this!'

O'Reilly grabbed the woman's wrist with her free hand and placed it in a leather strap fixed to the side of the bath. One of the other women let go the canvas and repeated the operation on the other side, so that the woman was now firmly held in a sitting position. Then the attendant returned to the canvas, taking one side of it while her colleague took the other. I saw it had a number of holes ringed with brass along each edge. The woman stopped her screaming and watched wild-eyed as the attendants stretched it over the top of the bath, beginning at the end where her feet were, putting the rings over a series of hooks which I now saw were fixed along the bath under the outside rim. The woman was fighting frantically, trying to get up, but of course she couldn't because of the wrist restraints, and when this proved to no avail she began thrashing about with her legs, which were

12

under the canvas and merely kicked uselessly against it. O'Reilly stood back now, arms folded, on her face the grim satisfied smile of the practised sadist. In a matter of half a minute the canvas was secured snugly over the top of the bath, the edges so tight it would have been impossible for the woman to get a hand through even if they had not been shackled. At the very top end there was a little half circle cut into the canvas and from this the patient's head protruded, but the opening was so tight she could not pull her head back down into the water and drown herself.

While this was happening the noise in the room was hellish, the woman's screams and curses alternating with bouts of calm, when she sobbed and pleaded first with O'Reilly, then the other women and finally with Morgan. 'Please, doctor, let me out, I beg you. Let me out and I promise I will be a good girl.'

This all came out staccato, for her teeth were chattering, leaving me in no doubt that the water was indeed as freezing as she claimed. When these appeals fell upon deaf ears, she began screaming again and pushing her knees vainly against the canvas, which was so tightly secured it moved scarcely at all.

One of the women went to a cupboard, took out a towel and gave it to Morgan. He dried his face and hands and tossed the towel to me and I did the same. Then he shrugged. 'We may as well go now, nothing more to be done here.'

He strolled over to where our jackets hung, and began putting his on and I followed suit. I must have looked puzzled and he said something that I could not catch because of the screams of the woman echoing around the room. He rolled his eyes and motioned toward the door. O'Reilly strode over to it and unlocked and opened it and we passed through.

The door clanged shut behind us with a finality that made me shiver and I thanked my lucky star that I was not on the wrong side of it, or one like it. The cries of the woman were instantly muffled and Morgan said, 'She will soon quiet down. The water is icy cold and rapidly calms the hot blood that causes these outbursts.'

'She seemed calm enough before she was put into the bath,' I said, forgetting myself and then realising I had perhaps sounded a note of protest.

He began walking swiftly, so that again I had trouble keeping up. 'Momentarily, yes, but she has been given to fits of violence, such as you witnessed a little of, ever since she arrived here a week ago. The hydrotherapy has a wonderfully quiescent effect. Another three hours in there and –'

'*Three hours!*'

I could not help myself. It was unthinkable to me that you could put someone in freezing cold water in the fall and leave them like that for three hours.

He stopped and looked at me, taken aback by my tone. Before I had time to think about it, I raised my hand to cover the bruise and was suddenly conscious of how I must appear to him, with my too-small jacket and my bashed-about face.

'I know it may seem harsh to the untrained spectator,' he said, 'but believe me it works ninety-nine per cent of the time. She'll be as meek as a newborn lamb after this, I assure you. And I'd go so far as to wager that after another three or four such treatments there will be no more violent fits. We will have her under control.'

'You mean she will be cured?'

He pursed his lips and moved his head from side to side, weighing up his reply. 'Well, not exactly. Not as you probably mean.' He began walking again, but this time slowly, as though the need to choose his words carefully forced him to slacken his pace. 'We must be sure of our terms here, Shepherd. Now, she will not be cured in the sense that she can be released and live a normal and productive life. Immersing her in cold water will not repair a damaged brain. So from that point of view, no, not cured. But think of what madness involves. Who is most inconvenienced by mental affliction?'

'Why, the sufferer, of course.'

'Not so, or rather not necessarily so. Often the patient is in a world of her own, living a fantasy existence, in a complete fog, and does not even know where she is or that the mental confusion she feels is not the normal state of all mankind. No, in many – I would even go so far as to say most – cases, it is the people around her who endure far more hardship. The family whose life is disrupted. The children who are forced to put up with bouts of abuse and violence. The poor husband whose wife tries to hurt him or turns the home into a place of fear. The parents who are too old to restrain a daughter undergoing a violent episode. And, not least, us, the doctors and attendants whose duty it is to care for these unfortunate beings. So not a cure for the patient, but one for everyone else, whose lives are made better because the illness is being managed.'

We continued walking in silence for a minute or so.

'So the patient can never resume her place in society, then?' I asked at last.

'I would not say never, no. After a period of restraint, of being shown again and again that making a nuisance or herself will gain her nothing, a patient will often become subdued. It is the same process as training an animal. The

15

fear of more treatment leads to compliance. In the best cases it becomes the normal habit. Oh, I know some may not like to admit it, but it's a tried and tested regimen. It worked for King George III of England, you know. He went mad, but after a course of such treatment the merest hint of restraint would cool his intemperance and he was able to take up the reins of government again for another twenty years.'

2

After our visit to the hydrotherapy room, Morgan took me on a brief tour of the institution. We began on the second floor, where the dormitories were arranged along a long corridor that must have run a good deal of the length of the building. Most of the women slept in large rooms accommodating twenty or so beds, although some were in smaller rooms, and a few were in isolation.

'It may be that they are violent or that there is something about them, some habit or tic that is a nuisance to others that makes them a victim of violence, or simply that they continually make a racket and keep everyone else awake,' Morgan explained. 'We try to keep things as peaceful as possible.'

Each sleeping area had a room nearby where two attendants alternately slept and kept watch. 'Is this to prevent the patients escaping?' I asked.

'Escaping? Escaping?' He looked askance at me. 'Good God, man, they cannot escape, because in order to do so they would first have to be prisoners. They are not; they are *patients*. They do not escape; they abscond. Or would do if we were to let them. Anyway, the sleeping quarters are locked at night so they cannot wander.'

I surveyed the length of the corridor and the many doors. 'What about the risk of fire? Surely if one broke out, there would not be time to unlock all these doors?'

He sighed. 'You may well be right. I have my doubts about some of the women we are forced to employ and fear that in such a case they would think only of saving themselves rather than chance their own lives getting the patients out.'

'I've seen a system where the doors in a corridor are linked and locked by a device at the end of the row that secures or releases them all at once.'

He stopped and stared at me. 'I know of only one institution that has such a system. Sing Sing prison. How came you to see it?'

I could only hope he didn't notice my momentary hesitation before replying. 'I didn't mean I'd actually seen it, sir. I meant that I had seen there is such a system. I think I read about it in the *Clarion* or some other newspaper.'

He resumed walking. 'I'm sure we cannot afford such luxuries. The state will fund these things for lawbreakers, but not, alas, for lunatics.'

I could not help clenching my fists at the idea that prevention from being burned to death in a locked room should be considered a luxury, but said nothing. I was not here, after all, to take up the cause of the lunatics.

On the ground floor we visited a long bleak room with bare wooden benches around the walls, bolted to them, all occupied by inmates, and in the centre a table covered by a shining white cloth, around which sat half a dozen attendants. The entire room was as spotless as the tablecloth and I thought what a good job the attendants must do to keep it so clean. I would later mock my own stupidity for this assumption. At either end of the table were two potbelly stoves, whose heat I could only feel from a few feet away when we approached them, but even if my own experience hadn't told me they were inadequate to the task of heating such a large room, I would have known because the women on the benches were shivering and hugging themselves for warmth. The backs of the benches were perfectly straight and you could tell they were uncomfortable from the way the inmates were forced to sit upright upon them, the seats being so narrow the sitter would simply slide off if she slouched. Each bench looked as if it would accommodate five people, which I could tell from the fact that every one had six women sitting on it and looked unpleasantly crowded. These inmates were all clad in the same coarse, drab calico garment I had seen on the woman in the hydrotherapy room. On one side of the room were three barred windows set at more than five feet from the ground, so that even standing, let alone sitting, it was impossible for any but an exceptionally tall woman to see out of them.

When I mentioned this to Morgan, thinking, but not saying, that it was a poor piece of design, he said, 'That's the idea. We do not want them looking out – it would be a distraction.'

I had to bite my tongue not to ask distraction from what, since the women had absolutely nothing to occupy them. There was no sound from any of them and they all seemed subdued, staring blankly into space, or down at the floor or even sitting with their eyes closed and possibly dozing, until they became aware of us, whereupon I sensed a ripple of excitement pass around the room.

A woman stood up and approached Morgan. She stretched out a hand and tugged his sleeve. 'Doctor, doctor, have you come to sign my release?' she said. She was old, perhaps sixty or so, with a bent back and a brown wizened walnut of a face.

Carefully, he lifted her hand from his arm as if it had been some delicate inanimate object and let it drop gently by her side. 'Not today, Sarah, not today,' he told her. 'Now be a good girl and sit down, for you know we have to see you can behave properly before there can be any talk of release.'

I was impressed he knew her by name – he'd told me there were some four hundred patients in the hospital – which made him smile. 'She's been here thirty years, since long before my time. She asks me the same thing on every occasion she sets eyes on me; she does not realise she will never go home.'

While this had been going on, other patients had taken their lead from Sarah and risen from their seats and a great hubbub of chatter had sprung up. In response to this disturbance the attendants rose from the table and busied themselves taking hold of those who were walking about and leading them back to the benches and where necessary pushing them down onto them. 'Now behave!' I heard one attendant snap at a young woman. 'Or you'll be for it later.' Instantly the woman turned pale and meekly went back to her place.

Eventually all the patients were seated again and after a few more stern words from the attendants, the chatter died down and silence reigned once more. Some still looked at us, with what seemed like great interest, but most resumed their earlier pose, and simply sat and stared empty-eyed straight ahead, not even making eye contact with the women sitting opposite them on the other side of the room.

'What are they doing here?' I whispered to Morgan.

'Doing? Doing? Why, man, you see for yourself, they are

not doing anything. This is the day room, where they spend much of the day. They will sit like this until it is time for their evening meal.'

'When do they have that?'

'At six o'clock.'

It was presently only four o'clock. I could not help thinking that if I were made to sit in total silence with nothing at all to occupy me, even if I were not off my head to begin with, I soon would be.

Morgan looked at me angrily, and I wondered for a moment whether I'd actually spoken my thoughts aloud, but being sure I hadn't, I saw I had irritated him by the tone of my questions. He took my queries as criticism of the regime, which, I began to see, they were, since I was so appalled by what I was seeing that I could not prevent a certain disbelief creeping into my tone.

'It is, as I said,' he paused to let go a sigh of exasperation, 'a question of management. If they were all doing something, they would be more difficult to manage. Any activity would have to involve something to do it with. If you allowed them books, for example, some of them would damage the books, or they would throw them at the attendants, or use them as weapons against their neighbours. And even if they simply read them it would not be good, for it would give them ideas. They have too many ideas already. It would be the same with sewing or knitting. Can you imagine the possible consequences of handing them needles? So removing potentially dangerous objects and maintaining an air of calm is essential for control. But also it is therapeutic. They acquire through practice the ability to sit and do nothing. It teaches them to be calm. If they can do this, then both their lives and ours are made easier.'

After this he took me outside via a rear entrance to show me the grounds. There were extensive lawns and an ornamental pond and beyond this some woodland. I felt a great relief to be out in the open air. I looked back at the hospital. It was a forbidding sight and I could not help thinking how daunting the first approach to it must be for a new patient. The style was gothic, with a fake medieval tower at one end and a round turret at the other. Much of it was strangled by ivy. The windows were small, which accounted for the gloom within, many of them merely narrow openings to imitate the arrow slits of an ancient castle.

Once again Morgan must have read my thoughts. 'Dismal-looking edifice, isn't it?'

I turned away from it. 'I fear no one could say otherwise. It looks as if it ought to be haunted.'

He began to walk away and I heard him mutter something that sounded like, 'Oh it is, my boy, believe me, it is.' I had the sense that he was talking to himself and did not think I could hear him.

I caught up with him just as we came upon a group of lunatics out for their daily walk. Still clad in their same worn calico dresses, each woman now had a woollen shawl and, bizarrely, a straw hat, such as you might wear on a day out on Coney Island, making the overall impression strangely comic. The women were lined up in twos, guarded by attendants.

As they passed us, a shiver of horror crept through me. My gaze was met with vacant eyes and inexpressive faces, while many of them jabbered away, seemingly holding conversations with themselves, or sometimes leaning toward their partners and talking animatedly, although in most cases the other woman appeared not to be listening, either staring mutely ahead or muttering away herself, lost in a conversation of her own. I saw too that these women were under restraint. Wide leather belts were locked around their waists and attached to a long cable rope, so that they were all linked to one another, a sight that reminded me of old illustrations I had seen of slaves being led from their African villages to the slavers' ships. I did a rough count and estimated there must have been around twenty women roped together in this fashion.

We stood aside to let them pass and I could see many of them had dirty noses, unkempt hair and grimy skin. My own nostrils attested that they were not clean, whereas I hadn't noticed any unpleasant smells amongst the other women in the day room and was surprised that there should be any now we were in the fresh air.

'Who are these women?' I asked Morgan.

'They're the most violent on the island,' he replied. 'They are kept on the third floor, separate from the rest. They are all extremely disturbed and their presence would not be compatible with the treatment of the others.'

As if to verify this, one of them began to yell, which sparked off a reaction in another, who commenced to sing, in a strangely beautiful and haunting voice, the old song 'Barbara Allen', and for a moment it felt as if the sadness of the song was a reflection of her state, but then others broke out in a discordant caterwauling, raucous stuff such as you hear in low taverns, and one woman added to the cacophony by mumbling prayers, while others stuck to simple cursing, casting oaths defiantly into the air seemingly at nothing or no one in particular, but to the world in general and what it had done to them.

The women were forced to keep to the footpaths and I

thought how they must have longed to kick off their shoes and run barefoot across the soft, elegantly coiffed grass. Every so often one of them would bend and pick up something, a leaf or nut or fallen twig, but immediately an attendant would be upon her and force her to discard it.

'They are not allowed possessions,' Morgan observed to me.

Possessions! What kind of hell was this where a fallen leaf was counted a possession? I could not help but be reminded of *Lear*, in which I had once played Edmund – who else? – and the old king's speech: 'Oh, reason not the need, our basest beggars are in the poorest thing superfluous.'

Following in the wake of this miserable spectacle of humanity, we passed a small pavilion, no doubt a vestige from the days when the asylum had been a private residence. On the wall was painted in elegant script 'While I live, I hope.' I shook my head at the irony of this; you only had to look at these poor women shuffling along to see there was no truth in it.

We wandered the grounds for the best part of an hour, during which I had several uncomfortable moments, as every now and then Morgan attempted to quiz me on my ideas for the treatment of lunatics, while at the same time ridiculing them without managing to convey any clue as to what these ideas actually were. I began to feel quite aggrieved that he should patronise me so and frustrated that I could not produce any counter-argument, and sensed myself losing control, which of course would have ruined everything. I held my tongue only with the greatest difficulty.

Morgan pulled out his watch. 'Dinner in six minutes. You may as well observe the dining hall.'

Back inside the hospital we looked on as the more violent inmates, still in twos, were marched through a doorway in shambling parody of a military manoeuvre. They were taken off to a separate dining room, Morgan told me, for they needed careful supervision while they ate. After they had gone, I followed him into the long, narrow dining hall where the rest of the patients were standing, behind backless benches on either side of plain deal tables that ran almost the entire length of the hall's centre. At a word from one of the attendants the inmates began to scramble over the benches and take their places upon them in such a disorderly fashion I couldn't help thinking of pigs at the trough.

All along the tables were bowls filled with a dirty-looking liquid that Morgan assured me was tea. By each was a piece of bread, cut thick and buttered. Beside that was a small saucer that, as I peered more closely, proved to contain prunes. I counted five on each, no more no less. As I watched, one woman grabbed several saucers, one after the other, and emptied the prunes into her own. Then, holding tight to her own bowl of tea, she stole that of the woman next to her and gulped it down.

Morgan watched and, when I glanced at him, lifted his eyebrow and said, 'Survival of the fittest,' and smiled.

Looking around the tables, I saw women snatching other people's bread and others left with nothing at all. All this Morgan viewed with such complete indifference that I began to despair of humanity, until I noticed one inmate, a young woman, not much more than a girl really, with long dark hair that fell down over her face, half veiling it, tear her own slice of bread in two and pass one portion to the woman next to her, who had been robbed of her own and who accepted it eagerly, showing her gratitude with a smile, the first I had seen in this place. At this moment, as if feeling the weight of my eyes upon her, the girl who had given away her own bread lifted her head and stared straight at me with a look that chilled me to the bone. It had a knowingness in it, as if she saw right through me and recognised what I was and observed something in me that enabled her to claim kinship. I was only able to hold her gaze for a short time before I had to look away. A minute or so later, I glanced back at her and, finding her eyes still fastened upon me, had to turn away and walk to the other end of the room.

While all this scramble for food was going on, attendants prowled up and down behind the women, not bothering to stop the petty larcenies, but tossing an extra slice of bread here and there when they saw someone going without.

When the bread and prunes had been consumed, which in truth didn't take long, for there was not much of it and the women were obviously ravenous, the attendants fetched large metal cans from which they dispensed onto each of the women's now empty plates a small lump of grey meat, fatty and unappetising, and a single boiled potato. You'd have thought a dog would have baulked at it, and indeed I don't think I ever saw a dog so poorly fed, but the women fell upon it as if it was the most sumptuous feast. A few, I noticed, grimaced as they bit into the meat, showing it to be as rancid as it looked, but managed to swallow it nonetheless. Everyone else devoured it as fast as they could chew it – and it was evidently so tough, this was no easy thing – and, when it and the potato were done, looked balefully at their plates as though they could not believe the meagre offering was already gone.

Afterwards Morgan and I had our dinner in the doctors' dining room. Although the dining table would have accommodated six people, there were only the two of us. I asked how many other physicians there were, at which Morgan shrugged. 'We do not have unlimited resources, you know. The state does not set great store on treating the mentally ill. We cannot afford to employ more staff or anyone more experienced than you. Which is fortunate for you. Normally someone just starting out upon a career as a psychiatric doctor might wait years for an opportunity such as you have here.'

'Indeed, I am very grateful for it, sir,' I said, deciding some humble pie as an appetiser would not go amiss.

'Especially with your old-fashioned ideas,' added Morgan.

Fortunately I was not called upon to explain them as just then our food was brought in, which quite captured Morgan's attention. There was a decent grilled sole to start, followed by a very acceptable steak and a variety of cooked vegetables. It was more than passable. I'd eaten worse in many hotels and it was certainly much better than the fare I'd had recently. The bottle of wine we shared was a luxury I hadn't tasted for a considerable time.

Afterwards there was an excellent steamed treacle pudding, followed by a selection of cheeses. When we had finished and rose from the table I took advantage of Morgan consulting his watch, which he seemed to do every few minutes, to slip the sharp cheese knife up my sleeve.

'Well, then,' said Morgan, 'you will no doubt be tired after all your travelling, not to mention your encounter with public transport, and I have some correspondence to attend to, so I will say goodnight.' To my horror, he stretched out his hand for me to shake, which of course I could not do because I had the knife up my right sleeve with its handle cupped in the palm of my hand. There was an awkward moment when

I did not respond and his hand was suspended in a kind of limbo between us.

He cleared his throat and, as smoothly as a trained actor overcoming a colleague's missing of a cue, turned the thwarted handshake into a gesture toward the door, as though that had been what he had intended to do all along, and we proceeded to it, where he paused and said, 'Oh, there's a small library for the staff, over near my office, if you should want to read before retiring. It contains mainly medical books.' Here he lowered his head and shot me a lightly mocking look. 'Some of them may inform you about, shall we say, modern treatments, but there are also some novels and books of poetry, should you simply want relaxation.'

I thanked him and said I would walk back in that direction with him to find something to look at before I turned in. Letting him go ahead, I slipped the knife into my jacket pocket.

We made our way along the passage that led to the main entrance in silence. The place had settled down for the night and the gas lamps in the corridor were turned low. From somewhere far distant above us came a soft moan that could have been the sorrowful cries of patients or perhaps the lowing of the wind. I shivered to think of those lost souls, for whatever reason not at rest, who even now would be wandering the night, keening at their fate.

At his office door Morgan pointed me along a passage that ran at right angles to the one running the length of the house that we'd just come along. 'The library is at the end of this passage, last door on the left. You'll need a light.'

The corridor was completely dark. He went into his office and emerged with a lit candle on a brass holder. He handed it to me, together with some matches. 'Not all the property is fitted with gas.'

We said goodnight and this time I proffered my hand in order to allay any suspicions he might have harboured about my reluctance to shake with him earlier. Once again his firm grip on my bruised bones invoked an involuntary grimace that I did my best to disguise as a smile. He went into his office and shut the door behind him, cutting off the light from within and plunging me into a twilight world.

Shadows brought to life by my feeble candle flickered on the walls and I could not see very far along the passage ahead of me. 'Darkness be my friend,' I said, although it didn't fit, because for once I didn't need its cloak to hide me, but saying it somehow made me feel less afraid, for I confess I was, although I could not have told you exactly why. There was something so eerie about the place, what with that constant distant moan, the misery of so many forlorn ghosts, that a depression settled upon me and began to seep into my very core. A book would do me good, to divert my thoughts to something sunnier, and I set off along the dim passage, although not with any great confidence. I could not help myself from creeping, treading softly, for the sound of my own footsteps bothered me as though they might be those of another, or perhaps for fear the noise might awaken some sleeping enemy as yet still hidden from me. Eventually I reached the end of the corridor and found the door to the library. It opened with a creak like a sound effect from one of those old melodramas in which it has too often been my misfortune to be involved.

It wasn't a very big room, only the size of a modest drawing room, which made me think reading and literature had not been a priority for whoever had had the place built as a private residence. All four walls were lined floor to ceiling with shelves of books. I walked around the room, casting the light of my candle over the spines. On first inspection their bindings all appeared old, foxed and mildewed, the gilt titles faded and their shine dulled. The place had the graveyard scent of mouldy neglect and I supposed the room and its contents had fallen into disuse once the place was turned into a hospital. Who here would want to read books now? The patients weren't allowed; Morgan had told me as much. The attendants had struck me as ignorant and uneducated, and that left only the doctors, and evidently not many of them had been of a literary turn of mind, because the dust on the shelves showed the volumes upon them had rested undisturbed for some considerable time. In one small section, though, I came upon books that were relatively new, the wood of the shelves cleaner, showing they had been taken out and put back. A closer look revealed they were all upon medical subjects, mostly to do with mental illness. I read their titles, which were so mystifying to me they might as well have been in Japanese, and I could not decide upon one to favour above the others and consequently, in the end, didn't examine any of them more closely. I was tired and not in the mood and, even though it would have been sensible to begin at once my education in my new profession, I understood myself sufficiently well to know I would not read anything about it tonight.

I went to the next section, which was comprised of the ubiquitous ancient worn stock, and here struck gold in a large, shabby volume and had no need to look further. *The Complete Works of William Shakespeare* in a handsome though battered edition. I set my candle down upon a small table and took the book from the shelf. It fell open at the

Scottish Play. I shivered. Was this a bad omen? It was certainly not what I would have chosen to read in such a setting and I was about to turn to something lighter, one of the comedies, when at that very moment my candle flickered. I felt the hairs on the back of my neck stand on end as from behind me came the plaintive creak of the door. There was the patter of bare feet over floorboards and I swivelled round in time to see a wisp of white, the hem of a woman's dress or nightgown, whisk around the edge of the door, its wearer seemingly fleeing after finding me there, and pulling the door shut behind her with such a slam the draught from it killed my candle dead.

It was pitch dark. I fumbled about, feeling for the candle, but succeeded only in barking my shin against some piece of furniture, drawing from me an involuntary oath. I shuddered at the sound of my own voice, as though if I only managed to keep quiet the intruder would ignore me, which, of course, was plain stupid of me. I remonstrated with myself for my cowardliness, asking myself why I, who had lately been in a far worse situation, was so fearful. I could only put it down to my being here, in this madhouse, where I should not have been, although I had every right to be here, so far as anyone else knew.

I felt about with my hands stretched out in front of me like a blind man, trying to remember exactly where I had set down the candleholder, but in my panic could remember nothing of the room. I told myself I must think clearly and sucked in a couple of deep breaths, got myself calm again and eventually laid my hand on the candleholder. I found the box of matches Morgan had placed on it and fumbled one out and struck it, the noise like an explosion in the dead silence of the night. I had great difficulty in applying the flame to the wick, my hand was shaking so. The match went out and I struggled to light another, the light flickering wildly as my fingers trembled. I steadied myself and at last the thing was lit. As visibility returned and the edges of the room fell into place, so my terror abated. I felt as if I had seen a ghost, and indeed it was not too fanciful to believe that I had. That fleeting suggestion of white dress, the patter of feet – it was all the stuff of tales of hauntings.

It was with some trepidation that I eased open the door, in dread of its rusty creaking. All this achieved was to protract the noise of its unoiled hinges, which took on the sound of a small animal, or some ghostly child perhaps, being tortured. As soon as there was enough of an opening, I insinuated myself around the edge of the door and shuffled my way along the passage outside, fearing that at any moment the spectre would come rushing at me and – and – and what? That's the thing about terror: it's the not knowing that gets to you and what your mind makes up instead. I stood still a moment, took another deep breath and rationalised what had happened. I had seen a hint of female garment. It was a woman and I was a strong fit man; what did I have to be afraid of? But then I began to think what woman it might be. The most likely was one of the attendants, of course, because by now the inmates were all safely locked in their dormitories (safely as long as there wasn't a fire!). But what if one should have escaped somehow? What then? What if she were violent? I shuddered at the thought of some madwoman launching herself out of the shadows at me and found myself twitching with every flicker of the candle flame, at every dancing shadow on the walls.

It seemed an age before I achieved the end of the passage.

The gas lamps in the main corridor had now been extinguished and there was no light showing under Morgan's door, so I guessed he must have retired for the night. The silence overwhelmed me because every instant I expected it to be broken by that other presence I had glimpsed. I made my way up the main staircase, treading as softly as I could, for it was old and as creaky as the library door and apt to groan a protest at every step. On the second floor everything was unfamiliar in the weak candlelight and I made several false turns before I found the right passageway and at long last made my way toward the safety of my room.

3

With a sigh of relief I closed the door behind me and leaned my back against it, sucking in deep gulps of air because I had, without realising it until now, been holding my breath for so long. I put a hand to my face and found my forehead was clammy. The bruise there seemed to be thumping away in time with my overworked heart. Several minutes passed before I was composed enough to put the candle down upon the writing desk, although my hands were still shaking. It took another few minutes before I felt confident enough of not injuring myself to take the cheese knife I had stolen from my pocket and set about the valise locks. The knife was very thin and the curl at the top of it made it ideal for the task, and the case and its locks were cheap. After no more than a couple of minutes I had triggered the springs of both locks and snapped them open. I took another deep breath to steel myself to lift the lid. What if the contents weren't sufficient for my basic needs? What if there were no spare shirts or linen? It was perfectly possible. They might have been in some steamer trunk in the baggage car for all I knew. I flung open the lid, and saw to my relief a pile of neatly folded shirts, underwear, socks, a spare pair of pants, a washbag containing toothbrush and powder, a hairbrush, a bottle of hair oil, a razor and so on. I lifted them out and found underneath a book, the boards well worn from use, the spine slightly torn. As I picked it up I realised I had put down the Shakespeare in the darkness in the library to look for my candle and in my terror never thought to take it up again, and so felt a little surge of pleasure that at least I had here a book to divert me from my gloomy imaginings. I took it up from the valise and read the title from the spine. *Moral Treatment* by Reverend Andrew Abrahams.

I tossed it onto the writing desk in disgust. Obviously some uplifting Christian work. Just my luck! I'd rather have had the Bible itself; at least the language is memorable and there's a rip-roaring story or two, not to mention a fair bit of adultery. But God save me from the sanctimonious religious writings of the present time, when men ought to know better. Still, at least it told me something about the sort of pious fool I had become.

Having nothing to entertain me, I got on with the necessary business of hanging up my clothes in the closet and laying out my toiletries on the chest of drawers. I put the valise under the bed, undressed and put on my nightshirt, which was just the kind of scratchy garment you'd expect from some Holy Roller, like sleeping in sackcloth, although after a short time it ceased to matter, for soon after my head hit the pillow, I was lost to the world.

I did not pass a peaceful night but was troubled by a succession of dark dreams. In most of them I was wandering along dimly lit corridors, haunted by shadowy corners from which, with no warning, and screams that froze the blood solid in my veins, women would fling themselves upon me, their faces hideously deformed, eyes black with madness, lips red as arterial blood, teeth bared like wolf fangs and dripping with hunger, their fingertips ending in long talons which raked my face, tearing at my eyes. I finally awoke from one of these nightmares to the sound of birds singing and light pouring in around the edges of the blind at the window, and although I normally have no time for Him, thanked God that at last day had dawned.

My nightshirt and the sheets were soaked with sweat. I wondered that I should have been so frightened to cause this and then worried that it might not be anything to do with my dreams but rather because I had suffered some serious injury in the accident, that perhaps the blow to my head had caused a fever of the brain.

I could hear footsteps in the corridor outside, doors opening and closing, the hollow echo of distant shouts, all the noises of a large institution rousing itself for another day, dreadfully familiar to me from the past few months but somehow different too. I threw back the blankets and got out of bed. There was no heating and it was cold, though not so cold as where I had just come from. I took off the nightshirt, found a cloth and a bar of soap in the washbag, poured myself a bowl of water and, after recovering from the shock of its bracing temperature, gave myself a thorough scrubbing. I examined the bruise on my forehead in the mirror and was glad to see it appeared less livid. This minor improvement was enough to give me a little surge of optimism and kindle the belief I might survive here for a while, that everything would be OK. I dressed in clean linen, shirt and necktie and pulled on the spare pare of pants. I sniffed the armpits of the jacket I'd had on, the only one I possessed, and recoiled at the stench of stale sweat. I opened the bottle of hair oil, which proved to be scented. There was no way I was letting the stuff anywhere near my head, but I shook a little into the armpit linings of the jacket and rubbed it in. The effect might make me stink like a French pimp but on the other hand it was to be preferred to yesterday's sweat.

I had no timepiece. The one I'd found in the jacket had been smashed in the accident and I'd thrown it away. So I had no idea of the hour, but it sounded sufficiently busy outside to think it was time I should be abroad.

I made my way downstairs and, coming across the maid who had first shown me to my room, I saw now that she was pretty and could not help noticing how long and slender was her neck, elegant as a swan's, surprising on so coarse a person. I asked where I might find Dr Morgan and she directed me to the staff dining room.

'Ah, Shepherd,' he said when I walked in, and I nodded self-consciously. 'Come and get some fuel inside you, we have another busy day.'

Breakfast proved a sumptuous meal, with devilled kidneys, grits, eggs, bacon, toast and preserves and a great pot of freshly brewed coffee, of which Morgan consumed a prodigious quantity, causing the pupils of his gimlet eyes to expand into an almost fanatical stare as he grew more and more animated.

Although I had put away a good amount of food the night before, I found I was still famished, which I blamed on my many months of deprivation, and busied myself getting as much down me as I could. The uncertainty of my lifelong career and especially my late unfortunate experiences had taught me never to presume too much where your next meal might be coming from but at every opportunity to fill your stomach against the evil day that was sure to be just around the corner. At the same time I could not help thinking of the miserable meal the poor wretches who were confined here had had last night and to feel more than a mite of sympathy for them. So preoccupied did I become by this that my attention must have wandered from what Morgan was saying, although he hadn't noticed and, carried away on a tide of caffeine, was rabbiting on at a furious pace, until suddenly something in his gabble flicked a switch within my brain.

'. . . the most tried and tested of modern treatments, the restraining chair, used so successfully on George III, only this is a much modified, up-to-date model, designed by myself. You'll soon forget your silly notions about Moral Treatment when you see the practical application of today's methods. It's no use harking back to the past . . .'

I sat upright. 'Sorry,' I said, 'I didn't quiet catch that. What did you just say?'

'I said it was no use harking back to the past.'

'No, before that.'

'I was telling you you will soon abandon those silly outmoded notions you have of Moral Treatment.' He looked at me. 'What is it, man?'

'Oh, nothing,' I said, waving a piece of toast in what I hoped was a casual manner. 'I just misheard you the first time, that's all.'

'Well, come on, aren't you going to argue with me? Put up your case, there's a good fellow, and then I can knock it down.'

I shook my head. 'No, no, not now, not at breakfast,' I mumbled. 'I can't think clearly when I'm not properly awake.'

So I was not such a pious idiot after all! The book in my room was to do with the treatment of lunatics and not a religious tract. If only I had taken the trouble to open it last night! As it was, I would have to dodge any further discourse on the subject with Morgan until I could slip away upstairs and take a look at the book. I could not hope to keep avoiding discussion about my beliefs; it was imperative I find out as soon as possible just exactly what they were.

Breakfast was accomplished on my part at an indigestion-inducing rate because Morgan had a good start on me with it and when he was finished kept consulting his watch and tut-tutting impatiently as a not very subtle signal to me to hurry up. I did not mean to leave the room without a full stomach, however, and stuffed the rest of the food on my plate into my mouth, bolting it down as fast as I could, with hardly any recourse to the action of my teeth or troubling to taste it.

I had scarcely swallowed the last morsel of bacon before Morgan was on his feet, pocket watch out and heading for the door. I scraped back my chair, mopped my mouth with my napkin, took a last regretful swig of coffee and trotted after him. As I caught up, Morgan stopped abruptly, so I almost cannoned into his back. He lifted his head and sniffed the air like a hunting dog. 'Can you smell anything peculiar?' he said.

I took a sniff myself and shook my head. 'No, sir.'

He shrugged. 'Hmm, funny that, could have sworn I smelt flowers. Rose petals if I'm not mistaken.' He peered at me suspiciously for a moment, which I returned with a blank face. He shrugged again, turned and walked on briskly. It seemed I had overdone the pomade in my jacket. I could not help wondering what my new boss was thinking of me now. I hurried after him once more, trying my best to hold in check what threatened to be a mighty belch.

* * *

The morning consisted of examining various 'difficult' patients. In one room we found O'Reilly and another attendant standing beside a thin, pale, fair-haired woman sitting on a stool. No sooner were we inside than Morgan's nose was raised and twitching again, and, even with the protection of my perfumed armpits, I could smell something unpleasant.

Morgan took a clipboard from O'Reilly and read through the papers on it swiftly. He handed it back to her without comment or even looking at her and advanced toward the woman. 'Now, now, Lizzie, what's this I hear? You've been playing with your excrement again.'

She looked up and gave him a wan smile. 'I have indeed, sir,' she said, 'and I enjoyed myself immensely.'

Morgan turned to O'Reilly. 'Completely unrepentant!'

'Yes, sir,' she replied. 'Bold as brass. It's been the devil of a job to get her clean again. We've had no cooperation from her at all.'

He sighed and looked back at the woman with the assumed sadness adults use when dealing with misbehaving small children. 'Very well, then, nothing for it but the chair. Longer this time. I did think we would not need it again with her, but I see now that last time we tried to rush things and did not give the treatment sufficient time to do its work.'

At the mention of the word 'chair' the patient's face blanched, something you would not have thought possible because it had been so pale already. 'Oh, no, sir, not the chair,' she protested, as the attendants took hold of her arms and pulled her from her seat. The woman resisted, trying to tug her arms free, but the attendants were muscular and strong and obviously better fed than she and they wrestled her toward a side door. Morgan strode swiftly around the group and opened it. At this the patient suddenly went limp and became a dead weight, forcing the attendants to drag her along, her legs trailing behind her, and all the while she was shouting and screaming exactly like a woman who has just realised she is about to be murdered.

Morgan went after them into the adjoining room, indicating with an impatient wave of his hand that I should follow. The room was bare save for a heavy upright wooden chair, which was bolted to the floorboards. The arms and legs of the chair were fitted with leather straps, with another stretched across the front of its high back. At the sight of the chair the woman came to life again and began fighting once more. The attendants hauled her into it, manhandling her calmly in the face of fierce opposition on her part, got her hands strapped to the arms and then proceeded to strap her ankles to the legs in spite of her kicking feet. Finally, they placed the strap attached to the chair back around her throat. A strap like that could strangle a woman, I thought.

All the time the woman was screaming and resisting with what little power she had. I really don't enjoy seeing a woman struggle. I have no liking for torture.

'If you leave me here, I will piss myself, I swear I will,' the woman shouted.

O'Reilly turned to Morgan, and raised an eyebrow. 'Gag?'

He nodded and she produced a piece of rolled cloth from her pocket, evidently made for the purpose, at the sight of which the woman stopped screaming and closed her mouth firmly, turning the lips inwards so you could not see them. Her panic showed in her eyes, which swivelled this way and that, desperately searching for some means of escape, like a cornered rat. The junior attendant went behind her, seized her head in an arm hold to prevent her shaking it around and with her free hand pinched the poor woman's nose tightly. Thus it was only a matter of time before she was forced to open her mouth to breathe, whereupon O'Reilly shoved the gag between her teeth while the other proceeded to tie it behind the woman's head.

After this, unable to move much at all, the poor wretch in the chair gave up the fight and her body slumped. No dignity remained to her and, lacking any other means of defiance, she carried out her threat and opened her bladder and urine began to drip from the chair and pool upon the floor below.

I watched in horror, appalled at what I was seeing, but Morgan seemed completely unmoved by the woman's plight, as did O'Reilly and the other attendant. All three were so extremely matter-of-fact about the whole affair, it was obvious it must be a daily occurrence in their lives. Morgan strolled back into the other room and retrieved the clipboard from where O'Reilly had put it down. Returning to us, he studied it, lifting the top sheet of paper, then the one underneath.

'I see we gave her only three hours last time.'

'That's right, sir,' said O'Reilly.

'I think then that this time we'll try six. That should do the trick.'

The eyes of the woman in the chair widened in terror at these words. It was her only method of expression. Morgan walked over to her and said, in a kindly tone, 'Now then, Lizzie, you may as well settle down because you are going to be here for quite the long haul. During that time I want you to consider the foolish behaviour that has led you to this situation and to consider modifying it so that you never have to find yourself here again. I hope that after this there will be no more soiling of yourself.'

He stood and smiled benignly, with the air of one who is conferring the greatest of favours, and as if waiting for some kind of response, though of course there was no way the unfortunate woman could give any, except to blink. Then, in that abrupt way he had of doing things, he turned to O'Reilly, thrust the clipboard into her hands and without another word marched out of the room. I caught up with him in the corridor.

'Six hours to be so restrained seems a terrible long time,' I ventured.

'You think so?' He stopped and looked at me with surprise. 'Why, not at all, man, not at all. Ten or twelve is sometimes necessary.'

'It seems so – so, well, harsh. Is there truly no other way?'

He looked exasperated. 'There we go again, with your old-style ideas. Ideas I may say that were formulated by a gaggle of well-meaning but ill-informed, completely unqualified Quakers, rather than doctors, and that have no basis in science. Come, man, let's have it out now, why don't we? I can't have you working here if you mean to challenge every-thing we do.'

I had no notion of how I had pushed him into this. His rage seemed out of all proportion to the objection I had made. His face was red with indignation, his cheeks puffed out, like an angry bullfrog. I thought his head was going to explode. I did not know what to say. It was not like drying up on stage, for I had no script. Indeed, I was not at all sure what my role here was. I tried to improvise but all that came out was a stammer. His features relaxed and his old calm smugness seemed to flow back. 'Well? Cat got your tongue?'

'I will gladly fight my corner, sir, only I would like the opportunity to reflect upon what I have seen here, if I may, and to formulate my reply carefully before making it.'

'Very well,' he snapped. 'Take all the time you want; it won't make any difference. We'll discuss it tomorrow.'

I breathed a sigh of relief. I would read *Moral Treatment* after dinner this evening and have whatever arguments it contained for my ammunition. As I followed him along the corridor, though, the thought came to me, why do I want to argue with him? Why should I of all people care so much about the treatment of these lunatics, I who was wholly ignorant of such things not twenty-four hours ago? Why put myself at risk by stirring the waters of this safe harbour, given what the consequences might be? But all that carried no weight. I knew I would continue on this course even though to do so lacked any sort of logic. What a piece of work is man! So full of contradictions. I thought not to find such compassion in myself. It troubled me to discover I knew so little of me.

We were now near Morgan's office and he begged to be excused as he had a letter he must dictate to his secretary, although I had the sense that this was a pretext, that he was still so angry with me he wanted to remove himself from my presence until he could calm down and reappear as his other, more familiar, urbane character. He was a man who did not like to lose control. I told him that as I hadn't after all visited the library last night, I would do so now.

It was strange how ordinary in broad daylight, robbed of its black corners and sinister shadows, the passage I had trod the night before was. The library, too, had lost the terror darkness had given it. There was nothing atmospheric about it now; it had only the air of a musty neglected storeroom and not even very much of the romance of books. I examined the dusty shelves and found they contained a good few novels, and several volumes of stories by one of my favourite authors, Edgar Allan Poe. For the moment, though, I restrained myself from taking one; there was enough horror about the place for me not to seek to add to it. I settled for the Shakespeare. Should a man ever find himself upon a desert island, it is the only book he would need and the only one he could not do without.

I returned with it to Morgan's office and hung about outside and shortly he emerged. He reached out a hand for the book and I surrendered it to him. He examined the title on the spine before flicking it open and regarding the list of contents, then he slammed it shut, releasing a little cloud of dust, and handed it back to me. 'Shakespeare, eh? Never could understand what all the fuss was about.'

Well, I thought, that is no great surprise. It would be difficult for a lover of the bard to show so little sympathy for others. Still, I did not want to take him on over this, not after our earlier spat. Save your battles for the things worth fighting for has always been my motto, so I merely smiled, like someone appreciating the confession of a venial weakness by a superior being. This evidently put me back into Morgan's good books and I realised he was a man who did not like to be challenged on anything. I've often observed this in those who are completely sure of everything they do. It's as if the exposure of any small chink in their certainty would demolish the whole edifice.

Morgan pulled out his watch. 'The boat will be in by now and we will have to review the new intake. They will be arriving directly at the examination room.'

We passed through the day room on our way there and, immediately Morgan opened the door, in contrast to the dead silence of the day before, were greeted by a great noise. I saw that at this early hour the inmates were not seated listlessly around the room as on the previous afternoon, but instead were on their hands and knees scrubbing the floor. I could have kicked myself for my naïveté in thinking it was thanks to the attendants that the place was spotless.

'The patients do the housework?' I asked, pausing to look at them.

'Yes, they do some of the physical work around the place, mainly cleaning in the mornings. The physical exertion tires them and makes them less violent and more compliant. In the afternoons they are fatigued from the exercise and more likely to sit here quietly. And it kills two birds with one stone. The place would not be viable if we had to pay for staff to clean it on top of everything else.' He began to walk away.

I looked at the women and was thinking how exhausting their chores must be on the meagre rations I had seen them consuming yesterday, when I noticed one of them had stopped her scrubbing and had sat back on her haunches and was staring at me. It was the young girl I had seen sharing her bread yesterday. Our eyes locked again and I began once more to feel uncomfortable but then, at the very moment I thought I should have to be the one to break the spell, her lips trembled into the suggestion of a smile, which I could not help returning. It was the first communication I had had with any of the lunatics.

I realised Morgan was nearly at the other end of the room by now and turned and hurried after him, but such was the impression made by those black eyes and that suspicion of a smile that they lingered in my mind the rest of the day.

4

The daily morning boat had delivered us three new inmates, judged insane by the doctors at the city asylum. One was an old woman, with untidy straggly grey hair, who sat in a chair, muttering away to herself and carefully picking imaginary fleas from her clothes, imaginary because she had been thoroughly bathed and reclothed at the hospital. She was just the sort of woman one saw about the streets of big cities all the time, begging and sleeping in doorways. I said as much to Morgan.

'Yes,' he replied, 'but that does not mean she isn't mad. A good percentage, if not all, of such creatures would not pass the test for sanity. It is their madness that has led them to their unfortunate situation. But the state cannot afford to treat every one of them.'

He asked the woman her name, to which she replied, 'Mary, Mary quite contrary,' and made herself laugh, a most hideous cackle that revealed she lacked a good few teeth; most of the survivors were blackened stumps. She stared at us a moment and then resumed her flea harvesting, giving it her full concentration as though we were not there. Morgan asked the attendant standing with us for the woman's history.

The attendant consulted a paper file she was holding. 'Persistent vagrant, well known to the city police. Her mind has been ailing for some time now, it seems, and it has finally got to the stage where she is a danger to others and to herself. She tried to take a lady's purse, being quite convinced it was her own. The police judged it not a simple matter of theft as the woman herself did not consider it stealing but taking back what was rightfully hers.'

'A diagnosis of senile dementia,' said Morgan, studying the notes. 'One that I agree with. And this one?'

The second woman was very young, perhaps twenty or so, and catatonic. Her eyes looked vacantly ahead of her. It was obvious nobody was home.

'May have smothered her baby, sir, although that's not certain,' replied the attendant, passing him more notes.

Morgan stood reading them for several minutes, then handed them to me. There was a coroner's report into the death of the baby that was inconclusive. The mother had been found in her lodging house sitting holding the body of the infant, which had been dead for several days. She had not spoken and was completely unresponsive to questions and so had been sent to the city asylum for an assessment, where she was judged insane and referred to the island.

Morgan approached her. He waved his hand up and down across her line of vision. There was no reaction. She did not even blink. He turned to me. 'Some pathology of the brain means it has failed to function properly. In all likelihood she killed her baby without realising what she was doing. Do you agree?'

I tried to read those lifeless eyes. 'Yes,' I said, slowly, 'but do you not think, sir, that it's possible the baby died by some

49

accident or illness and that the woman fell into this state through grief at losing her child?'

'There you go again!' It was said wearily. He shook his head. 'People do not go mad because they are upset, man. We all get upset but few of us become mad. Science shows madness has a pathological cause. There is some physical malfunction in the brain. You can require no better proof than this woman here. She shows none of the normal signs of grief, no weeping, no tearing of the hair. As you can clearly see, she is completely unemotional.'

I did not know what to say. I could not argue with his science. I had only the evidence of my own eyes and my knowledge of human nature. I thought of Lady Macduff and her frenzy after the murder of her children. I thought of Ophelia with her flowers, unable to be reached after the death of her father at the hand of her lover. And I remembered too the suggestion in the Scottish Play that the somnambulant queen has lost a child or is unable to have children. Does she murder Duncan because she is mad or does she go mad only because of the guilt of murdering him? I could not help thinking that Shakespeare understood what makes us humans tick better than modern science as related to me by Dr Morgan.

I was tempted to say all this but then, remembering my earlier diagnosis of Morgan's character, decided discretion was the wiser part. There was nothing to be gained by taking him on over this. He was not about to release the woman, and anyway, what was Hecuba to me?

We moved on to the third woman who, in contrast to the others, had an intelligent, alert expression. Before the attendant could say anything, she herself spoke. 'I have been sent here by mistake, sir. There is nothing wrong with my mind, I assure you.'

Morgan turned to the attendant and raised an eyebrow, saying to me in a whisper, 'They nearly all say that.'

The attendant looked at the notes. 'She caused a disturbance at the restaurant where she had previously been employed as a waitress. She'd been dismissed for being absent from work two days in a row.'

Morgan took the notes and looked them over. He raised his eyebrows. 'Quite an impressive disturbance, I see. Smashed the place up, threw a plate through the window, broke crockery, swore at the manager and screamed at the customers.' He lifted his eyes from the notes to the woman.

She coloured. 'I was not myself, sir. You see, my little girl – she's only two, sir – was sick, sir, and I was too worried about her to leave her and go to work. I sent word to explain but they wouldn't hear of it, sir. And so I lost my job and then I couldn't pay the doctor's bills.'

Morgan looked again at the notes. 'I see you assaulted the doctor, too.' There was a stern gravity about the way he said this, as though he named the worst of all possible crimes.

The woman looked down. 'I did, sir. I don't know what came over me. He wouldn't take my promise for payment for the medicine. He wouldn't give me anything for my daughter. My head was in a spin, sir. I lost control. But my daughter is better. She's being looked after by a relative now. And I'm all right, sir. I'm not crazy, really I'm not.'

'We don't like to use words like "crazy" here,' Morgan said kindly. 'What you are is mentally ill.'

The woman began to protest but he held up a hand to silence her and you had to admire the natural authority the man possessed, because she immediately fell quiet. She was smart enough to know that arguing might reinforce the diagnosis against her.

'You're mentally ill. It is not something to be ashamed of; it is a physical illness, no different from heart disease or diabetes. There are hundreds, perhaps thousands, of people in this great city who suffer setbacks and difficulties daily in their lives. They do not go smashing up restaurants. They do not attack doctors.'

'It wasn't really what you would call an attack, sir. I slapped his face, and then only the once, sir.'

'They do not attack doctors. The fact that you did these things, which mentally healthy people do not do, no matter how much pressure they are under, indicates there is something faulty in your brain. This is the best place for you.'

'But, sir, I cannot stay here. I must go home and look after my daughter.'

'Madam, stay here you must. You have been committed. Believe me, this is the right home for you at present. Here you will get the treatment you need.'

Tears ran down the woman's cheeks and she began wringing her hands. 'But sir, I – I –'

'There, there, calm yourself. Everything will be all right. It's a great shock to find yourself in a place like this, I know. But it is your best chance of becoming well again.' He smiled, handed the notes back to the attendant, turned to me and said, 'Right, let's be getting along now,' and made for the door.

'How long will it take?' I said, as I struggled as usual to keep up with him.

'How long will what take?'

'For that woman to recover her health and get back to her child. She seemed perfectly sane and sensible to me.'

He stopped and smiled at me patronisingly. 'To you, yes, because you have no practical experience. Here the woman is under no pressure, but what would happen if she were let loose in the world again and some little thing in her life went wrong? How many restaurants would she destroy then, eh? How many doctors would she beat up – or worse?'

I said nothing. I could see he would only grow angry again if I took him on.

'You and I would not behave so. At least I know I wouldn't, and I hope you wouldn't either. But she will do the same again because there is a pathological illness of the brain underlying her actions. It's a physical thing and not something that can be altered by "kindness". Now do you understand?'

This last question was rhetorical and he strode on. I stared after him. How easily I could imagine him smashing something or striking someone, there was the irony of the thing! I couldn't help but smile at his assuming me to be so peaceable too. Seeming, seeming! How simple it is to judge a sane man mad and a mad man sane! What a combination Morgan and I made. The lunatics had taken over the asylum.

I had an hour to myself before dinner and, although the Shakespeare called invitingly from my bedside table, settled down to read *Moral Treatment*.

The introduction itself was sufficient to make me understand Morgan's hostility. 'In the past,' wrote the Reverend Abrahams, 'a cruel and inhuman regime was practised against those unfortunates judged to be suffering from mental illness. They were treated more like animals than humans with souls. They were imprisoned, beaten, put under restraint and subjected to all manner of indignities. They lost all their rights and were often committed to institutions for life with no recourse to appeal. In most cases this treatment had no therapeutic value.

'In twenty years of dealing with the mentally ill, I have treated them according to my Christian principles, with the result that the vast majority have had their symptoms sufficiently alleviated to be able to take their places in society and lead a contented and useful life . . .'

This was so at odds with Morgan's philosophy that I found myself utterly absorbed. In the opening chapters Abrahams, who acknowledged himself a Quaker, explained the day-to-day running of his small hospital. Patients were treated as fellow members of the human race. They were kept busy at simple tasks such as gardening, sewing, carpentry and the like according to their tastes and abilities. During their leisure times they were encouraged to read, to take walks around the grounds, to play games both indoor and outdoor, including card games, chess, croquet and tennis; they were offered entertainment in the form of lectures, plays and musical gatherings. They were not made to feel different from the rest of mankind but wore their own clothes and were spoken to with respect by the staff. They were rarely locked up and only then on occasions when they were thought to represent a physical threat to themselves or others, which were rare. They were given wholesome and nutritious food. Above all, the people who looked after them, who were not doctors but ministers and trained nurses, talked with them regularly and listened to their accounts of what troubled them.

Under this system, according to Abrahams, the vast majority of his patients recovered, usually in a matter of months, and were well enough to be restored to their families. It was his firm belief that for most people mental illness was not a permanent state of being but a temporary crisis, brought about by some misfortune, which might be anything from a family death to a financial collapse. When handled with sympathy and kindness, patients recovered and became, with only a few exceptions, their former selves.

All of this was so reasonably argued, and put down in such a matter-of-fact way, with many examples of individual cases, that by the time I closed the book, I was already well on the way to being convinced.

5

Dinner found Morgan in affable mood. He discoursed upon his youth and his experiences as a doctor practising in an ordinary hospital, treating all manner of illnesses and injuries, and recounted anecdotes, some of which were genuinely amusing and others so concerned with the blood and gore often associated with doctoring that I didn't consider them conducive to enjoying my dinner, although I made sure I ate my fill anyway.

At one stage he asked me about myself, saying he would like to know a little of my history beyond what he had seen in my application for employment, that he knew all about my education at medical school, but nothing personal about me. I improvised easily the rest of my background, cheerfully killing off my father, an attorney, when I was ten, when he was trampled to death by an unruly horse ('You seem to have inherited his misfortune for accidents involving transportation,' Morgan interposed at this point, a remark I could not help thinking would have been insensitive had either of the incidents he was referring to actually happened), and disposing of my mother by means of the scarlet fever, which carried her off when I was sixteen. The result of recounting my struggles as an orphan was to see Morgan look at me with something like admiration, seeing me in a new light, as I described the various vicissitudes I'd endured as I single-handedly worked my way through school. The whole was a mixture of truth and invention. It was a technique I'd used so many times before, it came easily to me – creating the background for a character, the bits in between the lines that aren't written down.

'Bravo,' he said, pouring us another glass of wine and then lifting his in a toast that I copied. 'Your unfortunate past has been the making of you. It has provided you with grit and determination to work hard. It will serve you far better than being born with a silver spoon in your mouth and treading the primrose path.'

I beamed with pride, feeling very satisfied with my new self.

Back in my room I spent a long evening absorbed by more of *Moral Treatment*. It was not the sort of book I had been used to. Drama, novels and poetry had been my literary meat and drink, and I had some difficulty following all the arguments put forward in it, although my interest always picked up when I came across any case history the author included by way of example. It was always people that fascinated me. Facts are too malleable to make me have much respect for them.

I heard the clock strike midnight as I struggled through the second half of the book, yawning all the while. It was no wonder I was tired. There was the business of the wreck and the injuries I had suffered. Besides the blow to the head, I had sore ribs and an ache in my back that made it hard for me to sit comfortably, no matter how I tried to arrange myself. Then there had been all the stress to my nerves of arriving here, the pressure of being a new, untried employee, the battle within myself to keep in line, to overcome my obstreperous nature and not speak against the hard treatment of the poor wretches who were my fellow inhabitants of this place, separated from me by that most fragile of borders, chance. The wine at dinner had not helped either, so that at some point, notwithstanding my determination to plough through to the end of the book and prepare my arguments for the morrow, I must have fallen asleep.

I had the dream again, the one that always seems to return in times of trouble. I was back on my uncle's chicken farm, where I'd arrived the day before following the death of my mother. I'd never had a father; he'd run off before I was even born. I was eleven years old and my uncle had just strapped me because he'd told me I had to earn my keep and I'd refused to kill a chicken.

I stood before him, my pants around my ankles, my bare backside sore from the blows. I put a tentative hand behind me and felt something wet. When I inspected it, I saw it was stained with blood. My uncle watched me, breathing heavily, his belt swinging from his right hand. 'Well, boy, what's it to be,' he said, 'you or the chicken?'

'Does it have to be one or the other, sir?' I said. 'Is there not something else I may do to earn my keep?'

'There are plenty of other things you will be doing. None of them can be instead of this. You have to learn the business. You know Martha can't bear children. You can be like a son to us and then one day this farm will be yours. You have to be able to run it.'

I tried to look grateful. It was the first time I ever put on an act. I pretended to be a boy who wanted to spend his whole life on a chicken farm, with the scent of chicken shit clogging up his nostrils.

'Come on now, let's give it another try.' He began threading the belt through the loops on his pants.

I pulled up my pants, which hurt as they slid over the wounds on my backside. I tried not to cry. I could tell my uncle was not someone who would approve of a boy crying.

He went inside the big barn where the chickens were and came out holding a bird in each hand. He held them by their feet and they dangled helplessly, flapping their wings and clucking their heads off. I wanted to put my hands over my ears to shut out the noise but I knew it would be a mistake.

'Here, take this one.' He held out one of the birds. Gingerly I put both my hands around its legs. This made the bird even more agitated and the movement of its wings more frenzied and instantly I let go, but my uncle still had it so it couldn't get away. 'Get hold of it!' He was mad again now.

I bit my lip and took the bird, my head recoiling from it, but this time I had it firmly by the legs. I held it at arm's length. I didn't want it flapping against me.

'Now pay attention. It don't take but a second, so you need to watch nice and close, OK?'

I nodded. What I really wanted to do was close my eyes. This was the second demonstration. I had no wish to see another bird slaughtered.

He put his free hand around the hen's neck and released the other from its feet. Then he put that around the neck too. The bird's body was swinging, a crazy pendulum. 'Now all you have to do is twist, like so.' There was a soft crack and after a few seconds the bird stopped moving and hung lifeless from his hand. 'See, ain't nothing to it, son.'

I stared back at him. My chicken was going berserk, squawking its head off, and I felt sure it had seen the other's fate and knew what was coming. I wondered idly whether a chicken was really smart enough to figure all that out.

'Now you.'

I gritted my teeth. Bile rose up in my throat and I thought for a moment I was going to vomit over my feet but I managed to hold it down. I put one hand around the chicken's neck, got a good hold of it and let the feet drop.

'That's it, perfect,' said my uncle.

I put my other hand around the hen's neck. The feathers felt soft and warm, so warm. I could feel the bird's blood beating fast through my fingertips. I swear its eyes widened in terror, although I later discovered that a chicken's eyes couldn't do that. I shut my own eyes and twisted exactly as my uncle had shown me. The bird's wings were banging against me. I imagined my hands were huge and they were around my uncle's neck and that I was about to snap the life out of him so I wouldn't ever have to do this again. There was a click and after a last frantic flurry the bird stopped moving. Slowly I opened my eyes and saw its head was flopped over my wrist.

'That's my boy!' cried my uncle. I looked up at him and smiled.

'Come on, son,' he said, turning back toward the barn. 'We have another fifty to do today.'

* * *

As it always did, the dream jerked me awake. My fists were clenched around something soft and I opened my eyes and in the guttering light of my near burnt-out candle discovered my hands were squeezed around the pillow on which I'd fallen asleep. I was in a dreadful sweat. And then I heard the slightest sound and looked up from my fingers and saw a figure in the room, a woman in a white nightshift standing at the desk, her back to me.

I shot bolt upright. 'What in God's name –' I began and at that very moment the candle went out and the room turned black. I leapt from the bed and lunged for the figure but she was too fast for me and I grabbed only air. I heard the slam of the door and the patter of feet fading away along the corridor outside.

I stumbled to the door and out into the corridor. Everything was dark. I looked this way and that, up and down the passage, but couldn't see a thing, no glimpse of a person, no flicker of a light. I had no idea which direction the woman had taken. I stood still and held my breath and by some primitive animal instinct knew the intruder was there too and also holding her breath and immobile. And then, I guess when she knew she would have to breathe out and so give herself away, she was off, and the scamper of bare feet told me the way. I tried to follow but, unable to see even an inch in front of me, I was overwhelmed by the sensation that I was about to collide with something, even though as far as I could remember the corridor was clear of any furniture or other obstruction. My heart was beating fast and I had the constant fear of some harpy about to leap out at me and put her claws into my throat. I shuffled along, hands stretched in front of me to prevent collision with any unseen objects. I could hear nothing because of my own noise, so I paused, and there were a couple of footfalls ahead of me and then silence again. It was a cat-and-mouse game, with my prey waiting until I should move and the sound I made conceal her own movement. I felt my way along the corridor wall and eventually my hands met thin air as I came to a side passage.

I did not know which way to go and stood there shivering in the dark for what seemed like an age. If I chose wrong, she would escape me easily. I had the sense again that she was nearby, although she could surely have gotten far away by now while I had been fumbling around. I suddenly felt a fool because I realised she was playing with me, finding a macabre humour in the chase, letting me think I could catch her when she knew I could not. I strained my ears but everything was silent and then, just as I was about to decide at random and hope to pick the right direction, I heard the merest hint of another's breath, not far away. Instantly I took off, shuffling along to avoid tripping on anything, because I'd never explored this side passage. I heard the soft touch of feet gliding over bare floorboards only a few yards ahead of me and tried to speed up, but somehow my body would not let me, its fear of a collision with my prey too great. The hair on my neck bristled against my collar. My forehead was clammy from the terror of it all. Then, of a sudden, how or why I could not explain, I sensed she was just in front of me, a stretch of the hand – hers or mine – away. I steeled myself, took another step and made a grab, expecting to grasp warm flesh, and met instead something solid and cold that I realised was a wall.

I explored it with the palms of my hands, up and down and from side to side, but found nothing. The corridor ended in a solid wall. I was baffled. I turned and began to creep back toward the main passage. I held my hands out and felt the walls either side of me. The corridor was too narrow for the woman to have slipped past me without our touching. Her disappearance defied all logic. Then, I guess about halfway along this tributary of the main corridor, my left hand felt something different. Further investigation revealed there was a door let into the wall. I fumbled around and eventually met the cold metal of a handle. I turned it and pushed the door, which did not yield. It was evidently locked.

Still, at least the puzzle was explained. The woman must have flattened herself into this doorway and stood there while I crept past. That would have been the moment when I paused, sensing her presence close to me. And then, once I had gone by, she had returned silently to the main corridor.

I made my way slowly back to it and had just reached the junction when I heard a sound that made my blood freeze. A terrible distant laugh, my opponent braying her triumph. I knew it was useless to pursue her now, even had I had the nerve and inclination; she was too far off. I experienced a moment of frustration at her having toyed with me so and gotten the better of me, but it was subsumed by relief from the responsibility of pursuing her further. I returned to my room, where I found and lit another candle. I was so jumpy that the hiss of the match and the shadows dancing on the walls startled me. I almost expected the light to reveal the woman standing right in front of me. I had no key with which to lock my door, so took the chair from my desk and set its back beneath the handle. I knew I would do this every night from now on, to prevent another intrusion.

In my nervous state, sleep was out of the question. I picked up *Moral Treatment* and, without getting undressed, which I knew would make me feel more vulnerable, lay down on my bed and began to read. By the time the first light was stealing around the edges of the window blind, I had finished the book.

6

Next day, fired up with enthusiasm, I went to breakfast to do battle with Morgan, so convinced by the good reverend's arguments that I felt sure my employer could not fail to be impressed by them too. While he sat eating his breakfast in a leisurely manner, I used all my experience in making my case, presenting it as if it were the closing defence speech in some courtroom melodrama. From time to time I glanced at him and found him listening attentively, nodding his head now and then, which made me hope I was winning him over to my way of thinking. At last I had presented all my – that is to say Abrahams's – case and, falling silent, looked at him expectantly.

He sat smiling, and I thought I had carried the day, until I recognised it as the kind of smile one puts on to indulge a small child. At last he spoke. 'I have to admit I admire your enthusiasm,' he began, and I felt a glow of pride, but then he added, 'but I'm afraid it's misplaced. The ideas you espouse are woefully out of date. These things were tried years ago and proved to be a dismal failure.' I opened my mouth to protest but he held up a hand to silence me. 'Oh, I dare say you've read some of the claims these people make and no doubt they had a good outcome once in a while, but generally these theories have long been discredited. You see, these people were priests and unqualified do-gooders; they were not *medical* men. It's only comparatively recently that we doctors have become involved in the mental health problem. It's now generally recognised that insanity is not to do with social pressures and personal misfortune, but is a pathological problem. It's a physical disorder of the brain and, as such, must be managed. It cannot be cured so easily as you and the people who've influenced you think. Believe me, I've had years of experience and I assure you – who've had none – that I know what I'm talking about.'

I protested that surely he must agree that the way the staff at the hospital treated disturbed people could not be helping their condition. Did he not think, I asked, of trying a gentler method?

At that he began to grow angry and his face became red and choleric. 'How many attendants would we have to have for there to be sufficient of them to spend time chattering with the patients? Who will be playing music for them? Who will be supervising their games? Where is the money to come from to pay for the sumptuous feasts you wish to provide them with?'

We batted the thing back and forth until finally I could see that I was getting nowhere. All I achieved was to increase his ire. Finally, at the end of one of his tirades I decided enough was enough. I hung my head and said nothing. There was an awkward silence. It was Morgan who broke it. He cleared his throat and said, 'Look, I'm not an unreasonable man and I don't want to discourage someone who's just starting out in the profession. Here's what I'll do. I'll give you a chance to *prove* your ideas can work.'

I looked up. 'How will you do that?'

'I'll indulge you this far: you may take one patient, any patient you like, so long as it's not one of the violent ones. And you can treat her according to your notions. Separate her from the rest, give her different clothes, she can eat what the staff eat. She can have her own interests, although she'll only have you to play cards with or else she'll have to make do with solitaire.'

I was almost too stunned to speak. 'Y-you're serious?' I said at last.

'Completely.'

'Then thank you, sir.' I was grinning like a fool. 'That's incredibly generous of you. I truly appreciate the opportunity.'

'I should think so,' he said, picking up his coffee cup and taking a sip. He set it down and beamed at me. 'It's the chance to find out for yourself how wrong you are.' He began to rise from the table, even though I'd been so busy talking I'd had no time to eat anything. 'This afternoon you can select your guinea pig.'

Morgan strode along the day room, gesturing expansively with his arms at the wretches ringed around it. 'There you are, take your pick. Select one on whom to practise your experiment. Anyone you like, it's up to you.' He stood still, fingers in his vest pockets, smiling broadly, rocking back and forth on his heels, a poker player smug with a winning hand and enjoying himself immensely.

I looked at the sea of faces; many were muttering to themselves, others gazed into space, or dozed with their eyes closed, or fiddled with their fingers, or picked invisible bugs from their clothes, regarding their actions with intense fascination. Here and there I would find a woman staring at me, sometimes eagerly, as if she required only the merest nod from me to engage me in conversation, or, more often, fearfully, as though she thought I was about to whisk her off for a long cold bath or an afternoon tied to a chair.

I was at a loss. It was impossible to decide on one poor imbecile over another. The important thing was to select someone who would give me the greatest chance of success. Why, exactly, I could not have told you. For what reason was I allowing myself to become involved in this? What good could it possibly do me? It would not help my situation to antagonise Morgan, and yet I knew this was part of my motive. I could not endorse the man's bullish certainty that what he was doing was right. But another cause for acting as I did was that I was a professional and that this was what my part demanded of me. A man who has a book on Moral Treatment in his baggage and who puts its theories into a letter of application for employment, boldly it has to be said, given it obviously went against the current prevailing wind in the treatment of mental illness, would be bound to take Morgan on.

This was all true and very noble indeed – if it had been everything, but the bottom line, I knew, lay in myself, in my own make-up. I had always wanted to challenge authority, ever since that day with my first tender chicken neck, to wrest back the power from those who told me what to do, even though doing so inevitably drew attention to me. It is not what a man with my little foibles should seek to do.

'Well, come on, man! If you can't make your mind up then perhaps I should decide for you? I will pick one at random, yes?'

'No, give me another minute, sir, please.'

I paced slowly along the room looking at all the women along one wall and made the turn around the potbelly stove at the end and started back along the women on the opposite side. The more I strained to find one face that stood out from all the rest, the more one face seemed to merge into another. At one and the same time I felt sorry for them all, as a forlorn mass of humanity and yet also strangely detached because I could not find a single one I could imagine having any normal intercourse with. I decided I might as well give up and let Morgan choose, feeling suddenly hopeless about the whole thing. When regarded practically, in the flotsam and jetsam of society washed up before me, the very concept of Moral Treatment began to seem more and more fanciful. My eyes flicked from one woman to another and my confidence shrivelled and then, just as I was thinking this, I was stopped dead in my tracks.

It was the girl who had given away her bread. The one who had communed silently with me a couple of days earlier. Our eyes locked again and, as before, I saw an indefinable quality in them; madness, certainly, there was no doubt of that, for there was a primitive wildness about the way they stared, but there was intelligence too. Excitement pulsed through me like electricity. Not just my old, dangerous pulse, though that was there, to be sure, because the girl was attractive in her untamed way, but more than that. I could make something of this girl; she had the necessary clay to mould; she was crazy but also bright. Only one thing held me back: the familiar stirring deep within me, the quickening of the heart, the beat of blood in my temples. What if I succumbed to my ancient troubles here? It would end up costing me everything, that much I knew.

'Well?' Morgan was suddenly beside me, tapping his foot. 'That one? Is it to be her?'

The question alarmed me. It was the very one I had always

asked myself. All those other times. That way madness lay, and worse, I knew. Hold back, you fool, I told myself; don't ruin things now when you are safe. Don't do it, man, turn away now before it is too late.

I looked at the girl. She looked back at me. She tossed back her long dark hair as though to let me see her better. Her eyes were black and defiant.

'Yes,' I said slowly. 'Yes, let it be her.'

He beckoned to one of the attendants and spoke quietly to her, indicating the girl with a nod, which I took to be him asking for the patient's name and history. After a short conference with the attendant he came back to me and said, 'Very well, let's go to my office and look at her records. See what you've got for yourself.'

7

Morgan turned the pages of the file. 'Hah! Yes! I remember now. I fear you've given yourself a hard task. The poor girl cannot even communicate properly. Besides being mad, she's probably mentally retarded.'

He looked up at me and smiled, pleased as punch. The smile gradually faded as he saw he'd drawn no reaction from me. He'd expected me to be crestfallen at the news, whereas I did not believe a word of it. The girl's brain might be damaged, true, but even if he couldn't see it, the light of a sharp intelligence positively blazed from her eyes.

Disappointed, he once more studied the file. 'Hmm, let's see, not much to go on. Found in a state of distress wandering near the railroad depot three months ago. Refuses or is unable to tell anyone her name. We gave her the name of Jane Dove. We always call the unknowns after birds, for some reason, don't ask me why, and "Dove" seemed to suit her. No relatives have come for her. The police took her to the city asylum and she was judged mentally impaired and sent here. Origins and age unknown. She could be anything from, say, thirteen to around eighteen. Her height may make her appear older than she is, of course. She has no menses, which may be because she's young and hasn't started them yet or may not

71

signify at all, because it's common for mentally ill women to have delayed menses or for them to cease altogether.'

'You said she was mentally retarded, yet her expression strikes me as intelligent,' I ventured.

This produced a grim smile below the little moustache. 'Don't mistake madness for intelligence. Mental illness often displays a certain intensity that masquerades as it. This girl is illiterate. She is unable to read even simple words and cannot write her own name. She is linguistically backward, too, although whether this is because she was born with impaired faculties or the result of her falling ill later and losing her powers of speech it's impossible to know. Of course it doesn't matter, either way; the end result is the same.'

'She can't talk?'

'Oh yes, she can talk all right, but not in proper English. She speaks a kind of gibberish, mixes up the parts of speech, misses out certain words and so on. The staff have had problems understanding her, and she is unable to converse with the other patients, which of course has increased her isolation and not helped her condition.'

He tossed the file onto the desk between us and I picked it up and flicked through it. There was not much to add to what he had told me. There was a copy of the police report, which gave some brief details from the patrol officer. The only interesting fact here that Morgan had omitted to tell me was that the girl had been making a nuisance of herself accosting passers and asking them to help her. Various people had tried to assist her but had subsequently found her to be not in her right mind, as she became increasingly distressed, and some Good Samaritan had gone in search of a policeman. There were her admittance papers from the city asylum. The examination report from the doctor there, all of one page, concluded that the girl was insane, and sufficiently agitated to be a danger to herself or to others, and on that basis she had been sent to the island. Morgan's intake assessment was more of the same and you could easily believe he had simply copied the other one, accepting without challenge what it said and not making a proper diagnosis of his own. The sole new detail here was that he had commented on the girl's inability to speak normally and the difficulty he had understanding her. One thing, though, stood out. In order to test her literacy, and to trick her into revealing her identity, which she had so far refused to do or had been incapable of, Morgan asked her to sign her name. The girl became extremely agitated at the very suggestion and when he offered the pen to her she struck it from his hand, even though she had thitherto shown not the slightest inclination to violence. She had begun shouting, saying over and over again the same thing, 'Sir, I cannot read. I cannot read. You will not trick me into writing my name, because I incapable.' Morgan had underlined the last three words, obviously because of the odd use of language, and written 'sic' in the margin.

I made to hand the file back to him but he waved it away. 'No, keep it; you will need to add your notes to it. She's your patient now. I'll give you until the end of the year to discover for yourself how futile in practice your theories are. After that, we'll have no more unscientific nonsense about Moral Treatment.'

I swear his eyes twinkled as he spoke. If he was indulging me in this, I saw, it was not only for my benefit but for his own too. He drew great satisfaction, it seemed, from the prospect of my failure. As I hugged the file to my chest I thought I could have no better incentive to succeed.

* * *

The arrangement Morgan made with me concerning Jane Dove was that I could see her whenever I wished during my spare time and at any time during the working day so long as my regular duties were fulfilled. I could also prescribe my own regime for her according to my theories, providing that it did not put too great an additional strain on staff resources.

My responsibilities included supervising the daily exercise walk; assessing new arrivals, which I did first in conjunction with Morgan and was to do later on my own; judging when treatments including the use of restraints such as straitjackets and the chair were necessary; and overseeing hydrotherapy, as well as helping him make systematic progress reports on all patients. I was not allowed to visit the more violent inmates on the third floor until I had more experience. Morgan told me he would introduce me to them when he felt I was ready, although of course I saw them every day at exercise, walking on the rope.

Eager though I was to get started with Jane Dove, I needed first to put in place what was necessary to follow the precepts of Moral Treatment. It would be no use introducing the patient to a new routine of kindness and close personal attention if at the same time she was still suffering under aspects of the harsh system that ruled the hospital. So I needed to isolate her from the rest of the patients.

Fortunately I found that she already slept in a room on her own because she was a somnambulist whose nightly ramblings had disturbed the other patients in the dormitory where she'd been placed when first she arrived; consequently she now slept alone.

Next day, while she was in the day room with the other patients, I visited her room and found to my delight that, with an adjustment here and there, and a few additions, it would serve not only as a bedroom but as a sitting room, too. At the moment it contained a bed and a chamber pot and nothing else. I spent an hour wandering the hospital and discovered a good many rooms that were not used or at least hardly at all. From these I managed to requisition a good-sized rug, two old and battered but still serviceable armchairs and a small washstand complete with bowl, as well as a large chipped jug. In one of the unused rooms I found a couple of prints hanging on the wall, unnamed landscapes that looked as if they might be copies of English pictures, for they featured idyllic green countryside, complete with sheep. I thought them restful to a disturbed mind and had them taken up to the girl's room along with all my other finds.

I was in there arranging things in as pleasant a way as possible, thinking of it as a stage set and working out the most practical and pleasing place for the rug and where to position the armchairs, deciding where she would sit and where I, when I heard footsteps behind me. I looked round and found O'Reilly, the chief attendant.

'And what would you be a-doing of here, sir?' she said, her eyes sweeping the transformed room. 'Was you thinking of moving in here yourself?'

'No, not at all,' I stammered. 'This is all for Jane Dove. Didn't Dr Morgan inform you of our – our – little – uh – experiment?'

'No sir, he did not,' she snapped.

'Well, Jane Dove is to be my guinea pig.' O'Reilly looked baffled. 'The subject of the experiment. It is to try a different regimen, one based on Moral Treatment.' She looked more mystified still. 'It's something I'm anxious to put into practice here. The idea is to treat the patient with kindness, consideration and close attention, in general as much as possible like a normal person.'

'Ah, sir, but you see, they're not normal, are they?' I noticed for the first time how hard her face was, the hair tugged back into a tight bun as though to punish her features. 'They're mad. That's why they're here.' She smiled.

'I know that, of course. The question is how best to treat them. So they may be cured and returned into the world.'

'Cured? Let out, you say? Pardon me for saying so, sir, but I think it's you that's mad. Don't you realise they are never cured? Once they're in here, they're here for life. It's very rare for any of them to leave, sir. They're beyond that.'

I stood open-mouthed. Morgan had never told me this. He'd spoken of teaching the patients self-control, of suppressing their disruptive tendencies, of making them manageable. I had assumed this was so they could one day resume something resembling a normal life.

I gathered my wits together and made an attempt to pretend I'd known this all along. 'You don't believe they can ever be cured, then?' I said.

'No, sir, I do not. And you'll soon see, sir. Especially with this girl. She's a quiet one, but don't let that fool you. She's the maddest of the lot.' And before I could ask her to expand on this she flounced angrily from the room.

8

After this it was with some trepidation that in my spare time between the end of my working day and dinner that evening I ventured upon my first meeting with the girl, Jane Dove. It was essential I saw her before her bedtime, to prepare her for the transformation of her room. Otherwise, instead of helping her, the shock of entering it and finding everything altered might only confuse her more. For all I knew, she might not recognise it after the changes I had made and think she was back in her own home, wherever that was, or worse, be plunged into some fantasy in which she imagined she'd been abducted.

I had her brought to the small office that had been allotted to me. The attendant who escorted her was quite young, perhaps only eighteen or so, and, I noticed, treated the girl gently, speaking to her softly and kindly. I guessed she was not long in the job and, being naturally sympathetic, had not had this knocked out of her yet by the rigour of the place and the poor example set by most of the other attendants. I asked her her name. 'Eva Carlsen, sir,' she replied. She had a slight Scandinavian accent. I guessed she must have come here with her parents from Sweden or Denmark, probably when she was quite young.

I told her she should leave us and that I would call her to return the girl to the dining hall when I was finished with her.

The subject of my experiment stood before me shivering, waif-like in spite of her height – for she was tall, easily as tall as me, and would have towered over Morgan had he been standing beside her. Her eyes flicked this way and that, assessing the room, like a cornered wild animal looking for an escape route.

In as relaxed and kind a tone as I could manage, I said, 'Please be seated, Jane,' and gestured to the chair opposite me on the other side of my desk. She gingerly settled herself down, perching on the edge of the seat like a bird, ready to take off at the slightest sign of danger.

I gave her a warm smile. She did not return it but instead ran a finger around the inside of the collar of her dress, and began to scratch the top of her back, squirming awkwardly in the chair to reach the itch. I decided to wait until this operation was finished, but when it was she began scratching at the dress around her midriff. Eventually she stopped this, too, and let her hands settle in her lap. Only when she was perfectly still did she allow herself to look at me, or rather stare into me, with those black coals of eyes. I smiled again and said, 'Not the softest of materials, those dresses.'

She did not return the smile but leaned forward earnestly and said softly, 'Sir, they have calicoed my soul.'

I opened my mouth to comment on this peculiar use of words, which naturally jarred with me, being grammatically incorrect and seeming to confirm what Morgan had told me about her speaking gibberish, but closed my lips again without saying anything, surprised. She had used the noun 'calico' as a verb, which was technically not possible. But *was* it gibberish? In a weird way it made sense. It did what language is supposed to do, conveyed something to me. And something far more meaningful than merely confirming my remark. I was taken aback. What she had actually done was imply a comment upon the whole hospital system, as represented by the rough uniform it had clothed her in. The word suggested it had chafed her inner self, just as the garment she was wearing had her body. I somehow understood all that from her odd manipulation of this one word.

I decided this wasn't the time to tackle her about misuse of language. So long as I was able to understand her, correctness did not matter for the present, and there was always the possibility that if I made her self-conscious about it, she would cease to speak at all.

I shuffled some papers on the desk in front of me and pretended to study them to give myself time to think. 'Well now, Jane . . .'

'That is not my name.'

'No, of course not, but we have to call you something. Perhaps you would prefer us to use your real name?'

'Jane will do. After all, what's in a name?'

I wondered if this was a deliberate reference to *Romeo and Juliet*. It didn't have to be, because the phrase has long since passed into daily use, to the extent of becoming a cliché. The girl could easily have come across it without ever having heard of Shakespeare.

'What indeed?' I said. 'A rose by any other name would smell as sweet.'

She made no reply, but stared blankly back at me, giving me no idea whether the quotation was familiar to her or not. Was that a faint glint of defiance I saw in her eyes, or was I simply ascribing to her something that wasn't there? There was a long pause that grew more awkward for me as it went on and she showed no sign of wishing to end it. I cleared my throat again. 'Well, then, uh, Jane, let's try to fill in a few facts about you. Tell me, what brought you here?'

'A boat, sir.'

'Hah! That's right enough. We all came here by that means. Only way to get to an island.'

She considered this and I saw that she had not been making a joke. She had taken my question literally.

'You could skate here, sir, if the winter was very cold and the water froze.'

This was true but also completely crazy in the context of our conversation, or rather the conversation I was trying to have. I wondered for a moment whether she was mocking me, but when I examined her features they gave nothing away. I decided not to challenge her on this but to let myself be carried along by the flow of conversation. I would not do anything that discouraged her from talking or that suggested she was ill. In this way I felt she would become more talkative and I would find out more about her.

'And do you like to skate, Jane?'

She screwed up her mouth and put her head on one side, the way a chicken will, as though she needed to think about it. I presumed she was battling with her memory, trying to grasp something half-recalled.

'I think I do,' she said at last. And then suddenly her face brightened and she said, 'Yes, yes, I do. I am quite proficient on the ice, sir, although not so fast or elegant as . . . as . . .'

Her words disappeared into a mumble and then dried up altogether. She knitted her brows, troubled.

'As who?' I ventured gently, seeking to prompt her.

She shook her head, like a dog just out of the river shaking off water, as if to clear her thoughts. 'I – I unremember now. I think I used to skate around the lake on my own.'

There it was again, another made-up word, but again one that made perfect sense.

'The lake? And where was this lake, Jane? Can you tell me that?'

She thought another minute or so and then slowly shook her head. 'No, it was just a lake. That's all I know. It was surrounded by woods you had to walk through to get to it. They darked and – and –'

'And what?'

She lifted her head and looked straight at me. 'Do you believe in ghosts, sir?'

'Do you?'

She broke into a smile. 'You won't trick me like that. I asked you first. If I say I do and you do not, then you will think it another reason to call me mad.'

'I have not called you mad at all. Do you think you're mad?'

'Well, I am in the madhouse, so I suppose I must be. Although you are here too and you no doubt consider yourself sane.'

'That's because I'm a doctor. You're a patient. We're here for different reasons.'

She looked at me knowingly. 'Are we, sir? Are we really?'

Once again I had the feeling she saw right through me and her stare made me uncomfortable enough to lower my eyes to my papers and begin shuffling them again. Our little talk was not going at all the way I'd planned and I needed to bring it back on course. 'Now,' I said, all businesslike to enable me to ignore her question, 'you're probably wondering why I've asked you here.'

'Not at all, sir. I have long since ceased to wonder about anything that is done in this place. It all seems crazy to me.'

'All right, well, anyway, Dr Morgan and I have chosen you to take part in a trial of a different sort of treatment. You will no longer sit with the other women during the day but will be on your own, in your room. I have made certain alterations to it, to make it more comfortable, so you may use it as a sitting room as well as a bedroom. You will take your exercise separately, too, and mostly your walks will be with me, so that we can talk –'

'And what will we talk about, sir?'

'Oh, well, I haven't thought yet.' A nervous giggle trickled from my lips, making me feel foolish. 'Just, you know, anything that comes to mind. Anything you want to discuss.'

'Oh, I see.' She considered this a little. 'I will try to think of some things to talk about then, sir.'

I began to be exasperated by her manner. The way she took everything so literally. It frustrated me. I suppose I had expected gratitude that she was to be freed from the dulling daily routine of the place and that she would be flattered by my attention. Instead, I almost had the feeling she was making fun of me, teasing me for wanting her to be pleased.

'It's not another test,' I said. 'You don't have to have a list of topics prepared in advance. Just say whatever comes naturally.'

'And if nothing does, sir?'

'Why then, say nothing!'

She nodded to herself, considering this.

'You will also eat on your own, in a little room off the main dining hall. And you will be given better food, the same food as the attendants have, which is altogether more wholesome.'

She said nothing.

'Why do you not comment on what I've just told you?'

'You said to say nothing if I have nothing to say.'

I could not help a sigh of exasperation escaping from me and yet I wanted to laugh too. I tried again. 'Does it not excite you, the idea of proper food?'

'I have always had the appetite of a bird, sir. A little bird, that is, not one of the bad black ones, the rooks and the crows. Although now I shall eat all alone, like a crow.'

'I'm not sure I know the difference between rooks and crows.' I was glad of the opportunity to turn the conversation in the direction of light inconsequential chat.

'Oh, it's easy, sir. If you see a lot of crows together then they are rooks. And if you see a rook on its own, it's a crow.'

My laughter was genuine this time, for the joke was a good one, and she could not help smiling, her eyes sparkling, as if saying, You see, I'm a whole lot smarter than you thought, and possibly smarter than you.

'Oh, and so you will not be bored sitting on your own, I shall arrange for you to have some books.'

'That will be useless, sir, unless they contain plenty of pictures. Didn't they tell you? I cannot read.'

'You don't know how to read? Were you never taught? Really?'

She leaned forward slightly, confidential. 'It's the truth, sir, I promise you.'

'Well then, perhaps that will be part of our therapy.'

She recoiled. 'What do you mean, sir?'

'I will teach you to read. It's not difficult. You will pick it up in no time.'

She began to shake her head from side to side. The movement was so violent I feared she might injure herself. 'Oh no, no, sir, that impossibles. It's unpermitted. I am unallowed to learn to read.'

I was getting used to her strange manner of speech. 'Not allowed? How so? Who has said so?'

She didn't answer but looked sullenly at her hands, which were wrestling with each other in her lap. She began picking at the edges of the nails on one hand with those of the other. She was agitated in the extreme and it was as if all the bravado she'd displayed up to now had drained out of her. I did not push her. We sat in silence for a good couple of minutes. Finally she looked up at me from beneath her brows and said quietly, 'If you don't mind, sir, I think I should like to go now. I should like to alone in my room.'

I rang the bell and, after a couple of minutes, which we spent in silence, with the girl gazing intently at her fingers, Eva Carlsen reappeared. I told her to take the girl to her room and wait outside until the bell announced it was dinnertime. I explained where the girl would be eating, apart from the other patients. As they were leaving, I said to Eva, 'I would like you, whenever your other duties permit, to be responsible for looking after this young woman. She is not to be treated as the other patients. With her everything is to be softly, softly. No matter what her behaviour, it is to be met wherever possible with kindness, do you understand?'

She smiled and bobbed a little curtsy. 'Sir, I hope I am always kind to everyone.'

I laid a hand on her shoulder and returned her smile. 'I can see that. It's why I am asking you rather than someone else. I will speak to Mrs O'Reilly about it.'

9

Some days later I found myself sitting at breakfast, having just put myself on the outside of a fair meal of ham and eggs, and feeling pretty happy with life. Here I was, growing into my new role and with every prospect of a long run. I was comfortable; the lodgings and food were more than satisfactory; you could not call my duties onerous.

At first I feared my ignorance and complete lack of medical training would betray me, but I soon relaxed because it was not long before it became apparent to me that for all Morgan's bombast about scientific methods and his lectures on brain abnormalities, he didn't actually know much more about mental illness than the next man, even when the next man was me.

Although I could see that much of the work would rapidly become routine, like a popular play whose super-ficial appeal soon begins to wear thin, I had my Moral Treatment experiment to keep me amused and offer me some intellectual interest. I was pleased, too, with the character I had established for myself here. I could see I was respected and liked by everyone, except perhaps O'Reilly, a bully whose contempt for the patients naturally made her annoyed by what she saw as softness in the way

I handled them. But I could tell Morgan liked me and appreciated the obvious sincerity of my beliefs, even though he didn't agree with them. I was my own man, everyone could see, with my own ideas, and not just some docile lapdog.

So everything was going swimmingly and, provided I kept a lid on things and stopped my old nature from resurfacing and sabotaging me, I figured I could easily remain here until it was safe to leave. What could possibly go wrong?

The answer arrived a moment later when a servant came in with the morning post, which she handed to Morgan. He flicked through the envelopes without opening them and then said, 'Ah, here's one for you.'

My mouth was half open to say that was impossible – *it impossibles* – and wave the proffered missive away when I caught sight of the writing on the envelope and read the words 'Dr John Shepherd'. I took the letter from him and sat staring at it as Morgan opened one of his own and began reading the contents.

What an imbecile I was! Congratulating myself on my cleverness in making myself so comfortable here and over-looking something so obvious, something moreover that was now burning my fingers. Why had I not thought things through? Why had I imagined myself springing from the train wreck like a newborn? To let myself think that my life commenced here, with no preamble!

Morgan looked up from his reading. 'Well, go on, man. Aren't you going to open it?'

'What? Oh yes, yes of course.' I picked up his paper knife and slit open the envelope. Inside were a couple of sheets of writing paper, densely written in a neat, feminine hand. There was an Ohio address at the top of the page.

My Dearest John,

What is happening? Why have you not written? You promised to do so as soon as you were settled in your new position but it has now been nearly two weeks and not a word has reached me. My mind is a whirlwind of worry. Please, please write back the instant you read this and let me know you are alive and well. I am going out of my mind here with the worry of it all.

You will think me the very model of a silly wittering woman, I know, but my first thought was that it was out of sight out of mind. That once removed from your orbit I have ceased to matter in your life and am as little in your thoughts as you are the opposite in mine, that is to say, always, for I have no one else in the world but you. If such is the case, I must lose all hope for the future, for if after just leaving me you ceased to think of me, then what hope would I have after a month, or three, or six?

I could not account otherwise for your silence, until today, when we first had news in the Bugle of the recent railroad disaster. As soon as I saw the paper, my heart began to beat so fast I thought it would explode out of my chest and my head to pound, so that I had to sit down, on a bench right outside Mr Applegate's store, where I'd bought the paper after seeing the headline. It was several minutes before I could calm myself sufficiently to read the article. It was with my heart in my mouth that I commenced it, and when I came to the details of those killed and injured I could scarcely breathe, expecting as I went down the page to see the name John Shepherd jump out at me. I nearly fainted at the sight of 'John' followed by an 'S', but then found it was some other name starting with that letter. I finished it relieved not to see your name among the victims but then saw the note at the foot of the column that the list was incomplete because many of the dead and injured had not yet been identified. I immediately put on my cloak and set off to the railroad depot, where I consulted the stationmaster, Mr Wickets. He had no more information concerning the casualties than was in the paper, so I questioned him as to the possibility of your having been on the wrecked train, because naturally I have no idea of the different lines and routes of the railroad system. To my alarm, he informed me that the line in question was the one you would have taken from Columbus, although of course I had no way of knowing at what time and on which train you left that city. You had told me you had some purchases to make there before commencing your new employment and any one of a number of trains in the timetable was possible.

Please forgive the rambling nature of this letter. I am distraught with worry and cannot think clearly. I do not know how accurate the newspaper report was, if you are one of the unidentified bodies or among the injured taken to the hospital, or if you were even on the train at all. I pray God that you are safe and if so please will you wire me immediately to put me out of my misery, or if that is not practical – I know, at least I hope and pray, you are on the island and may not be able to telegraph – will you write back by express letter?

If I have not heard from you by Saturday, then I shall take the train east and come out to the island to find out for myself.

Please, please write and tell me you are safe. Even if my first foolish fears are realised and it is simply that you *no longer love me, at least, my darling, tell me that you live, that your heart still beats in this world, even if not for me?*

I love you and always will, dead or alive.

Your ever-loving fiancée

Caroline Adams

'Bad news?'

Morgan's voice came to me from far off, as when someone wakes you and interrupts a dream. 'What?' I said, looking up, half delirious.

'I said, is it bad news, old man? You're as white as a ghost.'

My head was swimming. I couldn't speak. This was a thunderbolt, striking out of the blue, that could ruin everything and even destroy me. My first thought was to jump up from the table, run to my room, throw a few things into my valise and hurry down to the jetty before the morning boat left and return with it to the city. And I almost did it, until reason took over and I closed my eyes and took a few deep breaths, the way I always do with stage fright. Do not panic, I told myself; there will be a way to handle this. There must be.

I felt a hand on my arm and opened my eyes, to find Morgan peering at me. 'What's wrong, old man? You don't look at all well.'

'Sorry,' I muttered, 'it's nothing. Just a bit of food went down the wrong way. Couldn't get my breath for a moment there.'

He shrugged. 'Well, you do tend to bolt your food like a man who's been starved for a month. You need to slow down a little.' He pulled out his watch. 'Although not too much:

it's seven minutes after eight and we really should be making our rounds in another eight minutes.'

I stuffed the letter in my jacket pocket and wiped my mouth with a napkin. 'Yes, of course. Shall we go now?'

10

It was a difficult morning with the letter burning a hole in my pocket. It was all I could think about. I longed to take it out and read it through again. I needed to find an answer to the problem or plan my flight; I could not simply sit and do nothing and wait for this woman to arrive.

Once or twice I was wrenched from my anxiety by Morgan speaking to me impatiently and realised he was repeating himself because I'd not heard him the first time. It was obvious he was growing frustrated with my distractedness and I had to force myself to concentrate on my tasks. But halfway through the morning he wanted to consult something in his office and while he was busy there I asked his secretary, who sat outside, when I would have to have a letter ready by if I wanted it to go next day. She said the daily boat left at nine and I would need to have it in the mailbox on the wall in the hall before eight thirty, which was when the letters were collected. I asked her some more about the postal service and worked out that provided my letter was in the box next day it would reach Ohio in time to forestall Caroline Adams's visit.

It was in this agitated state that, after the morning round, I slipped away to see Jane Dove in her room. There was no response when I knocked on the door, so I opened it tentatively, thinking she might be asleep. Instead I found she had moved one of the armchairs so that it faced the window and was sitting watching the mist rolling off the river and across the lawns. She appeared to be in a trance and seemed not to register my presence.

I cleared my throat. She jumped and turned and stared at me. It was as if it took her a moment to swim to the surface from her immersion in her reverie.

I gave her a smile. 'Where were you?' I asked gently.

Her brow furrowed, like one trying to grasp something, to identify some distant memory, as if attempting to decipher what was written on the missing page of a notebook from the impression the pencil has left upon the page beneath it.

'I – I was by a lake but I could not see the water on account of the mist. I could hear the rooks cawing.'

And indeed, as she said this, I realised I could hear that very sound from outside now. It was obvious the two things, the mist and the sound of the birds, had triggered some recollection in her, presumably of her home. Sensing this might be an opportunity to lift the curtain of her amnesia, I pulled the other armchair over and sat down facing her, our knees almost touching. She wasn't looking at me but was once again gazing out the window, and I understood she was seeing not the hospital grounds but that other unknown place.

'What else?' I asked softly. 'Can you tell me anything more about what you saw in your mind's eye?'

She made no answer and we sat like that for a good minute until finally she shook her head and came out of her trance completely and looked straight at me, seeing me properly at last. 'It's gone. I can't see it any more. I don't know if it was real. It feels like a dream.'

I had a sudden inspiration. 'Perhaps it was the lake upon which you skated?'

She considered this a moment. 'Or perhaps I dreamed that too.'

We sat in silence once more and then I said, 'What have you been doing with yourself all morning? Are you not bored?'

'It is better than day-rooming it with the others.'

'You prefer being alone?'

She smiled. 'I prefer armchairing to benching.'

There it was again, that strange use of English, that verbing of nouns, but once again it made perfect sense. It communicated, which is surely all words are meant to do.

'I think it is not good for you to have nothing to do,' I said. 'My feeling is you are more likely to recover your past by some stimulus that reminds you of it, as the mist and the rooks did just now. But sitting here struggling to do so strikes me as not being the best way to do it. You need more ideas put into your mind to provoke recollection.'

She looked at me blankly.

'I've decided I will teach you to read.'

Immediately she shrank back into her chair, clasping its arms so tightly with her hands that her knuckles showed white. Her expression was one of horror. 'Oh, no, no, sir. Not that. I have alreadied you about that. It is strictly unallowed.'

'Who *unallowed* it? Who?'

Her grip loosened as she thought about this. She bit her lip and finally shook her head. 'I unremember that. I only know it is.'

94

I pondered this a little. She seemed so terrified by the very thought of learning to read I decided it would serve no purpose to push the matter. 'Very well, we'll leave that for now. I will say only one thing. Books and reading are good for the human mind. They are the very bedrock upon which all education is founded. They are the fount of culture. Whoever has told you otherwise, whoever has forbidden you these benefits, cannot be a good person. Think it over; you may come to change your mind.'

Her expression did not alter and we sat again without speaking, until at last, ever conscious of the time as I had become under the regime of Morgan's constant clock-watching, I rose and said, 'I have asked Eva to visit you for half an hour of her spare time. She will bring some needle-work to keep you occupied.'

Her face relaxed. 'I unremember if that is something I can do but I have a strong feeling it is not.'

'In that case Eva will instruct you. It is part of the Moral Treatment to keep you occupied. It does not do for the mind to dwell on things.'

She made no reply but turned her head and looked out the window again, exactly as she had been doing when I came in. 'I will see you again soon,' I said, pushing back my chair and getting to my feet. She did not respond and I found that when I went out I instinctively closed the door quietly behind me so as not to disturb her meditation again.

For the rest of the day I was preoccupied with the letter from Caroline Adams, so much so that during the exercise hour I hardly spoke to Jane Dove. She in turn seemed to be lost in her own thoughts. It was only when the bell rang to signal that the session was over and we were turning back toward the building that she broke the silence. I realised it was the first time she had ever initiated a conversation between us.

'I was thinking . . .' she began, then stopped and licked her lips nervously.

'Yes . . . ?' This was said gently. She had never so far ventured to tell me any of her thoughts and I did not want to pressure her, which instinct told me would only make her clam up. I continued walking beside her, looking down at the ground, as if what she had to say was of no consequence at all to me, unless she wished it to be.

She cleared her throat. 'I was thinking about what you said concerning reading.' She paused and I simply nodded to encourage her to continue. 'As I have told you, it is unpermissioned. But *looking* at books is not.'

I was, I admit, slow to follow and my response was crass. 'But there's not much point if you can't read.'

She stopped and turned and looked me boldly in the face. 'But some books have pictures in them, do they not? I think I would like to study the pictures.'

This was an interesting development and no mistake. 'Very well, we will go now to the library and see what we can find.'

On the way I tried to make up for my earlier ignoring of her by engaging her in conversation, even though all I seemed capable of was the most pathetic kind of small talk. After all, what does one say to a lunatic one hardly knows? I asked her how she found her room and whether she was enjoying the better food now, to both of which she replied enthusiastically and gratefully, although I could tell only half her mind was on what she was saying. I saw she was eager to get to the library.

Once there, I indicated the bookshelves with a sweep of my arm and told the girl to help herself. I said I, too, would look for books with prints or colour plates in them. I began at the shelves where the non-fiction books were ranged – but not the medical, which I did not feel at all suitable for a young woman or likely to be beneficial to anyone with a mental affliction. After flicking through a few volumes, I came across a book of Audubon's pictures of birds in gorgeous colour plates and quite lost myself in admiring the vividness of the hues, the reds and yellows of exotic parrots and the lifelike rendering of the creatures, and so failed to pay attention to what the girl was up to. I suppose this was because I was not a trained medical man; I had not learned to put the patient first. Thinking about it, I do not know whether as a human being I ever learned to put another person before myself.

Eventually, though, I looked up from the bird book, eager to show it to her, since I was excited to find something that so exactly answered our purpose, a book full of beautiful and colourful images that would give her great pleasure to sit and study. To my surprise, I saw the girl was over at the shelves containing fiction, staring into an open book she had in her hands.

'I doubt you'll find much there,' I called across to her.

She looked over her shoulder at me. 'On the contrary, sir, I have goldstruck. There are many books here I should like.'

I closed the Audubon and, still holding it, walked over to her. She held out the book she was looking at and I saw there was a black and white print on the page. I put the Audubon under my arm and took the other book from her. The picture showed a little girl sitting on a beach, and behind her an inverted boat with a chimney emitting smoke poking up from what had once been the hull and was now the roof.

I recognised it immediately as the Peggotty house from *David Copperfield* in the original Phiz illustration.

'Yes, that's something.' I flicked through the rest of the volume. 'But there aren't many pictures, considering it's such a long book.'

'There are enough for me,' she replied. 'And the length of the book unconsequences; I will not be looking at the other pages.'

I closed the Dickens and swapped it for the Audubon, which I opened, flicking through the pages, revealing a cascade of colour. 'Would you not prefer this? The whole book is made up of pictures; there is more for you to look at.'

She eyed the book suspiciously. 'I think I would rather the other one.'

'Are you sure? Why would you not like this?'

'Does it contain a picture of a rook?'

I consulted the index, found that it did and turned to the appropriate page. I held it out to her.

She turned her head away. 'In that case, I should unlike it. I unlike rooks. I would unlike to sit in my room and look at a picture of one.'

I became exasperated. 'But that's craz—' I began and then realised that this sort of oddness was only to be expected; the girl was here, after all, because she was mad. 'Forgive me. The point I'm trying to make is that just because there's a picture of a rook in the book, it doesn't mean you have to look at it.'

'Ah, but, sir, I would know it was there.'

I sighed. 'Very well.' I swapped the books over again. 'But what is the use of this other book that has pictures to illustrate a story, one you cannot follow without reading it?'

'I may not be able to read it but I can sit and look at them and make up my own stories. I can look at the picture of that funny upside-down boat and try to imagine the kind of people who live in it. It will while away many an hour for me, up there, alone in my room.'

I wondered for a moment whether this would be good for her, sitting and making things up, fashioning for herself a fantasy world to retreat into, when surely what I should be doing was getting her to engage with real life. But when I saw her looking at me with such an eager expression, eyes shining bright, cheeks flushed with excitement, the pulse beating in that lovely long white neck, I hadn't the heart to refuse. Besides, I had spent my whole life taking people into worlds of make-believe for a few hours here and there and who was I to argue it might be bad for them? Didn't we all need to escape the harsh realities of the world sometimes, and didn't this poor girl more than most?

I smiled. 'All right, you can have that one.'

She laid her fingers on the back of my hand, the one that held the book and said, 'Oh thank you, thank you, sir. I cannot tell you how I grateful you.'

We stood like that, her hand upon mine, like a butterfly that had landed there, saying nothing, until of a sudden it became awkward and, at the same instant, we both snatched our hands away.

11

This progress with my special patient gladdened me for all of twenty minutes after I had left her in her room and then, once again, I felt an undertow of dread as I remembered the business of the letter. I racked my brains for what to do. The first thought was to flee immediately, but the problem was, where to? Although I was reasonably certain I was officially dead, that would not prevent a policeman recognising me. I had insufficient money to hide myself away for long. Shepherd had had very little cash upon his person. As for coming by any more, my former profession was closed to me for ever. I could hardly put myself on display to the general public and not expect someone to recognise me after all the newspaper coverage. And anyway, it was like any other trade, a small world in which everyone knew everyone else. Even if I could manage to disguise myself in some way it wouldn't help. In my line, name and reputation were what got you work, things I had built up over years of hard graft. Without them I would have to start at the bottom again and I might go months without landing something.

No, my only hope was to do what had sprung into my mind immediately after the train wreck, as soon as I looked in Shepherd's jacket pocket and found the letter from Morgan offering him a job at the hospital. To lie low here, amass a little capital and then, when everyone had all but forgotten me, head out west to some obscure place where no one knew me and look for some new enterprise. In the meantime, all I had to do was to control myself, to make sure I did not get into any trouble of the old sort, which so far, I congratulated myself, I had been able to do. It looked as if the survival instinct had triumphed over all my normal – or should I say abnormal? – inclinations.

So there was nothing for it. One way or another I had to solve the problem of Caroline Adams. If she received no reply to her letter, she would show up here next week and all would be up. But how could I reply to her? The handwriting would give me away.

In the course of my often precarious career I've once or twice been forced to forge another person's writing and reckoned I could do so now, if only I could find a sample of Shepherd's hand. So as soon as dinner was finished I made my excuses to Morgan and slipped away to my room. There I turned Shepherd's valise inside out. I examined every bit of it. I even took my razor and made a slit in the lining just on the off chance he might have hidden something there, although what and why I did not know. Nothing!

I went through the clothes, item by item, but they held no surprises. Then I remembered there had been a few pencilled notes in the margins of *Moral Treatment* and took it up and began feverishly thumbing through it. I studied them long and hard but they were simply scrawled phrases from which it would be difficult to formulate an individual style. They offered no reliable guide to how the man wrote a letter in pen and ink, nor would I have the least idea how he signed his name. I struggled for a while, examining each note in turn, comparing the individual letters and even taking a pen and copying them one by one, trying to assemble them into a viable script. I had just begun to think I might be getting somewhere when I was thrown into utter despair as another thought occurred to me: how did I even know these notes were Shepherd's? He could have borrowed the book or been given it by someone else who had made the marginalia. I tossed my pen down in defeat. How could I forge what I had never seen?

Then I recalled my first day there, in Morgan's office, when he picked up the letter from his desk, the letter I was supposed to have written. He must still have that letter now; he was such a fussy, precise, methodical man it was not at all possible he would have thrown it away. Ergo all I had to do was get hold of it and copy the writing. I leapt from my chair in jubilation and then at once slumped back heavily onto it as I realised that gaining possession of the letter was easier said than done.

The first thought I had was to simply go to Morgan and ask for it. He could hardly refuse. The trouble was I couldn't come up with any justification for doing that. He'd be bound to ask me why I wanted it and there was no logical reason. No, if I wanted the letter, I would have to steal it.

I lay on my bed in a real funk for the next couple of hours waiting for everyone to retire for the night. I listened as one by one the sounds of the place faded – patients wailing, their unearthly ghostly caterwauling, and the attendants barking out their orders and remonstrances – until there was nothing but the occasional lone cry, and the creaking of the house putting itself to rest, settling down upon its ancient complaining joists, accompanied from outside by the whispered comments of the wind.

When I was quite sure no one was about, I rose from my bed, lit a candle and set about my task. I had spent much of the last few hours making an inventory of the contents of my room in my head, trying to think whether it contained anything with which to pick a lock – a pin or needle perhaps – but nothing had occurred and I cursed myself for having returned the cheese knife to the kitchen. Now I went through the same search physically, looking in every nook and cranny, without any luck. In the end I set off on my quest with no great hope. If Morgan's office were locked, then I would fall at the first hurdle.

Once again the night-time corridors of the old house filled me with dread of what might lurk in its dark corners, my hair on end at the moaning of some distant lunatic, and from without, the answering hoot of an owl. I shivered at the thought of how close I had come to death, how recently we had rubbed shoulders twice, how he had had his icy hand upon my collar, only for the most spectacular piece of chance to allow me to wriggle free. In the near blackness now, part of me knew that this was not the end of the matter, that he might be here in the shadows, biding his time until the right moment to claim me came.

I reached the front hall and Morgan's office. As I stretched out my hand for the doorknob, it shook uncontrollably, like a sick old man's. I almost dared not touch the brass for fear of failure, but there was nothing for it and in the end I gripped the handle and turned – and lo and behold the door swung open. It had not been locked. I told myself what a fool I had been to let myself get so worked up about it. After all, why would Morgan want to lock his office? It was out of bounds to the patients, which left only the attendants, and since it almost certainly contained nothing but records and papers, what interest would they have had in poking about in it? Which left, of course, only me.

I stepped inside, closed the door gently behind me and set to work. There were four wooden filing cabinets along one wall and I placed my candleholder on top of the first and started in on it. As I had expected, everything was as meticulously arranged as Morgan's appearance, as neat and tidy as his necktie or his moustache. In the first cabinet I found the patient records, in alphabetical order. The next seemed to contain all the administrative paperwork for the hospital. There were lists of purchases of food and clothing, copies of contracts with suppliers and so on. This might hold information that could be useful to me at another time but was not what I was after now. My heart leapt when I discovered that the third cabinet contained correspondence. The final file in the top drawer of the three ended at 'H', and thus I figured 'S' would reside in the bottom one and skipped out the middle. My surmise proved correct and I began flicking through the files, finding Shackleton, Shadrack, Sheedy and . . . Shipton. There was no Shepherd. I went back to the beginning of 'S' and worked my way through every bit of paper in it. Perhaps Morgan had misfiled it, or rather not Morgan, you could not imagine him ever making such an error, but the secretary who would have done the filing for him. I knew it was a long shot but I was desperate. It wasn't there. Despondently I closed the drawer and proceeded to the fourth and final cabinet, knowing it would surely be a waste of time. I saw at once it was what I was looking for; the files in it were related to the staff.

I was flicking through them, looking for 'S', when the name O'Reilly jumped out at me. I stood still and listened for a moment. Utter silence. In spite of the danger I was running, I couldn't resist taking out the file and looking through it. There were a couple of letters of reference, and I was surprised to find these were not, as you might have expected, from other mental hospitals or even medical establishments. One was from a hotel, where she had worked as a chambermaid, the other from a county jail, where she had been employed as a turnkey, which I supposed might give her a qualification of sorts to work in a mental asylum, but did not explain how she had risen to the position of chief attendant. Reading her record, I found details of her salary which struck me as seeming about right for the work involved, and I was just about to close the file when I saw a note: 'June 1893. $20 payment for "special services".' Below that was another, the same amount only this time labelled 'July'. I turned the pages and found these payments went back some two years, regular as clockwork every month, the only alteration having come some six months ago, when the payment was increased from $15 to $20. What 'special services' could O'Reilly be providing that commanded such a huge sum? All I could think of – perhaps suggested by the term 'special services' – was something of a carnal nature, except that Morgan was much too fastidious for anything squalid and, it had to be said, O'Reilly was too unattractive both in appearance and person to be the object of anyone's lust.

My mind was in a whirl and I had almost forgotten where I was when I suddenly came to my senses. Had I heard something? I wasn't sure. I could not risk being caught here simply because of idle curiosity. Whatever O'Reilly and Morgan had going on between them was none of my concern. It did not affect my situation. The important thing now was what I had come for. I stood still and breathed as softly as I could for two or three minutes, until I decided there'd been nothing after all, or perhaps only some sound made by the wind outside, and so deemed it safe to continue my search. I replaced O'Reilly's folder and moved on, hoping to find my own staff file, but when I reached the letter 'S' there was nothing for Shepherd.

I closed the cabinet and asked myself what a file about me would contain. I had been here such a short time, after all. All there was written down about me was contained in that one letter of application and perhaps a copy of Morgan's reply to it, and there probably wasn't enough for him to have started a file on me yet. If that were the case, that the letter had not been filed away, there was only one other place it might be: still on Morgan's desk.

I took my candle and placed it there. I sat down in Morgan's chair to give myself his view of it, so that all the papers were the right way round and easy to examine. There were plenty of them. I began leafing through. They were mainly letters and, since a letter was what I was searching for and I had no idea what it might look like, I had to go over them one by one, reading just enough of each to make sure it was not from the person I was supposed to be.

I was engrossed in this, completely absorbed by my task and oblivious to all else, when I felt a sudden chill. I don't know if my ears had picked up some noise so slight I did not register it consciously, or if it was some so-called sixth sense. Most likely the latter, my primitive animal instinct for survival, which had always somehow gotten me through, even in the tightest of spots, or when I took the most fool-hardy risks. Anyway, all at once I knew there was someone – or, and I shuddered to think this, some*thing* – behind me.

Someone had come into the room and was right now almost upon my shoulder. I could feel his or her hot breath upon my neck.

I was afraid to turn, dreading to encounter something supernatural. Yet that might be a blessing, I saw in a flash, because if it was Morgan, everything was lost. If he caught me here like this, he'd probably call the police and all would be up with me. There was complete silence and yet I knew someone was there, and moreover I had the certainty that whoever it was knew that I knew because I had interrupted my examination of the papers and was now sitting motionless. I spun the chair round and found myself staring into the face of a woman. And what a face! Her black hair was a wild storm around her head, and her eyes were red-hot coals, as if she had come straight from Hell to drag me back there with her, a place, it has to be said, where I most certainly belonged. Her skin was as white as a corpse's and her lips as scarlet as arterial blood. As our eyes locked she cackled, thrust out her hands and grabbed me by the throat.

I was paralysed. I could neither move nor think. Her nails were talons and bit into my flesh. She was tall and muscular and her arms strong as any man's. Her huge hands squeezed my windpipe so hard I struggled for breath. I felt the life drain out of me. She let out another hideous laugh, sending a blast of foul breath into my face. I felt myself going under and knew I had to do something before I lost consciousness altogether. I swung my legs at her, made contact with my feet and pushed hard, so the chair toppled backwards and me with it as she was forced to release her grip. I was on my feet in an instant and as she came at me pushed the toppled chair at her so she fell over it. She managed to right herself and stood looking at me, coiled and ready to spring at me again.

But she made no move. Instead she bared her teeth in something that was . . . what? A smile, yes, and an awful one, but not just that. A threat, but more than that too. Truth is, I'd never seen anything like that frightful expression on the face of man or beast and the courage I'd had a moment before vanished. I ducked as she made a feint with one of her hands toward me, but it wasn't me that she was after. She carried on the move, sweeping her arm across the desk and toppling the candle. It caught the papers there and set them alight.

She let out another dreadful laugh and then turned and ran out the door. I stood frozen to the spot, too terrified to have any notion of pursuing her. I was relieved when the door slammed shut behind her. I don't know how long I stood like that – probably only a few seconds, although it seemed an eternity at the time. It was the fire that brought me to. Everything on Morgan's desk was ablaze, the flames already a foot high. I tried to smother them with my hands but only got a burn for my trouble. It was a serious conflagration and if I couldn't get it under control the whole house would be in danger. I slipped off a shoe and began frantically beating out the flames, as pieces of burning paper flew into the air and drifted to the floorboards. It must have been all of five minutes before I had the fire tamed and finally stamped out the last embers, plunging the room into darkness.

It was then that I heard voices in the hall outside, and recognised Morgan and O'Reilly.

'It's your fault for leaving the door open,' I heard him snap.

'She's as crafty as she is crazy,' came the equally ill-tempered reply. 'You try handling her, if you think it's so easy. She can't have gone far. I'll have her back in a jiffy before anyone else is awake.' I heard her footsteps hurrying off.

The door was thrown open and light flooded into the room. Morgan stood in the doorway holding a lamp. His jaw dropped when he saw me. 'Shepherd, I did not expect to find you.'

I thought fast. 'I – I heard a noise, sir. Footsteps outside my room and strange laughter. I thought one of the patients had escaped. I followed her down here. She attacked me. She knocked over my candle. I'm afraid it's made a bit of a mess of your desk.'

He stepped into the room and merely glanced at the desk. He didn't seem too concerned about it, which shocked me; because of his obsession with neatness and order I'd have expected him to be angry or at least upset.

'It doesn't matter. What about you, man? Are you all right? It seems she got her claws into your face.'

I felt my cheeks. The right one was wet with blood and I could feel a gash running its length. I made an attempt at a wry smile. 'And I was just getting over my brush with the cab, too.'

'Yes,' he said, distractedly. He walked over to the desk and set the lamp upon it.

'Who was that woman?' I asked.

He flapped a hand in the air. 'Oh, nobody. She's just one of the – one of the – one of the patients from the secure ward. She's given to these attacks. We have to watch her all the time. She's wily, though. The worst combination, a highly intelligent, violent lunatic. It's not the first time she's done something like this. Anyway, nothing for you to concern yourself about. Do you want me to take a closer look at that cut? Doesn't appear to be too deep.'

'No, it's OK. I'm sure it's only a scratch.'

'Well, then,' he said, as he surveyed the charred debris on his desk, 'I suggest you get yourself back to bed. Thank you for your intervention. If you hadn't been so sharp, she might have burned the house down.'

I didn't point out the illogicality of this; the candle had been mine. 'Can I help you clean up the mess?'

'No, I'll sort it out, thank you. Better get yourself some sleep. We have rounds at 8.07 tomorrow, remember.'

As I went to leave, I glanced down at the desk. A piece of blackened paper caught my eye, a fragment about an inch square, the only surviving corner of a sheet of paper, the rest of it turned to ash. I could just make out the words 'John Shepherd' and below them the number '103', obviously the beginning of an address, and below that the letters 'Col', which I took to be the beginning of 'Columbus'.

12

It was only when I was back in my room and beginning to recover from my ordeal with the madwoman that I became aware of a pain in my hand and then remembered how I had burned it. Luckily the burn was small and it was my left hand anyway and even a greater injury wouldn't have affected me too badly. Being right-handed, I would still have been able to write up my patients' notes. I poured a little cold water into my basin and was just bathing the burn when I had a eureka moment, not in the bath like Archimedes, perhaps, but at least while bathing.

Drying my hands quickly, I rushed over to my desk, took out paper and pen and began to write. I put the address of the hospital at the top of the page.

My Dear Caroline,
  Thank you for your letter, which has only just reached me. I am sorry for not writing before but . . .

As I wrote, though, something in the back of my mind niggled me. Something was wrong, but I couldn't think what. And then it hit me. It was all too neat and would never convince. I screwed up the paper, tossed it into the wastebasket, took a fresh sheet, transferred the pen to my left hand, wrote out the hospital's address once more and began again, writing with great difficulty, for I was not accustomed to using that hand anyway and now every letter hurt because my fingers were sore from the burn.

My Dear Caroline

Thank you for your letter, which reached me today. I am sorry not to have been able to write before. As you feared, I was on the train involved in the wreck and I was indeed injured. Before you become alarmed at this, let me assure you that none of my injuries is serious, life-threatening or permanently disabling. The main damage was to my hands. My right hand suffered some broken bones and is in a plaster cast, so will be of no use for some time. The left incurred severe bruising and a sprain to the thumb. It is only today that the bandages have been removed, enabling me to use it to write you. This will explain to you the unfamiliar script. It is deuced difficult to write with the wrong hand anyway and the bruising makes it well nigh impossible, but I wanted to ease your fears.

I have to go now; the pain is too intense to continue longer.

At this point I paused. I had no idea how to sign off. Would Shepherd have put his full name? Unlikely. 'John' alone seemed most probable but I couldn't be certain. And what if he employed some pet name, or some secret symbol shared only between the two of them? In the end I decided on a simple 'J'. The writing in the letter had grown increasingly shaky and illegible, partly deliberately, as an excuse for

112

keeping it short, since the more I wrote the more I was likely to give myself away, but also because it was painful writing with my wounded left hand, increasingly so the longer I went on.

I read the thing through once more and had almost decided it would do when it hit me like a freight train. A catastrophic error, nothing short of a complete giveaway. It was entirely possible that Shepherd had been *left*-handed. I could not believe my stupidity at not having thought of this, and could only put it down to all that I had been through this night and my fatigue. In spite of the pain, I made myself copy out the whole letter again, but substituting 'my writing hand' for 'my right hand' and 'the other' for 'left'. When I'd finally done, and read it through, this seemed a bit stilted, but not enough to be odd to anyone who didn't already suspect some deception.

As far as I could see, there wasn't anything more in the letter to arouse anyone's suspicions. I had made the writing as much like printing as I could, devoid of any individual style. If nothing else, it would keep Caroline Adams off my back for a while and buy me some time, perhaps until I was ready to make my escape to the west, although that seemed unlikely, but if not, then at least until I could figure out what to do about her.

Wanting to get the thing out of the way and not to have to think about it any more, and still being so enervated by the events of the last couple of hours, I decided I would take the letter down to the hall and put it into the mailbox. I screwed up the first two versions and tossed them in my wastebasket, put the finished letter in an envelope and addressed it. Dawn was well on its way and I figured I could manage the trip downstairs without a candle.

I was at the top of the main stairs when I heard voices below. A man and a woman were arguing. Creeping slowly down the first flight of stairs, I made them out to belong to Morgan and O'Reilly. I had seen Morgan annoyed before, when I had seemed to criticise his therapeutic regime, but although he had been short with me then, he had never raised his voice. He was a man who liked to maintain control, not just of others and his environment, but also of himself. Why, on one occasion, he had gone off into his office especially to prevent himself giving vent to his anger, to put himself out of my presence until he cooled off. Now, though, he was positively yelling. What was even more surprising was that O'Reilly was giving as good as she got and yelling back.

I tiptoed down to the first floor to try to find out what it was about.

'It's not what I pay you a fortune for,' came Morgan's voice.

'I sometimes think there's no amount of money could make it worth it,' was O'Reilly's reply.

'Oh, well, if that's your way, then I'm sure there are plenty who would disagree.'

'That's as maybe. But would they keep their tongues to themselves too?'

At this Morgan grunted and then there was silence. Guessing the conversation was drawing to a close, I scuttled down the gloomy passage that led to the library and secreted myself in the dark recess of a doorway.

I heard Morgan's voice again. It was quieter now and I couldn't make out the words, but all the anger had gone from his tone and he sounded resigned. A moment later I heard the door of his office open and close, and I watched from the shadows as O'Reilly headed for the staircase. I waited a little while, not daring to move in case Morgan came out too and caught me, which might make him wonder how much I had heard. After ten minutes he emerged and went up the stairs, with a weary tread not at all like his usual smart step. I waited a couple of minutes more until I was quite sure he was out of the way, then crept from my hiding place, posted my letter and went to bed myself, knowing even as I undressed that I had a rough night in store. I knew I would dream again of the chicken farm, as I always did when I was agitated, and of Caroline Adams, and without doubt, before I woke, I would feel the grip of the crazy woman's fingers around my throat.

13

Next morning I was somewhat sluggish after the busy night I'd had and the disturbed sleep I'd passed, which had been every bit as bad as I'd anticipated. I was slow and ponderous in the carrying out of my duties. Morgan did not appear at breakfast and sent a note saying he would be occupied all day and would see me at dinner and asking that I manage things as best I could on my own.

The extra workload meant it was afternoon before I even thought of poor Jane Dove. When I did, I saw it was nearly time for the exercise period and decided I'd collect her from her room and take her out myself, and coming across Eva on the stairs on her way to collect Jane, I told her she need not bother today, I would do it instead.

When I knocked upon Jane's door there was a momentary delay before she replied and bade me enter, only a second or two, but enough to make me wonder why. I opened the door and found her sitting in her armchair. Her hands were in her lap, clasping *David Copperfield*, which was closed. On the floor beside the chair was some embroidery, a cushion cover by the looks of it, evidently still in its infant stages.

'Hello, what are you up to?' I asked.

'Oh, I have been looking at the pictures in the book, sir, and now I am looking out the window.'

This struck me as too pat but I let it pass.

'And what stories have you made from the pictures so far?'

She blushed. 'Oh, nothing that would interest you, sir.'

'On the contrary, I should very much like to hear about them.'

She eyed me warily. She *suspicioned me one*, she would have said. 'I have decided the people who live in the upside-down boat are seafaring folk. In my story they are simple fisherfolk.'

'You see, you were wrong, because that *is* interesting. In the novel that's exactly what they are. They're called –'

She held up a hand in protest. 'No, sir, pray don't tell me. If I know just a little of what the story is meant to be, it will restrict me in what I can invent. It will spoil it for me.'

'Very well,' I said.

There was a pause. For want of something else to say, I picked up the embroidery from the floor. 'I see Eva has been instructing you in sewing,' I said.

'Yes, she patients, but I'm afraid she is wasting her time. I have never been any good at needlework.'

'How do you know?' I said.

This startled her. 'How do I know?' she repeated. She was flustered, as if the question had touched upon some buried memory. Her face was a struggle of trying to remember.

'What is it?' I said at last, hoping to free the memory for her.

It was a mistake. In a moment her expression had resumed its composure. 'Why, sir, just look at the confusion of stitchery in your hands. You only have to see that to know

117

the person responsible was not and never will be able to work a needle.'

At that moment the bell for exercise rang and I told her to get her shawl and come outside with me. When we were in the fresh air I tried to open up her thinking about her past life with remarks that I hoped would seem nothing more than idle conversation.

'What do you think of the grounds here?' I asked as we strolled toward the river.

'They pleasant me,' she replied simply.

'Are you fond of the countryside?'

'Is this the countryside, with the town just across the river?'

'I was not necessarily talking about this place. I meant the countryside in general.'

She considered this. 'I like grass. And trees. But I unlike rooks. Spare me the cawing of rooks.'

'What do you think of when you hear a rook?' I said. 'What do you see?'

She looked me in the eye, a sardonic smile playing about her lips that seemed to say, You will not catch me out like that. 'Why, what do you expect me to see? I see a black bird with a black beak, which is why you will never see a rook at night.'

I gave up trying to grill her for the moment. I decided to take another tack, which was to engage her in casual conversation and wait for her to let something slip. Although why did I think of it that way? Because she was resisting remembering anything? Yes, that was certain, but also because I had the uncomfortable feeling that she perhaps recalled far more than she was letting on.

Just then, I saw the women from the third floor on another

path that intersected with ours, bound together on their rope, a shuffling centipede of humanity. We reached the junction at the same time and Jane Dove and I stopped to let them go by. I always found these women grimly fascinating and could not keep my eyes off them. It occurred to me that the madwoman from last night would be among them and so I examined every face closely, hoping to take another look at her, this time when she was under restraint and calm and not in the middle of a frenzy.

The women passed us, one by one, until finally the last had gone. Some cast their eyes to the ground under my scrutiny, but many stared back, studying me as intently as I was studying them. None was the woman from last night and I wondered what had become of her. I resolved to ask Morgan about her at the first opportunity.

I returned my attention to Jane Dove and found her watching the retreating line of these most sorely afflicted patients. Her expression was like a frightened child's. It was obvious, *it obvioused*, she was seeing the possibility of one day finding herself in the ranks of these wretches. I noticed her stance was very erect, as if instinctively she was separating herself from the women, who were mainly bent and huddled, as though they were ashamed of their dementia. Her neck, I thought, was long and white and smooth, most like a swan's.

At dinner Morgan tried to be his usual bustling self, all smiles and confidence, but I sensed something had gone out of him. In spite of the energy he put into the conversation, the brusque way he handled the serving dishes and the ferocious efficiency with which he chewed his food, the lines on his face were deeper etched today and he looked tired. I guessed his sleep after the incident with the madwoman had been every bit as disturbed as my own.

I longed to know more about her, but it was difficult, because as he sat himself down he said, without looking at me, 'Thank you for what you did last night, Shepherd. You were extremely vigilant and helpful.'

I opened my mouth to put a question to him about the madwoman but, before I could get a word out, he went on, 'Now, tell me about your day. I gather we had some new arrivals?'

With his evident desire to put the subject to rest it was impossible – *it impossibled* – to repeat my query and I was obliged to forget my curiosity and report on the new patients the boat had brought. He interrogated me about them at some length in what I felt was unnecessary detail, which I took to be him shifting me even further from the events of the previous night.

As soon as we had exhausted the topic of the newcomers, he was ready with more inquiries about how I had managed in his absence, moving from one subject to another as soon as the first was done with. Eventually, however, he ran out of things to ask and there was a pause in the conversation during which we both ate in silence.

'Sir, about that woman last night –' I got no further, as he waved a hand dismissively.

'Don't give it another thought, my boy. Just one of those things we have to put up with from time to time in our line of work.'

I wasn't to be so easily put off. 'Of course, it's just that I didn't see her at exercise today with the rest of the third-floor group.'

He let out a little laugh, which seemed out of place, given

the subject and what had happened only a few hours earlier. 'Of course not! You can't expect her to settle down straight away after something like that. She's under restraint. It will be some time before she is calm again. I couldn't think of letting her outside until I'm quite certain it's safe. You were on the receiving end of her violence yourself last night; you wouldn't want her to attack someone else, would you?'

'No, of course not.'

'Quite.' And with that the conversation was closed.

Something about all this was very queer indeed and yet Morgan had effectively slammed the door on any more discussion of the woman. The only other source of information was O'Reilly, although I knew this was a long shot; she was not at all well disposed toward me on account of what she saw as my mollycoddling of Jane Dove. She clearly disliked there being an area of the institution, even though it was only a single patient, over which she had no control. I knew all about pecking orders from my time on the chicken farm. I understood that, although I was a doctor and O'Reilly merely the chief attendant, she saw herself as above me in the hospital hierarchy.

Nevertheless I resolved to give it a try; there was always a possibility she would let something slip. I duly sought her out next morning, 'chancing' to come across her in the hydrotherapy room where I knew she would be. Fortunately I found her alone, waiting for a patient to be brought to her.

'Oh, Mrs O'Reilly,' I said, as though surprised to find her there. 'I was looking for Dr Morgan.'

'He is never here at this time.' She looked me straight in the eye as she said it. We both knew that I knew this.

'Well, I think I will stay and supervise the treatment,' I said.

She shrugged. 'As you wish, sir. It's completely unnecessary. I am quite capable of managing on my own. I've done it more often than not.'

'Oh yes, of course. It's more for my own instruction. I didn't mean to question your competency for one moment.' I paused. 'In fact, I was most impressed by it the night before last, the way you brought that woman under control.'

She shrugged again. The compliment didn't touch her. 'It was nothing. I've done such things dozens of times.'

'She did seem especially violent,' I ventured. 'Has she been here long?'

She stared at me. 'We have lots of them like her, believe me, sir. There is nothing special about her, nothing at all. You need not concern yourself about her.'

I was trying to think of another way of opening up a conversation on the woman after this rebuff, but she spoke before I had the opportunity. 'And how is your hand, sir? I believe you received a nasty burn.'

I held up my hand. 'Not really. Painful at the time and still a bit sore, but no lasting damage.'

'Still,' she said, her expression impassive and completely unreadable, 'it was lucky it was your left hand and not the right. It might have stopped you writing otherwise.'

I swear I saw the shadow of a smile pass over her lips, but it was gone before I could be sure. There was something triumphant about her bearing and I felt a sudden emptiness in my stomach. I remembered the abortive letter to Caroline Adams. I had dropped it in my wastebasket after I copied it out. Had O'Reilly somehow seen it? Had she been in my room, or looked through my trash? Or was this just paranoia that I had somehow caught from being among so many who suffered from it? Was being here driving me out of my mind?

'Now, if you have no objection, sir,' said O'Reilly, still looking me in the eye, 'I must get on. I have things to arrange before the patient arrives.'

If what she'd said was a challenge, threatening to ask why I had written a pack of lies about having a broken hand to a woman called Caroline, it was not one I could take up. I could hardly accuse her of going through my trash without exposing my own duplicity. I should have torn the abandoned letter to shreds. Why, oh, why had I not done so?

14

In the coming days I began to enjoy the time I spent with Jane Dove more and more. I looked forward to our sessions together. Partly this was because she was the only person on the island with whom I could be something approaching myself. I did not have to keep up the act with her as I did with Morgan. But mostly it was due to the nature of the girl. She had a quick and lively mind and a sharp, irreverent sense of humour. Most of all, like Desdemona with Othello, I fell in love with the language that she used. As I had surmised almost from the beginning, her way of speaking was anything but the gibberish Morgan had pronounced it to be. He'd made a cursory examination of her, as he did of all the patients, and concluded that her odd patois lacked rhyme or reason, whereas I soon realised it not only made sense but, in a peculiar way, even had some advantages over standard speech.

She invented new words from old, often by changing the way they were used. She said 'We outsided' rather than 'we went outside', or 'I downstairsed' in place of 'I went downstairs', both of which I found perfectly clear and actually more economical than the conventional expression. She coined new words that had a power all their own to convey the mood of a place, for example, when she called the day room, where she had been compelled to spend her former days sitting unoccupied for hour after hour, 'a dullery of disregard'. I could think of no better way to convey its atmosphere, both the boredom of those abandoned women, and also the neglect, that they were left like that because no one truly cared about them or whether they were unhappy.

Gradually, as we talked together, I found myself imitating her. This wasn't simply a conscious intention on my part to create a greater intimacy between us, although it had that in it, but rather because I could not help myself. Her way of speaking was infectious. I would say to her, 'You've aloned all morning, did that difficult?' and she might reply, 'I have always own-companied, it unbothers me.'

When I made my first attempts at this way of speaking, I thought I detected a glint of laughter in her eye, although I could not be sure of it, nor whether if it were there she was delighting in having converted me to her 'gibberish' or was privately mocking me because she found my attempts at copying her feeble.

She certainly corrected me when I broke the unstated, instinctive rules her language demanded, not openly, for it was never verbally acknowledged between us that we were communicating in this way, but simply by pretending not to understand me, and, if I did not then correct myself with something that adhered to the proper form, she might say, for example, 'Oh, you mean you unheard me.'

There was a hitch, though – there is always a hitch – which was that I began not merely to speak in her way of speaking but to *think* in it too. It was so easy and natural, and besides it had something in it that took pleasure in words for their own sake, in the funny ways a person can twist them and play with them, just as the best poetry often does, and it began to be automatic to me. Once or twice I even caught myself using it with Morgan, saying something like 'I've forwarded to dinner all day', which would have been Jane Dove's shorthand for 'I've been looking forward to dinner all day', but luckily Morgan didn't seem to notice, although nevertheless I concentrated on trying to keep separate the way I spoke to myself or Jane Dove and the way I talked to anyone else.

As we *languaged* alike I began to hope Jane Dove might so *comfortable herself* with me she would begin to give more of herself away. I could see she had amnesia. It *obvioused* from the way she sometimes struggled visibly to retrieve some lost memory and from the evident distress it caused her when she failed. At the same time I could not help suspecting she remembered more than she let on, but I couldn't figure the reason for this secrecy when, after all, she knew I was trying to help her. But, as a person who has always put on an act, not just in my working life but at every other time too, I understood how subterfuge becomes a habit that is hard to break. Was it possible that in her former existence she had carapaced herself with this hard outer shell for some reason and that she now continued to maintain it without any longer knowing why?

Jane Dove now became my main interest, outside my own safety and survival, of course. Once I was accustomed to the routine of the hospital regime, there was little else to amuse me. The more time I spent with this swan-necked girl, the more I liked her and the more curious I grew about her previous life and determined to achieve some kind of breakthrough with her. This was fuelled by Morgan's attitude to her, his mocking way of referring to her as my 'guinea pig', his sneering appraisal of the very idea of Moral Treatment or any aspect of it. Although he made a joke of it, occasionally he demonstrated an impatience with the whole experiment, mainly on the increasingly frequent occasions when I lingered too long with Jane and arrived late for some therapy – by which I mean half drowning or tying up one of the unfortunate patients – that he and I were meant to be administering together.

From all this I could tell he would not tolerate me continuing the trial indefinitely. There was another time constraint too, because even if Morgan did not put an end to the whole thing before I had achieved some real success, my own situation eventually might. There would come a moment when I would have to make my move. I could not hope to keep up this masquerade for ever, nor would I want to. Even if it *safed* to remain at the hospital, it was not the kind of life I could live permanently. And the longer I remained, the more I *comfortabled* here, the likelier I was to be unmasked.

As if to confirm that *head-in-sanding* would not do, that events would inevitably overtake me, one morning Morgan handed me another letter at breakfast. I recognised the hand immediately as belonging to Caroline Adams. The only good thing about this was that she was so far Shepherd's only correspondent. I put it in my pocket for later, as I did not want any reaction in my expression to prompt a stream of questions from Morgan. I need not have worried; he was already looking at his watch and eager to get on with the affairs of the day.

When I was at last able to sneak off to the sanctuary of

my own room, I tore open the letter, ripping the envelope as if it had been this troublesome woman herself, and *anxioused* my way through the rambling pages inside.

My Dear John

Should I even use that word 'My'? Am I still entitled to do so? I confess I do not know. My mind has been in turmoil ever since I received your letter this morning. It brought me great relief and yet great anxiety too. How is it possible for two such conflicting emotions to reside in the same breast? I do not know. Naturally I was over-joyed to find you alive and well, especially after the shock of receiving a letter addressed in an unfamiliar hand. (How is your poor hand? I do hope it is on the mend. While I am anguished by the thought of you being hurt and in pain, I thank God that it was no more than this when so many others suffered far worse injury and some even lost their lives.)

But as I read your letter my joy began to drain away, like water down a drain. It was so cold, so unemotional. Where were those endearments that you know I so treasure in your epistles? Where was the mention of how you were missing me? Why did you not use your special name for me, when you always have before? Why did you not tell me something of your new life, your hopes and fears for it, and for how it may help our future and enable us to be together? It was as if the whole thing had been written by a stranger. And then at the end, that heartless signing off, no expression of love, none at all. Instead of anything warm and loving, just that cold and heartless 'J'. It was like an initial on a tombstone to me.

I tell myself to give you the benefit of the doubt,
that it was difficult for you to write with an injured
hand and that the absence of a final tenderness and
that brusque signature are nothing more sinister than
indications of fatigue, that you were physically
incapable of writing more. I tell myself all this, but I
do not convince, I am not persuaded. Reassure me, my
darling boy, that I am being a weak and foolish girl,
please, I beg you, although I hardly dare ask since I
fear that, finding yourself in a new place and a new
life, you have discovered you do not want anything of
the old, or at least one part of it, the part that was me.

Please, please write by return and set my mind at
rest. Or, if it is the other, then show me some mercy and
put me out of my misery.

With love
Caro

My brain was in a whirl. Those words 'written by a stranger' cut me to the quick. How close she was to realising the truth! My subterfuge had worked but only just. I had to get rid of this stupid young woman, get her off my back, and fast, before she began to put two and two together and came up with the right answer.

The rest of my day passed in a fog, as my mind kept returning again and again to the letter. Morgan lost patience with me more than once, saying, 'Come on, man, pay attention. Keep your mind on the job, I'll not have sloppy work.' As though there was a better way to fasten some sobbing wretch into a chair! I could have strangled the man, he annoyed me so, demanding my concentration when all I wanted was to steal away and work out a scheme to divest myself of this troublesome lover. Even Jane Dove could see something was wrong, saying to me as we walked the grounds during the exercise period, 'You have somewhere-elsed me all day.'

At last it was evening and I watched darkness invading the grounds, great shadows stealing across the lawns, with a sigh of relief and not my usual dread. I rushed through dinner and Morgan *unobjected* when I departed as soon as I'd swallowed the last mouthful; I think he'd *enoughed* me for one day.

Once alone, I reread the letter and considered what to do. There was only one option. I had to break all ties with Miss Adams; nothing else would serve. I had thought it might be amusing to string her along for a while, but now I saw it would not answer. Apart from anything else, how long could I plead my injured hand as an excuse for my unfamiliar handwriting? Sooner or later the break would have to be mended. And even before that time came, with every letter there was the risk I would give myself away by perhaps not understanding something she referred to, not being able to show any knowledge of our shared life, or simply by employing an expression that Shepherd himself would never have used.

I sat at my desk and took up my pen, beginning 'Dear Miss Adams'. I had decided it *necessaried to brutal her* from the start.

Dear Miss Adams,

I am afraid it is with great regret that I have to tell you that unfortunately your anxiety about our future relationship is not misplaced. I wish it were not so, really I do, but that is not the case. Believe me when I say that I did truly think I loved you and thought I meant

everything I said to you in our moments alone together,
those little endearments you mention which I can no
longer bring myself to utter (I was beginning to enjoy
myself now!).

    I think it was the train wreck that changed my mind.
The brush with death made me examine my life and
the course it was upon and see that it would not do.
For me, at least, it was a happy accident because it
stopped me blundering into a situation which would
have ended in disaster for us both and I am certain
would, at some future time, have hurt you far more
than will this letter now.

    I end by thanking you for your past affection for me
and with great sadness at the unhappiness this will
doubtless cause you, through no fault of your own. I hope
and pray that any such distress will be short-lived. You
are a wonderful girl and someday will make some fortu-
nate man very happy, only just not me, your obedient
servant

    J

I put down my pen with a sigh of satisfaction. It was as
though a great weight had lifted from me, or the shadow of
some evil angel had passed over me and sought another
victim. I read the letter through. It left her no room for
manoeuvre. It did not matter if she chose to write back;
there would be no need for me to reply, nothing odd about
my silence. I wrote her address on the envelope, congratulating myself on the knowledge it was the last time I would
ever have to do so. The matter was over and done with and
Caroline Adams was now no more than a footnote in
Shepherd's history.

I went downstairs – *I downstairsed* – to post the letter in the mailbox, whistling a merry tune to myself. As I rounded the turn of the stairs I nearly bumped into O'Reilly who was coming up.

'Ah, it's you, Mrs O'Reilly.' It was stating the obvious but then that's what one does in such a minor awkward situation.

'It's nobody else, sir.' She had an annoying way of putting me in my place and making me feel a fool. 'Been writing a letter, have you?' She nodded at the envelope, which I held to my chest so she might not read the address.

'So it seems,' I replied. Touché.

She held out her hand. 'Let me post it for you, sir.'

'Oh no, I couldn't trouble you to do that.' I clutched the letter more closely still. 'Anyway, you're on your way up.'

'I just remembered something I forgot to do downstairs, so it's not any trouble at all,' she said and stretched her hand out further.

I held the letter tighter still, for I really had the feeling she might actually snatch it from me. It was as ridiculous as a children's game, as if I were holding it above my head and she leaping up and trying to get it.

'Yes, that's very kind, but I'm on my way to the library, you see, and I have to pass right by the mailbox on the way.'

She dropped her hand and nodded. Checkmate. 'Very well. Goodnight then, sir.'

We stood there awkwardly for a moment, in each other's way. Finally I said, 'Well, go ahead, then. You said you had to go back downstairs for something you'd forgotten.'

She smiled her sinister smile again. 'Ah yes, sir, so I did. But I've just realised, I don't need to after all.'

I flattened myself against the banister rail and, with a nod of acknowledgement, she stepped past me. I turned and watched as she glided up the stairs exactly as I'd always thought a ghost might walk. I went down and mailed my letter. I did not go to the library. O'Reilly – if she was watching – and I both knew what the game had been about, so what would have been the point?

15

In the following days I noticed O'Reilly was becoming increasingly casual in her behaviour toward me, almost to the point of insolence, even in front of Morgan. One morning he arrived in the hydrotherapy room, where we were preparing a woman for treatment. He looked surprised as he came in and pulled out his watch.

'This woman was meant to be in the bath seven and a half minutes ago. What is the reason for the delay?'

Before I could say anything, O'Reilly said, 'We were waiting for Dr Shepherd, sir. He was meant to supervise. Only I think he was delayed by his special patient.'

This earned me a scowl from Morgan. 'First things first, Shepherd. You need to get your priorities right.'

I merely nodded and scowled myself as, when Morgan took the patient's notes from O'Reilly and began to study them, she regarded me behind his back with something like mockery in her eyes. I was putting a brave face upon things, though, for I had heard the emphasis with which she had referred to me as 'Doctor Shepherd'. It reinforced my fear that she had *wastebasketed* me, found my discarded draft letter to Caroline Adams and guessed the truth about me.

Afterwards I told myself I was being silly. Of course the letter showed that I was duplicitous toward my erstwhile fiancée, but it didn't necessarily indicate that I was not who I was supposed to be. I told myself this, but I was not reassured. Everything in O'Reilly's demeanour toward me now – the lack of due respect, the mockery, the talking about me to Morgan while I was there as if she were above me in the pecking order – indicated that she had something on me. The question was, was she going to use it, and, if so, when?

I began to hate her lean and hungry features, her bony face, her scrawny chicken's neck. I had made an enemy, without ever actually doing her any wrong. What I had to do now was find a way to stop her hurting me. The woman's interference could, after all, cost me my life.

Such was her insolence, I would have loved to teach her a lesson once and for all, but I knew that that way madness lay. I would simply bring down upon myself exactly the consequences I feared she might cause. I spent hour after hour lying on my bed, head resting on my hands, staring at the ceiling as the shadows crawled across it and dark descended outside. It was no use; there was no obvious way out. O'Reilly was a powder keg that might blow up at any moment. It seemed I *powerlessed* to predict when that moment might be or to prevent it when it did.

But a few days after the incident in the hydrotherapy room, I was walking with Jane Dove in the grounds at exercise time when I saw in the distance the women from the third floor. It occurred to me that I hadn't inspected them since the day after the incident with the madwoman in Morgan's office, when I had tried to get another look at her but found her absent from the group. I thought she must have rejoined it by now and I determined to seek her out.

I was only half paying attention to what Jane Dove was saying – a rambling story she had extrapolated from the picture of Miss Havisham in *Great Expectations*, the book she had now moved on to after inventing stories for all the illustrations in *David Copperfield*, although, of course, she did not know the name of the woman in the picture – and I changed direction suddenly to one that would lead us to encounter the top-security patients. Jane paused in her patter, evidently surprised at the way I stepped across her to veer off in this new direction, but then, not getting a reaction from me (I was too focused upon my mission), she resumed her tale. A hundred yards later, as I had judged we would, we had to wait while the line of roped women crossed our path, exactly as they had before, and Jane stopped talking as we both watched them. Glancing at her, I saw a shadow of fear pass over her face, and you didn't have to be a psychiatrist to know she was again considering the possibility that she might one day find herself in the ranks of these wretched specimens. It was but a momentary thing and I did not have time to study her because I needed to scrutinise the faces of the women as they went by. Once again I looked carefully at each and once again I drew a blank. The madwoman was not there.

I wondered if my mind was playing tricks upon me, if in the heat of the moment in Morgan's study I had been too terrified to notice the woman's features properly and commit them to memory, but I immediately dismissed the idea. I knew the picture of her face was etched in my mind with acid; it would be with me until my dying day – along with some other women's faces, of course. I wondered, then, if perhaps the woman's expression had been so distorted by the frenzy she was in as to make her unrecognisable now in the shambling blankness I saw upon the faces of the women before me, the deadness that represented some kind of repose. But that notion, too, seemed fanciful. Even allowing for the difference in situation, the drama of that night, the routine of this exercise walk, there wasn't anyone here who looked the least bit like that mad fiend.

As the last woman went by us, I stopped the attendant who was bringing up the rear of the procession.

'Yes, sir?'

'Tell me, would you, where is the other woman from the third-floor ward?'

'Other woman, sir? I'm afraid I don't know who you mean. These are all the women from the secure ward.'

'All? Surely not? Is there no one sick or under extra restraint somewhere?'

She *puzzled me one*. 'Why no, sir, they're all here, all present and correct. There is no one else.'

I nodded and she hurried off to catch up with her charges. I stood staring after them. 'Strange,' I said to myself. 'Passing strange.'

'What?' asked Jane Dove. 'What is strange?' and I realised I had spoken the words aloud.

'Oh, nothing,' I replied, giving her a cheerful smile – *cheerfulling her one* – 'now, you were saying about the old lady in the wedding dress?'

'Oh, sir,' she said crossly, 'you have not been listening, have you? That was some time ago. We have moved on since then. We are in a rowing boat now.'

'Very well,' I said. 'Recommence rowing.'

She did, but I fear she must have found me as inattentive as before. I had a lot on my mind.

* * *

137

My first thought was to ask Morgan once again about the missing woman. Assuming the attendant had been correct – and she'd been very definite in what she said – then Morgan had lied to me. The madwoman (I thought of her as such, although, of course, they were all mad here) was not on the violent ward, even though she was extremely violent, as the scratches on my cheek and the burn on my hand testified. So where was she?

Moreover, the attendant I'd spoken to seemed to have no knowledge of her. She'd stated emphatically that there was no other woman upstairs. And yet I was pretty sure that if I asked Morgan about the woman and mentioned her not being at exercise, he would tell me the same as before, that she was under restraint because she was still too disturbed to be returned to the others.

I thought back to that night and how agitated Morgan had been. I remembered the conversation with O'Reilly that I'd overheard, his fury with her and the way she'd answered him back, something I had never heard her do before. Then there was that twenty dollars a month mentioned in her file, an absolute fortune for a woman like O'Reilly. Whatever the secret was about this woman, there was no doubt the two of them were in it together. I began to see this was the source of O'Reilly's self-assurance and arrogance. I also saw it might be an avenue to explore as a means of breaking her hold over me. If I could just find out more, I might use it against her to counteract what I suspected she had on me.

That evening I looked in on the dining hall when the patients were having their evening meal. It was a thing Morgan and I took turns in doing. The attendants were perfectly capable of managing the meal on their own, but Morgan liked to maintain a tight rein on everything. He thought our appearance would keep everyone on their toes and stop standards slipping.

I saw O'Reilly at the head of the hall, her eyes scanning the tables in front of her, ranging up and down each, like a bird of prey selecting its next victim. I was at the other end of the hall and she acknowledged my presence with a nod, the slight inclination of her head somehow conveying so exactly the way she regarded our relationship that I could not help thinking the woman was wasted here; she would have earned a fortune on the stage. Then she carried on with what she was doing, as if I were not there. I watched her and thought what a smug predator the woman was, a jumped-up queen in her little empire who needed taking down a peg or two.

I was wrenched from these thoughts by a dispute at the table closest to me. Two women were squabbling over a piece of bread, one of them hugging it to her breast and the other attempting to pry it from her. Suddenly the one with the bread took one hand off it and fetched the other a hefty slap across the face.

I signalled to the nearest attendant, who hadn't noticed the affray, and she rushed over, pulled the women apart and gave the one without bread another slice. The woman took it resentfully and shot the other woman a smouldering look and I was riveted for a moment, wondering if she was going to slap her back. I found myself quite excited at the prospect of a lively fight, with plenty of womanly biting and scratching. But nothing happened and the affair fizzled out with both women too busy eating to continue the ruckus. I looked up and across the hall. O'Reilly was gone.

I strolled the length of the hall and worked my way to where she had been standing, thinking that in the noise and confusion, with the patients talking and cackling and arguing and appealing to the attendants who were rushing here and there, I'd simply misplaced her and would spot her again in a moment. But no, my first thought had been correct: she was gone.

I left the hall and wandered out into corridor. I went into the day room. Empty. I had no idea how long O'Reilly had been gone. I paced around, looking everywhere I could think she might be, but there was no sign of her. Eventually I walked the length of the building but still didn't find her. I decided to go back to the dining hall. She still wasn't there. I went out through a door on the other side of the hall this time, which led into the back corridor that ran parallel to the main corridor at the front, and began walking along it and almost immediately met O'Reilly coming toward me. I nodded and carried on past her so as to avoid any suspicion that I'd been looking for her. All the way along the corridor I could feel her eyes boring into the back of my head, but when I finally looked over my shoulder, she wasn't there.

I had never been in this part of the building before. There was nothing here that had anything to do with me, and my presence here must have made O'Reilly suspicious. As far as I knew, the passage led to the kitchens, the laundry room and storerooms, places where I had no concern. Perhaps O'Reilly had gone to one of those. But then I came upon something that made me think that, no, she had not. Something that interested me greatly. What I found, near the end of the corridor, were the back stairs.

Was I being fanciful, or had O'Reilly disappeared from the dining hall to go upstairs to her very own 'special patient'? Had she slipped away to deal with someone over whom she had a particular charge? Had she perhaps gone to the kitchen and helped herself to a portion of food, to take somewhere to a woman who was locked away all on her own? My heart beat faster. I had stumbled upon some mystery here, that was for sure.

Later, lying on my bed, reading my Shakespeare, I began to draw a lesson from *Hamlet*. It was no use prevaricating, waiting for something to happen to me, because if I did, that thing would be bad. I had to be the one calling the shots. I had to take control of the situation or all would be lost. I resolved I would follow O'Reilly secretly and discover the truth.

16

Next day it was Morgan's turn to look in on the patients' supper, and a good hour before the meal began I managed to get away and slip into the back corridor. I made my way along it to foot of the back stairs. I was tempted just to head up them on my own, rather than wait for O'Reilly, but decided it was not a good plan. For one thing, what would I do when I reached the third floor? I would have no idea where to go, where the woman I was looking for might be. Not only that, I would have O'Reilly coming up behind me and might find myself trapped with no convincing explanation for being there.

I looked along the corridor and saw a door a little further along. I walked over to it and tried the handle. It proved to be unlocked and, opening it, I found the room in darkness, for it had no window. The dim light from the corridor showed it to be some kind of storeroom, with shelves along two of the walls, all empty. There was dust everywhere, which told me it was not in regular use. I slipped inside and pulled the door to behind me, leaving it open perhaps half an inch, through which I had a perfect view of a bit of the corridor and the bottom of the back stairs. All I had to do now was wait for supper to begin and then hope that halfway through it O'Reilly would sneak away as she had the day before.

I had a fairly tense time of it. After I'd been there half an hour I heard women's voices coming along the corridor toward me. I pulled away from the gap in the door and held my breath and prayed they wouldn't notice it was open. It was a couple of attendants and they were so busy talking about some expedition to a dance hall they were planning that they didn't notice the door was ajar or think it significant if they did, and went on by. I let out my breath and resumed my vigil.

Nothing happened for what seemed like hours and I grew so weary of standing I sat myself down on the dusty stone floor and was just beginning to think I was on a fool's errand when I heard brisk, clipped footsteps in the corridor and knew without looking that they were O'Reilly's. Once again, I held my breath.

The footsteps grew closer and closer and then stopped. I guessed O'Reilly was at the foot of the stairs. There was a long silence and I heard a creak, which I knew must be her setting a foot on the bottom step. After that there was another long silence. I could hear my heart beating. Had she gone up the stairs or was she still there? I had no way of knowing. I couldn't hold my breath any longer and let it out as quietly as I could. I decided to risk a peep around the edge of the door to make sure O'Reilly was out of the way and that the coast was clear. I eased my head round so my eye could see through the gap and straightway pulled it back. O'Reilly was standing at the foot of the stairs, one foot on the bottom step, the other on the step above it. I took another peek. She was holding a tray on which I could see some crockery and a glass of water. I could smell food, roast beef, unless I was mistaken, better fare than the thin soup and rancid cold meats the women in the dining hall would be tucking into at this moment. O'Reilly stood still as a statue, head slightly cocked, like an animal listening for its prey.

I moved further back into the storeroom, away from the door, and listened. I heard the creak of the stair again and thought for a moment this meant she had resumed her ascent, but then came the sound of her steps along the corridor again. She moved slowly and once more I took a deep breath as she passed by my door and the footsteps retreated along the corridor away from the stairs and the way I had come. It was no use putting my eye to the gap in the door now, because it faced the wrong way to see her. I listened while the footsteps went slowly, tentatively you might have said, further away. Then abruptly they were coming toward me again, and were now short, quick steps that stopped right outside my door. The door was pulled shut, I heard a clink of metal and then, to my horror, my absolute horror, the sound of a key turning in the lock.

The footsteps marched quickly away again. My instinct was to cry out, to shout that I was locked in, but I held myself back. How on earth would I explain what I had been doing here in the first place? It was impossible to think of any reasonable excuse for skulking in an empty storeroom. I listened as the sound of the footsteps grew more distant and then stopped. I heard again that creak of the stair and guessed O'Reilly had gone up. I was left alone and trapped in the dark.

With no window, the room was pitch black. I had a box of matches in my pocket. The box was half full. I took one out and struck it on my shoe and looked at the door. I tried the handle but, sure enough, it was firmly locked. I held the match up and looked around the room, foolishly allowing myself to hope there might be another door that I somehow hadn't noticed. Even a cursory glance told me there was none. I went to inspect the shelves in case there was anything on them that might help me pick the lock. Before I could get to them the flame of the match burned down to my fingers and I dropped it. I fumbled out another and lit that. In its eerie glow I looked at the shelves on one side of the room, which proved to contain nothing but cobwebs. I turned to the other side but my match went out again.

At this rate I would soon run out of matches. I lit another and saw something I had missed in my first look at the room. A book, quite a large volume too. I just managed to make out the title on the spine when the match fizzled out. I lit another. *The Complete Works of William Shakespeare.* Well, who would have thought it? What book would I have chosen if I had been told I must be locked in a room with only one? Here it was.

It was covered in dust and I blew it off, forgetting myself for a moment and blowing out my light too. Here was an irony and no mistake. To be in solitary confinement and to have the best book a man could want for company and yet no light to read it by. This was an exquisite form of torture indeed!

I felt inside the book. The pages were as thin and insubstantial as they always are in large books such as *The Complete Works* and the Bible. I lit another match and looked in my box. I would soon be deprived of light at this rate. I looked again at the book. What I was about to do was sacrilege, but there seemed to be nothing else for it. I thumbed through the list of contents. It was an unfamiliar edition.

I began to make a choice and then the match went out.

I made up my mind, lit another precious match and found *The Comedy of Errors*. I had the book open at the first page of the play and found the last one. When my match died, I steeled myself, apologised to the spirit of the great man and ripped out the whole of the play. It troubled me more to desecrate this book than any of the things I had done in this life, although I knew it ought not.

I put the book down on the shelf and then took a leaf from the torn *Comedy*. I rolled it and then twisted it to make a spill, then another and another. I carried on until I had finished the whole play. I cannot tell you how bad this made me feel.

In the dark I arranged my spills in a line along the shelf, then struck a match and lit one. As I had hoped, it burned slowly and lasted longer than a match. It gave me more chance to look around.

One after another, scene by scene, act by act, I burned my way through the *Comedy*. Apart from the shelving, I was looking at bare walls; there was not even a fireplace and a chimney I might have tried to climb up. But then why would anyone have wanted a fire in a storeroom? I crawled over every inch of the floor, on the off chance there might be some trapdoor or manhole, but there was nothing. I even looked at the ceiling in the forlorn hope of an opening, but there was none. I was well and truly trapped.

I sank to the floor with my back against the door. There was only one way I was going to get out and that was if someone released me. But I knew that could not happen by chance. It was obvious the room hadn't been used in ages. How likely was it that anyone would happen to visit it just now? There could be no accidental rescue. Or any other kind either, unless I made a rumpus to attract attention, as no one knew I was there.

Or did they? Why had O'Reilly chosen that moment to lock the door? Was it because she had noticed it was slightly open when it was normally kept shut and in shutting it thought she might as well lock it too? That was more than possible. She had that perfectionist efficiency about her; it was one of the things that I, who am entirely the opposite, slipshod and laissez-faire, disliked about her.

Or had she sensed my presence? Had she been alerted to the possibility of my being in the storeroom after having met me in the corridor the day before, when I had no business to be there? There was no way of knowing.

I had no idea what to do. If I did nothing, then I would starve to death. Even if I stayed long enough to be missed and a search was initiated for me, it was unlikely anyone would look here. The only way out was to bang on the door and attract the attention of someone passing along the corridor. This would lead to all kinds of embarrassment and awkward attempts on my part to explain how I came to be here, but if it were done it were best it were done quickly. The longer I left it, the bigger deal my absence would become and the still greater fuss would be made about how I had happened to be locked in the room in the first place.

I decided I needed to think things through before taking this inevitable action. There must be some plausible excuse I could come up with. I sank once more to the floor and put my head in my hands. I could feel the blood beating in my temples. I thought how if I only had O'Reilly in here with me now, I would show her how dangerous an enemy she had made, and then, unaccountably, I fell asleep.

Heaven knows how long I dozed. I woke in darkness

completely ignorant of where I was and in a blind panic. I thought it was the henhouse where my uncle used to shut me up to punish me for transgressions when he couldn't be bothered to strap me. I put my hands upon the floor and could not understand why it was not covered with the thick parquet of dried chicken excrement. The smell of the stuff singed my nostrils. I could feel the chicken feathers in my mouth, in the back of my throat, choking me, suffocating me. I could not breathe, the stench was overpowering, I screamed my head off. I clambered to my feet and felt for the wall. I groped along it and found a door, my hand was upon the handle, I turned it and tugged at it – and the door swung inwards. I was free.

As light poured in from the corridor I came to my senses and realised where I was. Had I really screamed? I could not be certain, though I was pretty sure that I had. I listened. There was no sound from outside. Slowly I peeped around the edge of the doorframe and looked in both directions. There was no one. I stepped quickly outside and gently closed the door behind me. I had no notion of the time but guessed I must by now be late for dinner with Morgan. I began to hurry along the corridor, then remembered how dusty the room had been. I looked down at myself. My jacket and pants were covered in dust. In the dim light of the corridor I must have looked like a ghost. I began to brush down my pants. I took off my jacket and beat it furiously. I didn't have any explanation ready for how I'd gotten so filthy. The air around me was clouded with dust that got up my nose and sent me into a paroxysm of sneezing. It was a good few minutes before my clothing looked reasonably decent and all the sneezing had stopped.

I straightened myself up, put my jacket back on and

hurried to the front corridor and ran full tilt along it and almost bundled into O'Reilly and one of the attendants as they came around a corner. She gave me a supercilious smile. 'Ah, there you are *Doctor* Shepherd. Dr Morgan has had people looking all over for you. You're very late for your dinner, you know. Where *have* you been?'

I simply stared at her. We both knew where I'd been. I hadn't been certain that she had deliberately locked me in the storeroom because I wasn't sure then that she knew I was there. But it was obvious to me now she must have known I was inside. Why would anyone else unlock the door and not open it and look inside? The puzzle was why she had let me go. Why had she not humiliated me in front of Morgan and the whole hospital, as she could have done if she'd waited until I made a racket screaming to be let out? One look at her face told me all I wanted to know. She had imprisoned me as a warning, to tell me not to meddle in things that were none of my business. Little did she know me, though, or what she was taking on.

I dodged around the two women and hurried on my way, but O'Reilly called me back. 'Oh, Dr Shepherd . . .'

I stopped and turned around. 'Yes?'

'Forgive my mentioning it, but you have what appears to be dust on the seat of your pants.'

I arrived in the doctors' dining room a good half hour late. Morgan was just finishing his main course. I saw his watch was open on the table beside his plate. 'Ah, there you are, Shepherd. You're thirty-two minutes late, you know. Where on earth have you been? If it's that Moral Treatment business with the girl that is messing up my schedule, then I shall have to think again about allowing it.'

I decided the best form of defence was attack. 'Oh, no, sir, it was nothing at all to do with her. I went for a walk outside and sat down under a tree and I must have dozed off. I haven't been sleeping too well since – well, since that night when I found the woman setting fire to your desk.'

I knew this was not a subject Morgan would want to revive. He avoided my eyes and then indicated his plate with his fork. 'I asked the kitchen to keep some supper warm for you. First-class meal tonight. Great favourite of mine; you'll enjoy it.'

I sat down and my food was brought to me. I looked down at my plate and knew right away that I wouldn't be able to manage even a mouthful. It was fried chicken.

17

Next day it snowed. It was by now mid-November and Morgan and I sat at breakfast watching through the window as the heavy flakes began to carpet the lawns in front of the house, and he said, 'That's all you're going to see for the next few months. Take my word for it, it'll be like this until February now. It's the same every year.'

I could have told him how little it bothered me, how anything that increased our isolation here was welcome to me, even though I had no coat. I realised Shepherd must have had one with him, because the day of the accident had not been warm. But he had obviously taken it off for the train ride, the wagons being well heated, and he must have stowed it in the rack above his seat. I didn't blame myself for missing it when I took his valise. I'd had hardly enough time to exchange clothes with him before people arrived on the scene; I was lucky to have gotten away as I had.

Later that morning I visited Jane and found her kneeling upon her armchair at the window watching the snowflakes falling. She heard the sound of the door and turned toward me excitedly. 'Oh look, sir, look. It's snowing!' It was said with all the delight of a child.

'Yes, I know,' I said, smiling back. She resumed gazing out the window.

'The lake will be frozen. We'll be able to skate.'

'But, Jane,' I said, tentatively, because I did not want it to be too much of a shock, 'don't you remember? There is no lake here.'

'No lake . . . ?' She sank back on her haunches, her brow corrugated into a frown. 'No lake? But how will we be able to skate?'

There was an awful silence, somehow made worse by that eerie quiet that always seems to descend with snow. She began to cry. I strode over to her and put an arm around her shoulders. She buried her face in my chest. Her frail frame was racked by great sobs. We were like that some few minutes. I could feel her heart beating against mine. She was as warm as a freshly killed hen, and almost as limp and lifeless.

When the sobbing at last began to subside I said, 'What lake were you thinking of, Jane?' There was no answer. 'Try to picture the place, Jane,' I said. 'Tell me what you see in your mind's eye.'

'It's the lake I told you about before, sir. In the trees, in the woods.' Suddenly she let out a little cry and pulled away from me, the knuckles of her right hand in her open mouth. Her eyes were wide open and wild, staring at something far beyond this room.

'What, Jane, what is it? Tell me what troubles you.'

'Something bad, sir, something bad happened.'

'At the lake?'

'Yes, but it was not my fault, I swear it, sir. It was not my fault.'

'Did someone fall through the ice? Is that it, did the ice

152

break and someone skating upon it fall through and drown?'

She chewed her knuckle furiously, eyes still off someplace else, and then all at once her head collapsed onto her chest and she whispered, 'I – I do not know. I can't see, sir. I can't see anybody falling through the ice.'

I wanted to push her further, to urge her to keep looking into her mind, but I held back. I sensed her sanity was close to breaking point here, whether with the sheer effort of trying to remember or because deep down she feared to do so, I didn't know. So I said nothing, but put my hand on her shoulder, and stroked it gently, my fingers touching the downy hair on the back of her neck.

'It's all right, Jane,' I said softly. 'Nobody blames you for anything. You are not there now. You are here with me and I will keep you safe and warm.' At which she threw her arms about me and buried her head in my chest once again. Even through my clothes, I could feel her sharp little nails digging into the flesh of my back. I wanted for her never to let me go, but after what must have been at least a couple of minutes I forced myself to break away, gentle as I could. I had to. The old feelings were flooding back.

At this separation she grew more distressed again and I almost did not know what to do to calm her. My great fear was that she might go into some kind of fit, start screaming perhaps, drawing the attention of any attendants who happened to be near. I was particularly worried about O'Reilly. In such a case I had no doubt that Morgan would be only too delighted to pronounce my trial of Moral Treatment a dismal failure and bring it to an immediate halt. I did not think I could bear to see poor Jane Dove returned to the ranks of living dead, condemned to sit in silence every morning, staring mindlessly into the endless night her future would become. And to be honest, nor did I think I could stand it myself, to lose her lively company; she was the only friend I had in this godforsaken place, the only thing that made it possible to endure here.

'Come now, quiet yourself,' I said in as cheery a voice as I could manage, for I was trembling on the brink of the precipice here. 'Let's have a little of the bard, what do you say?'

She managed a weak smile and wiped away her tears with the sleeve of her gown. I had lately begun reciting parts of Shakespeare to her, acting out bits of plays, taking upon myself all the characters and distinguishing them one from another by assuming different voices. It had proved a great success, much more so than I had expected, for although Jane was only young, she had taken to the great man's works immediately, and made no difficulty of understanding the language. For me it brought back all the pleasure of my profession, even though I knew that part of my life was gone for ever; I relished the joy of performing and, if I'm honest, the thrill of showing off.

At first I did this only in the early evenings before dinner, when I had time to return to my room and collect *The Complete Works*, but then Jane suggested I leave the book in her room. At first I resisted because it meant I did not have it myself to read at night, and it was of no use to her when I wasn't there because the book had no illustrations, but she pointed out that leaving it there would mean that even if I popped in on her for a few minutes between duties I would be able to act out a scene or two for her delight, and so in the end I acquiesced.

Now I took up *Hamlet*, already her favourite, and acted

out the wonderful scene with the prince and Rosencrantz and Guildenstern, the witticisms and wordplay of which I was confident would banish her unhappy mood. Sure enough, the great man did not let me down now and soon her tears were dry, her face began to lose the blotchy redness that comes from crying and she was laughing away in spite of herself. I had just finished the scene and she was clapping and pleading 'Encore, encore' (which I had taught her was the actor's reward for a good performance) when I remembered I had meant to be there only a few minutes, having just dropped in on my way between tasks. With no timepiece, I had no idea how long I had been with her, except that I knew it had been too long. Seeing she was now more or less all right, I told her I would have to go and rushed from the room.

I was supposed to be helping Morgan assess the new arrivals and went quickly to the examination room, where I found him in the middle of examining a patient. He was making his own notes, which was normally my task, standing over a desk to write down his observations instead of calling them out to me. He looked up angrily when he saw me and tossed the pen down on the desk. 'At last!' he snapped. 'Take over the notes, if you please.'

We finished the examination of the three new patients in a silence as frosty as the weather outdoors. As soon as the women had been taken away and we were alone, he said to me, 'What explanation do you have for being so late, sir?'

'I'm most terribly sorry, Dr Morgan. I quite lost track of the time.'

'You were with your *special patient*, I presume?'

155

I paused. I did not want to admit it but I had no choice, since it was obviously so. I nodded.

He stood up and put his hands behind his back and began to pace around the room. Once again I had the feeling that he was trying to get control of himself, that he feared his anger taking him over. I could not help wonder what experience had led him to suppress that side of himself so. Was it the madness he witnessed daily that made him resist any primitive wild impulse in his own nature? I felt a certain sympathy with him in this. I of all people knew only too well how hard it was to contain the beast within.

At last he stopped his perambulations right in front of me, lifted his head and looked me straight in the eye. 'I said we would continue this experiment only as long as it didn't interfere in your proper duties.'

'I know, sir. I'm sorry. It won't happen again.'

'You're right about that, because I am calling a halt to it now.'

'But, sir,' I said, 'I think I'm making progress and it would be unfair to stop the thing out of hand without assessing it.'

'Unfair?' His eyes bulged. 'You think it would be unfair? I call it damned unfair to let another man do the work you're paid for, don't you?'

'Yes, sir.' I hung my head meekly. Experience had taught me it was better to humble myself when he was in such a mood than to argue with him, which only made him more irate.

He recommenced his pacing. Eventually he stopped and stood staring out the window at the snow, which was still falling fast, his back to me. 'All right, you have a point. It's no use stopping it in a moment of annoyance. I will inspect your progress first. I will expect to notice measurable improvements, though. For one thing, the girl must not be talking gibberish. And for another –' here he turned and looked me in the eye again, 'for another, I expect that she will – at least a little – be able to read.'

There was a hint of a smirk as he said this. I could feel his eyes laughing at me. My heart sank inside me. There was a chance I might help Jane Dove to moderate her speech before him, but it would *impossible* me to persuade her to attempt to learn to read, and, even if I could, to accomplish it within the very short time that would be all I would be allowed before he examined her. He was hardly going to let me extend the trial another month.

'Very well, sir,' I replied. 'And when would you like to see the girl?'

'I don't want it to take up any more working time than it already has, and certainly I can't waste mine on what I know to be such a . . . such a . . . lost cause. Let's say Sunday, shall we?'

I tried not to look too crestfallen as I nodded agreement. It was already Tuesday.

18

It was not until the afternoon exercise that I was able to see Jane Dove again. It was not the best situation for a serious discussion, especially one I knew would be unwelcome to her; we were both shivering, she in her thin dress with only a knitted shawl over it as an acknowledgement that winter had truly announced its arrival and I for my part with no coat. I had only a muffler, which Eva, who had seen my plight, had given me, and an extra undershirt, undergarments being the only items of clothing Shepherd had been abundantly equipped with.

In an effort to keep warm, we walked briskly along the footpaths the gardeners had cleared early on, a task that fully occupied them with the continuing heavy snow. After exchanging a few pleasantries with my charge, when I scarcely knew what I was saying, much less what she replied, I stopped abruptly and stood stamping my feet and clapping my arms about me in an effort to keep my blood circulating. 'Jane, I have to talk to you about something serious,' I said.

Her face fell. 'What is it, sir? You are leaving this place. I knew it, I felt it coming.'

I managed a smile. 'No, no, not that at all, although, of

course, I shall have to leave one day, but not yet awhile, I hope.'

It was her turn to smile.

I plunged on. 'But unless you can help me – help yourself, that is – then it will amount to the same thing as far as you are concerned.' I told her about Morgan's ultimatum.

She became very agitated, twisting the ends of her shawl round and round in her hands. 'It impossibles, I cannot do it.'

'I know it's a tall order by Sunday, but you're intelligent and quick-witted. You'll be able to pick up enough reading to placate him.'

She looked me straight in the eye. 'No, sir, you misunderstand. When I say it impossibles I am not talking of my capabilities, but of what is allowed. I am unpermitted to learn to read.'

'Who says? Who forbade it? Whoever it was cares so little about you they have left you here to rot.'

Confusion took hold of her features. 'I – I can't remember who, sir. When I try to think of it a fog descends upon my mind. I can see nothing. I only know that if I am discovered reading, I will lose –'

'What? What will you lose?'

She hung her head and shook it slightly and whispered so soft I could scarce hear, 'Everything.'

I resumed walking. It was the only way I could manage to control my frustration. My face was suddenly hot in spite of the freezing weather. I was moving so quickly now she had to trot alongside me to keep up.

'Sir,' she said, 'wait a minute. I have an idea.'

I stopped and *resentfulled her one*. 'Well?' I was not hopeful.

Her cheeks were red. Her panting breath turned to mist

in the cold air. 'I will *pretend* I can read. That will be all right.'

'How can you pretend? How do you think you'll be able to fool an educated man like Dr Morgan?'

She looked arch, something I had never seen in her before. 'Oh, but sir, I am very good at pretending. And I think I know a way it may be done.'

The whole idea was so fantastical; I didn't even bother to ask what she had in mind. Instead I sought to end the discussion by pointing out the – to me – obvious flaw in the stratagem as a whole. 'If you pretend to read, will it not just be the same as actually being able to? If whatever relative of yours who banned it ever shows up here, they'll be told you can read.'

'Yes, but in that case, sir, I will not need to remain here any longer and will have no further need to please Dr Morgan. And so you will be able to reveal our ruse, that I can't read after all, but that it was something we worked between us to save me from being put back with all those mad people when I am not mad.'

I could not help the sigh of exasperation that escaped me. The number of patients here who had told me they were the only ones who weren't crazy! 'And how do you propose to bring it off, eh? Tell me that?'

She smiled and I could not help noticing how fetching she looked, as flirtatious as some society women I'd known. 'I will learn a passage from a book, get it by heart and then I will reel it off while looking at the book and appearing to read from it. Dr Morgan won't suspect a thing, because it won't even occur to him that someone might do that. I will learn perhaps a couple of really long passages. I have a wonderful memory, sir, you will see.'

'Jane,' I said. 'You can't remember who you are. You can't even remember your own name.'

There was a long pause. 'Florence,' she said.

'What? You're telling me that's your name? You knew all along?'

She looked down at her feet, avoiding my eyes. 'It came to me just now. When you said that, about me not being able to remember it, it just jumped into my head.'

She lifted her eyes and looked straight at me, *defianting me one*. We stood eyeballing each other. I again had the feeling she was lying but somehow I could not bring myself to challenge her.

'All right, *Florence*,' I said. 'This is indeed a breakthrough. When I tell Morgan, he will have to admit I'm making progress with you. It will help our cause.'

She turned away and resumed walking slowly, looking at the path upon which fresh snow had fallen even as we talked. 'I – I would rather you said nothing to him about the name. I uncertain it is what I'm called. Perhaps it came to mind simply because it was a name I happened to like.'

I *impatiented her a sigh*. 'But, don't you see, it's just the sort of ammunition we need.'

She stopped and gave me a look as icy as the weather. 'If you tell anyone else, I shall deny I ever said it.'

'Well then, on your own head be it. I can do nothing for you. You will have to embrace your fate.' And I stalked off, furious with her. All the way back to the building I thought how stupid and ungrateful she was, after all I'd done for her, to throw away her chances of recovery because of some silly secret she felt bound to keep.

∗   ∗   ∗

Later, though, on my own, in my room before dinner, when my heat had cooled, I began to think that perhaps she had something after all. Maybe there was a way in which we might fool Morgan. I loved the audacious duplicity of it, the cleverness of the deceit we might practise upon him, and by the time I left my room and was hurrying to Jane's, my heart was thumping in my chest with excitement.

What surprised me was that she seemed to be expecting me. Oh, she made a good show of being humble and contrite after her earlier defiance, but I noticed she did not offer to give ground. I behaved as if nothing had happened and pretended I had not been cruel to her. 'I've been thinking over what you said, about pretending to read. How did you think to work it?'

'Well, sir, we will take this book, *Great Expectations*, and you will read the opening part of it to me, a little at a time. I will repeat what you say after you and we will do this until I can say it on my own without you prompting me, and then we will move on to the next little bit and so on until I have a sizeable chunk I can say from memory, enough to fool Dr Morgan.'

'That's good, very good. But what if he's not convinced? What if he selects another passage for you to look at?'

'I have thought of that possibility, too, sir. To this end, we will break the spine of the book. After my reading of the beginning, if he wants more, I will close the book and hand it back to him. When he opens it, it will naturally fall to that page.'

'Hmm, I'm not sure I like that. What if it doesn't?'

'Then, sir, as I take the book from him, I will turn to the window as if to get better light and let it fall to that page while my body is blocking his view. He will never notice it's a different page.'

I stared at her a long moment.

'Well, sir, what do you think?'

'I think,' I said, 'that you are a crafty little minx.'

'Oh, sir,' she said, with a nod of her head to one side, 'I will take that as a great compliment, coming as it does from you.'

It was only later, after dinner, when I was alone and those words of hers came back to me, that I asked myself what exactly it was she had meant by them.

After that we went at it with a will, working on the opening of *Great Expectations* and a passage from later in the book when Pip meets Herbert Pocket in London and is instructed on the manners of a gentleman, a passage which had made her laugh when I first read it to her. We broke the back of the book in that place. She was a quick learner. We did as she'd suggested, I giving her a sentence or part of it at a time and then she sitting beside me and repeating it parrot fashion until she seemed to have it by heart.

Of course, the opening chapter of *Great Expectations* is one of the greatest pieces of writing in all literature, in part because it has such natural rhythm, which makes it easier to memorise than most bits of prose. But even so, she amazed me because she was so good at retaining what she had heard. She said she kept repeating the words over and over to herself when she was alone, and this was evident because I found that at the start of each new session she seemed better schooled in her pieces than when we had ended the time before. When she was ready to put all the separate sentences together and to attempt to speak the whole passage in one go, she insisted on sitting holding the book in front of her, 'reading' from it as she would do for Morgan. I was most impressed at the way she did this, for very cleverly she thought to run her eyes from side to side, as if they were following the lines of words on the page as she had seen me do, to give the effect that she was actually reading rather than staring at a load of meaningless symbols and parroting something learned by heart. What an actress, I told myself, to be so naturally attuned to stagecraft, to have imagined herself so wholly in the part.

It was a frantic week and we spent every moment we could on our task, with me squeezing a few minutes here, a quarter of an hour there, from my busy timetable to cloister myself with her and work away at it. I confess I felt quite exhausted from the stress of it all, whereas she seemed strangely serene, utterly confident in her ability to bring the thing off.

At last Sunday came and I prepared for the day with a sinking heart. As I dressed I couldn't help thinking of all that was at stake. If Jane or Florence or whoever this strange girl was didn't manage this seemingly impossible feat, then my position here might be ruined. It would be obvious to Morgan that she and I were in cahoots, that I had tried to deceive him. How then might he begin to perceive me? Might the scales fall from his eyes as he realised I was not the straightforward person he had thought me to be? Might he suspect me of falsehood in other areas too? Might he begin to wonder about my identity altogether? On that frosty morning I shivered as I thought on all this and, I tell you, it wasn't only because of the cold.

19

The weekends were a kind of holiday in the hospital, if only in the sense that we took a break from routine. After Saturday morning there were no therapies, although sometimes if a patient became troublesome she might have to be put under restraint for the protection of herself and others, but this did not need either Morgan or me. Technically we were off duty from midday Saturday onwards, although the rule was that one of us was always on hand in case some emergency arose.

In the afternoon the patients' stultifying routine was relaxed. In the day room the cover was taken off an old upright piano that stood in one corner and a member of the staff would play popular tunes upon it, and sometimes patients too, the ones who could be trusted not to damage the instrument. The pianist would play dance tunes and the patients were permitted to dance with one another, or on their own if they wished, as some of them did, standing swaying about in time to the music, lost in whatever worlds their minds inhabited.

Observing these sessions was like watching dolls come to life. Deadpan expressions became animated, sullen looks turned to smiles, lifeless eyes shone brightly. There was a hubbub about the place that gladdened the heart to see and convinced me that the philosophy of Moral Treatment was right; if we only treated these poor women with kindness and made an effort to engage them in real life, they would respond by becoming so much more human, more like their former healthy selves, and have a better chance of being cured.

Of course, it was not all plain sailing. Often one of the women would grow over-excited by the dancing, the lack of restraint and the noise, and play up or become hysterical. Sometimes a collision on the dance floor would lead to an argument or even a physical fight. There were disputes over the piano and squabbles about which tune should be played next. All of this was ammunition for Morgan, when I ventured to suggest that an improvement came over the patients with the more relaxed regime, to argue back that it was all right for a limited time but would always eventually end in tears.

On Sunday morning there was a service in the hospital chapel that everyone was expected to attend, staff and patients alike. Morgan himself read the lesson in something of a drone that I'm sure was calculated to be soporific, so as not to arouse the emotions of his audience but to maintain them on a manageable level. So well did he succeed that his discourse was always punctuated by snores from the inmates. Afterwards we sang hymns, with one of the attendants accompanying on the chapel organ, old favourites like 'Shall We Gather at the River' and 'Rock of Ages'. There was a certain lack of reserve in the way these were rendered, with many of the women overly lusty in ringing out the words and others so out of tune as to provide myriad descants.

Luncheon was much looked forward to by the patients, for they were given proper soup followed by some decent roast meat, not a great quantity but not fatty or rancid like the normal fare, and there were a few vegetables too. The meal was always consumed with a lively buzz of conversation, which was not only on account of the food itself, but also in anticipation of what was to follow, because that was when visitors were allowed.

On this particular occasion, it was almost as if the patients' Sunday excitement had transmitted itself to Morgan, so much did he seem to be looking forward to his examination of Jane Dove. I swear even his moustache was bristling with anticipation, and he was like some animal eager to devour its prey as we walked along the corridor to her room.

When we entered, Jane was sitting in one of her armchairs. She stood up awkwardly and dropped him a half curtsy. Morgan nodded at her and then looked about at the arrangement of the room, the pictures, the sorry-looking furniture, the battered armchairs, the scratched table, the well-trodden rug, and said, 'Well, this is a surprise, I'm sure. I had no idea we were running a luxury hotel here, absolutely no idea at all.'

I managed a thin smile at this; it was better to indulge his humour than challenge him, which would only upset him and prejudice him even more against poor Jane. I looked at her for signs of nervousness and was relieved to see she appeared calm and in control of herself. It was a complete contrast to the turbulence I felt within my own breast, but then it was always much more difficult to rely on someone else rather than yourself; you never knew when they might let you down.

Morgan gestured to Jane to resume her seat and then settled himself in the other armchair facing her. He gave her a broad smile. 'I understand from Dr Shepherd that you have made the most marvellous progress under his new regimen.' His voice dripped sarcasm.

'Sir, I have tried my best to improve myself,' she said innocently, as if taking him at face value.

As I stood behind Morgan where he could not see me, my jaw must have dropped open. I had never found humility to be one of Jane's attributes.

'Very well then, let me hear you read.'

Jane looked about her as if in search of something suitable. On the desk were *The Complete Works* and *Great Expectations*. I walked over to it and picked up the latter and held it up, 'What about this, Jane? Can you read a little of this for Dr Morgan, do you think?'

'Yes, sir, I will try.' She looked sweetly at Morgan. 'But you must make allowances for any mistakes, sir. I have not long learned.'

Morgan nodded. It was obvious he anticipated some half-baked disaster. I handed Jane the book and she opened it at the beginning and began. 'My father's family name being Pirrip, and my Christian name Philip, my infant tongue . . .'

Her voice was clear and she 'read' with great expression. What was especially clever – a thing we had not worked on together – was that every few words she would stumble over a word and then correct herself, or pause and stare hard at the book, her lips moving to herself as though she was trying to spell out the letters before continuing. I stole a glance at Morgan and saw, as he watched, the smugness vanish from his face and something akin to admiration replace it. Outside we could hear the chatter and laughter of the visitors who had just arrived on the boat. It somehow magnified the quiet and tension in the room.

But Jane seemed oblivious to it all. At the end of the first paragraph she paused and looked up at Morgan. He waved a hand at her. 'Go on, my dear, go on.' I wondered for a moment if he suspected the trick that was being played upon him, but Jane handled the situation perfectly, unable to prevent – or so it seemed – a little smile of triumph appearing, as if she was pleased with herself at reading for him, and then immediately stumbling on the next word, taking some time, it seemed, to work it out, which had Morgan leaning forward in his chair in anticipation of having caught her out, but then sinking back as she managed the word and went confidently on.

After another few lines he held up a hand. 'That's enough of that,' he said. 'Now I'd like to hear you read something else, if you please.'

My heart was in my mouth. Jane shot me an anxious glance. This is what we had hoped would not happen, that she would have to rely on the trick with the broken back of the book. For the moment I was unclear whether Morgan intended her to move to another passage of her own choosing or if he meant to take the book from her and find another piece himself. Before I could find out, there came a knock at the door.

'Come in,' said Morgan, somewhat impatiently, obviously annoyed at the interruption.

The door opened and Eva's head appeared around it. 'Oh, Dr Morgan,' she said. 'Sorry, sir, I did not know you would be here.'

'Well, I am. What do you want, girl?' he said brusquely.

'It's Dr Shepherd I wanted, sir,' she said.

'Is there a problem?' I said.

'Oh, no, sir,' she replied with a smile. 'Not a problem at all. You have a visitor, sir. A young lady.'

My mouth fell open. My legs turned to water and my head swam. I thought I was going to faint. 'A young lady?'

'Yes, sir. She's waiting downstairs in the staff sitting room.'

I turned to stone. I could neither speak nor move. Morgan swung round in his chair and looked up at me and said, 'Well, go on, man. You had better go and see to her.'

'B-but –' I stammered.

He waved a dismissive hand. 'Don't worry about us, man. I can take care of things here on my own. Off you go now, doesn't do to keep a lady waiting.' He sounded like an indulgent father.

I managed to get my feet going and shuffled over to the door, moving like a man in leg irons. It was only as I was going out that I remembered Jane and caught the look in her eye that cried out, *Please don't abandon me!* I could not even think about her now. She and her future had suddenly become the least of my problems. I summoned the weakest of smiles and turned away.

Outside Eva was waiting for me and set off ahead of me. I was in a blind panic and my instinct when we reached the bottom of the stairs was to head out of the front door and run, but no sooner did the thought enter my mind than I dismissed it. Run where? There was no escape. I was on an island.

As Eva turned into the corridor that led to the staff sitting room, I stopped and said, 'Just a minute.' I was trying to buy time, give myself breathing space in which to gather my wits, think of a way out. 'Um, did the lady say who she was?'

'Yes, sir. A Miss Adams. That was the name, I believe.'

I nodded as though registering this. Well, who else could it have been? No other person had written to Shepherd since I'd been there and nobody besides Caroline Adams seemed to know he was there. My head was swimming. Discovery was inevitable. I thought, the woman is expecting Shepherd to walk in the room and knows I am not he and Eva thinks I am Shepherd – how do I reconcile this? It was vital to prevent them seeing me at the same time. 'Eva, it's all right,' I said, 'you can go and get on with your work. I don't need you to announce me.'

'If you're sure, sir –'

'Quite sure, thank you.'

She turned and walked back toward the stairs. I took out my handkerchief and wiped my brow. I was in a cold sweat. At the foot of the stairs Eva paused and turned to look back at me, her expression one of concern. I put on a smile, which seemed to satisfy her and off she went back upstairs.

20

I looked along the corridor, one way and then the other. It was clear. In the distance I could hear the buzz of conversation from the room set aside for the patients' visitors. Caroline Adams would have come over on the boat that brought them. I hurried along to the staff sitting room and knocked on the door. A faint feminine voice answered, 'Come in,' and I opened the door, slipped inside and closed it smartly after me.

'Oh!' The woman standing before me took a step back, surprised. She was tall, attractive, with auburn hair that was set off by the green of her coat and a pert little nose that somehow suggested to me that there was no nonsense about her. I saw at once that her clothes were elegant and tasteful but also not new. The nap of her coat had hints of shine about the cuffs. It was evidently not her money that Shepherd had been interested in. She had a battered fur stole about her shoulders that looked as if it had been taken from some moulting animal. She shrugged it back, as the room was warm, revealing, I was intrigued to see, a white ribbon around her neck, which was itself as smooth and pale as alabaster. I imagined it would feel cold as marble to the touch of my fingers.

'Good afternoon,' I said. 'Miss Adams, I presume. I understand you're expecting Dr Shepherd?'

'That's right, although he will not be expecting me.'

'Evidently not, I'm afraid. He's fully occupied with patients all day. Perhaps I can help. I'm Dr Gargery.' It was the first name that jumped into my head, straight out of Jane Dove's reading of *Great Expectations*. I felt a stab in my stomach at the thought of how I'd abandoned poor Jane to endure her trial with Morgan alone. For all I knew, without me to help, she might already have been consigned back to the living death of the day room. Then I thought that it didn't matter, not if I couldn't find some way out of the fix I was in. Unless I could wriggle free from it, there would be no one to conduct experiments in Moral Treatment upon poor Jane. The very idea of it would be discredited along with me.

I pushed the thought away and concentrated on playing the new role I had assumed and immediately felt a frisson of excitement. I would have relished this switch of characters, from a dead doctor to one who had never lived, were it not for the constant fear that someone – Morgan, perhaps, O'Reilly, maybe, or any other of the staff – might come into the room at any moment and call me Shepherd.

I saw she was staring at me. 'I beg your pardon, but what did you say your name was?'

My mind was suddenly blank. What name had I told her? I couldn't think. Calm down, I said to myself. Think. All that came to mind was Jane Dove reading to Morgan. Why had I thought of that? Then I remembered, *Great Expectations*. 'Gargery,' I said.

She looked at me hard. I felt myself wilting under her scrutiny. I was hot under my collar and put a finger around the inside of it to loosen it.

'Is there something wrong?' I asked at last.

'I'm sorry; I didn't mean to be rude. It's just that you seem so familiar. It feels as if I have met you before somewhere. Were you ever in Ohio?'

'No, never, but people are always telling me I look like someone else. I have that kind of face.' There was a pause. She seemed satisfied by my explanation. I cleared my throat. 'As I was saying, I'm afraid Dr Shepherd is terribly busy all day and will not be free until long after the boat takes you back.'

At this amplification of the bad news, Caroline Adams was silent and stood chewing her bottom lip.

'Perhaps I can help?' I said. 'Forgive me for intruding but Dr Shepherd – John – and I have become great friends and he's confided in me about, well, your situation.'

'Oh!' Red spots blossomed on her cheeks.

'Pray forgive me. Perhaps I should not have said anything.'

She burst into tears. 'Oh, no, no, not at all.' She let out a half-strangled sob. Then she fiddled in the little reticule whose handle she had looped over her wrist and pulled out a handkerchief and wiped her eyes and blew her nose. I waited while she composed herself. She faced me bravely. 'I should not go on so, I know. But I have no family, no one else in all the world but John. I suppose you think I am a foolish girl, chasing after him like this.'

I made a feeble gesture with my hands, which neither dismissed the idea nor endorsed it, and she went on, 'It is just that his last letter to me was so strange.' She pulled an envelope from the reticule and I thought she was going to show it to me, but instead she waved it at me. I could see my scrawl on it. 'It wasn't at all like him. I don't recognise him in it, not one bit.'

I put on a grave expression. 'Well, of course he has some difficulty writing, still, on account of the injury to his hand.'

'It's not the handwriting; I understand about that. It's – it's – well, the complete lack of feeling. The coldness.' She glanced out the window at the falling snow and shivered. Her voice trembled. 'It was not a letter I ever expected to receive from the man I loved.'

A tear rolled down her cheek and she shook her head, unable to go on. I walked over to her and laid a hand upon her arm. 'Please,' I said, 'don't distress yourself.'

She took out the handkerchief again and gathered herself once more. 'I am making an idiot of myself. What must you think of me?'

'I assure you I do not think anything ill of you, Miss Adams, quite the reverse, in fact. I – I have – but no, I mustn't say anything. It's not my place at all. Although what was said to me was not specified as being in confidence, it was perhaps so de facto, in that it was never imagined that this meeting here today, between you and me, would ever take place.'

Her head perked up and she looked me in the eye. 'What exactly has John told you?'

She seemed at once both anxious to know and fearful of finding out.

I was only half a line ahead of her in the script, only there wasn't a script of course. I had to make it up as I went along, always tailoring my answers to the questions she fired at me. I opened my mouth but nothing came out. I was trying to think where to go next. Just then I heard footsteps approaching in the corridor outside. I forgot about saying anything. Indeed, I could not have spoken; it was impossible even to get my breath. Those were a woman's footsteps and I thought if it's O'Reilly and she comes in then I may as well string myself up here and now and save the state the trouble. Caroline Adams and I stared at each other, the tension near unbearable for her, I realised, at the prospect of the ending of our tête-à-tête just when she was on the verge of making some discovery, the explanation for Shepherd's behaviour she had come for.

The footsteps reached the door and went on by without pausing. We both waited as their echo died away in the distance. I still hadn't thought of anything to say.

'Listen,' I managed finally, taking the break in the conversation caused by the footsteps as my cue, 'we cannot talk frankly here because the room is in constant use and we are bound to be interrupted.'

'Is there somewhere else we can go to be more private?'

I made a show of thinking hard, wrinkling my brow, a ham performance, but then what was this if not some ghastly melodrama? 'Not really . . .' I began, then gave a tentative nod toward the window, 'except outside, and it doesn't look too welcoming out there.'

She tossed her head. 'Oh, I don't mind a bit of snow. The cold doesn't bother me in the least. Can we find a quiet spot outside?'

'Oh yes, the grounds are quite extensive and everyone else will be inside on a day like this. There's a gazebo around the back where we can shelter a little.'

'Very well, then, if you're agreeable and kind enough to spare me a little more of your time, let's go there.'

I quite admired her at that moment for her bravery and determination. She would endure anything to get her man.

I walked over to the door, with her behind me, opened it and peeped out. The coast was clear.

'You seem rather cautious,' she said. 'Is there some problem?'

'Well, it's best I'm not seen with you. I wouldn't want it to get back to Shepherd. John, I mean.'

'Oh. Well, perhaps I should go along on my own and meet you somewhere outside.'

'Capital idea! Here's what you must do: follow this corridor to the main door, the one you will have come in by. Go outside and turn left around the outside of the building and keep walking until you're at the back. I'll go out by the back door and meet you there.'

'All right.'

I stood aside to let her pass and she began walking along the corridor. After ten yards or so she suddenly stopped and looked back and said, 'Dr Gargery?'

Instinctively I looked over my shoulder, thinking she must be addressing someone behind me, forgetting that Gargery was me. Luckily I remembered in time before it registered with her. Although, why should she notice? Why on earth would this woman think I was anyone other than who I said I was? I smiled. 'Yes?'

'Thank you.' She mouthed the words almost without uttering them, obeying the need for secrecy, and then she turned and went off along the corridor. I stepped back into the staff sitting room, shut the door behind me and stood with my back against it. My whole body was quivering. I shuddered out a sigh. So far so good. I'd gotten her into a place where it was unlikely we would be seen together. Or if we were, only from a distance, and to any observer we would simply be Dr Shepherd and his young lady visitor. Everything could yet be all right so long as she didn't speak to anyone, because then the game would certainly be up. This meant that somehow I would have to spin out the couple of hours before the boat left, taking the visitors back to the city. It would not be easy. I could hardly expect her to wander around in the freezing weather for so long, especially now the snow was coming down thick and fast. Yet letting her back indoors would put me in peril again.

Then I realised that even if I brought it off, kept her occupied and away from others all that time, it wouldn't solve the problem. This was a determined woman and no matter what cock-and-bull story about Shepherd's motives I offered her, she would not be satisfied until she had had a showdown with the man himself, and that, of course, was impossible – well, at least in this world. And then sooner or later the truth would come out and I would be exposed. Even if I avoided discovery this time – and that was still looking far from certain – I probably couldn't survive another such episode. I had to find a permanent solution, or, if that couldn't be managed, at least one that was longer-lasting than merely until her next visit. All this was going through my head as I opened the door, checked that everything was clear, ducked out and made quickly for the back door. If anyone happened to be looking out a window somewhere, they wouldn't see me following in the footsteps of Miss Adams.

The sky was a lowering threat and the snow continued to fall. I found her under a tree, like some ghost in the dim light, for the afternoon wore on and the sun was losing strength. I summoned a feeble smile.

'But you haven't a coat,' she said. 'You'll catch your death.'

'I don't feel the cold,' I lied, wondering how I would keep my teeth from chattering. Great white flakes fell upon us, settling on our heads and shoulders, threatening to turn us into snowmen. 'Let's walk away from the building. It will lessen any chance of bumping into someone and will help keep us warm into the bargain.'

The grounds were naturally deserted, as I'd hoped, but at the same time the complete absence of anyone else pointed up the madness of our enterprise. Even the lunatics were not crazy enough to be abroad in such conditions. I began to trudge in the direction of a small area of woodland. It was three or four hundred yards away. I was thinking about taking her all the way to the edge of this side of the island, to the black water there, but I saw almost at once that would be no good; it would only lead to more questions.

'Can we not talk as we walk?' she said.

Our feet were crunching through snow several inches deep now as the path we were on petered out. No one normally walked in this part of the grounds. They weren't cultivated at all, there weren't enough gardeners, and this area was left more or less to nature.

'I thought you mentioned a gazebo?' she said. 'I don't see any sign of one.' She was puzzled rather than worried.

I pressed on ahead of her, leaving her no option but to trail along in my wake. 'Yes, I'm not too familiar with this part of the grounds but I think it's over here somewhere.'

'But Dr Gargery, must we go on? The snow is getting so deep.'

'Let's get into the wood, at least. We can't talk here; we might still be visible from the building. We can be private

179

under the trees and they'll shelter us from the snow.' I went on and a moment later heard the crunch of her feet behind me.

After another five minutes we were battling through snow a foot deep. I ploughed on, willing her to follow, determined not to stop now.

'Dr Gargery, Dr Gargery,' came her voice from behind, 'are you sure this is wise? The snow is getting deeper. My skirts are getting soaked.'

'Only a little way now.' I could hear the fake cheeriness in my voice. 'The ground will be clear once we're in the woods; you'll see.'

I carried on as fast as I could and she had no choice but to follow. Eventually I was in amongst the trees. She staggered in after me, panting, water dripping from her hat. The ground here was only lightly dusted with snow, protected by the trees all about us. I turned to face her.

She stood brushing the snow off her coat. I stared at her. It was deathly silent, that special kind of silence when it snows, every sound muffled. At last she must have felt my eyes upon her, because her hand stopped mid-movement and she looked up at me.

'Dr Gargery, what is it? You look so strange.'

I didn't say anything. I was thinking how tantalising was the small hint of flesh that I could just make out above the collar of her coat. I was remembering how white and smooth was the skin hidden beneath that collar. I was relishing the thought of that silky white ribbon.

'Dr Gargery,' she said again. 'What's the matter? Why are you looking at me in that way?'

I said nothing. I took a step toward her. Her face was all alarmed now.

'Dr Gargery, why don't you speak? You look so very peculiar. What are you doing? I don't like it. Please, sir, take me back to the hospital now; you're frightening me.'

There were only a few feet between us. I took another step. She began backing off, taking a step back every time I took another forward, until, although she didn't know it, she was almost touching a tree behind her. Of a sudden I took three swift paces and she retreated and came up against the tree. I reached out my hands and seized her by the lapels of her coat, ripping them apart, scattering buttons around us like shrapnel.

'No!'

She opened her mouth to scream, which of course I could not allow. I let go the coat and seized her by the throat to keep her quiet. She was too shocked to say anything anyway. Her lips moved soundlessly, mouthing what she thought was my name. I got my thumbs into her throat and squeezed with all my might. Her eyes began to pop out the way their eyes always do. She sank to her knees. I applied more pressure and she somehow managed to release a half-strangled squawk and I whispered, not unkindly, 'Keep calm, my dear, for I have to tell you everything is all right. Very soon now, in less than a minute, less than half a minute in fact, you will be with your beloved John Shepherd for ever.'

A great shudder went through her body, and then it became limp. I was shaking myself, as you do in these situations. I must have drifted off somewhere and came to with the awareness of her dead weight pulling on my wrists. My hands were still clasped around her neck. I let go and she fell forward against my legs. I took a step back and she collapsed onto the thin carpet of snow. I felt hot and sweaty and took out my handkerchief and wiped my brow.

She had fallen with her head on one side. Her face was purple and contorted. I hate that and avoided looking at it. I bent down and felt around the back of her neck, where the white ribbon was tied. I calmed myself with deep breaths until my hands had stopped trembling and I was able to undo the knot. I slipped off the ribbon and put it in my pocket. It was just a piece of ribbon, nothing to connect it with her. I wanted to have something of her, to remind me of that moment when I held her fragile life in the whim of my fingers.

More myself now, I began to think what I must do. I looked all around. Everything was quiet, and I was reassured that no one had witnessed what I'd done. I walked back to the edge of the wood and peered out between the trees. It would soon be dark. I needed to hurry. I returned to what had been Caroline Adams and was now a piece of dead meat. I could not leave her here where she would be in plain sight if anyone came into the wood. I bent down and took up the reticule, whose strings were still looped around her wrist. I rifled through the contents. There was my letter. I slipped it in my pocket. I helped myself to the small wad of dollar bills; she had no need of them now. There were a few coins, which I did not bother with, and a little note-book that I thought might contain information that would identify her, so I took that as well. It was too dark now to be able to read it here. After making sure there were no other papers in the reticule, I closed it and left it tied to her wrist.

Squatting on my haunches, I got my arms beneath her, lifted her and staggered to my feet. She was a tall woman, heavier than most, but I had that almost superhuman strength that always comes at such times. I carried her to the far side of the copse and out of it, staggering as my feet sank into the snow. I trudged on for forty or fifty yards and then the snow grew deeper still. I realised there was some sort of dip in the ground here. I let her drop and then fell to my knees and began scooping out snow, working furiously until I'd made the hollow some couple of feet deep. I rolled the body into it and then began heaping snow back over her. With the help of the snow falling from the sky she was soon completely covered. Thanks to the depression I had made, there was no telltale mound; the surface was smooth and level.

I backed away. I took off my jacket and, walking backwards, drew it from side to side across the trail of my footprints, more or less erasing them. It was probably an unnecessary precaution, because falling snow was covering them fast anyway, but it meant that even should my footprints from the building to the little wood remain, no one would be able to track them further. Once I cleared the other side of the wood, I put my jacket back on and made my way as fast as I could toward the building.

By now it was near enough dark and, with the sky full of snow, there was neither moon nor stars. I had just reached the back of the hospital when I heard voices, coming from the direction of the front door. I made my way along the side of the building and peeped around the corner. The visitors were leaving and were walking up the drive toward the river to get the boat. I had a sudden moment of panic at the thought of the boat. Would Caroline Adams be missed when she did not return with the rest of the passengers? Then I relaxed. There was no one who would be making the journey back on the boat but those who came on it. The trip itself was so short it was unlikely Miss Adams would have had time on the way out to strike up an acquaintance with another visitor who might notice her absence going back. She had told me herself she had no family to miss her. I was pretty sure I was safe.

I looked out across the grounds at the way I had come, the few feet nearest the house now illuminated from the lights within. Snow continued to fall. Caroline Adams would rest concealed within her icy cocoon until the spring melt. And by that time I intended to be well away from here, several hundred miles out west.

I hadn't time now to stand here ruminating on all this. Jane Dove! I hadn't thought about her for a single moment in the past hour. My heart sank and even the triumph of having the interfering Miss Adams out of the way was deflated at the thought that Jane might have been found out, our deception discovered, and that in all likelihood I was about to be summarily dismissed and sent on my way into who knew what danger. I hurried inside.

My clothes were a mess, of course; I was pretty soaked through. I went up to my room where there was a fire lit ready for my evening there. I took off my jacket and pants and draped them over chairs as close to the fire as I dared, to dry them. I put on Shepherd's spare pair of pants. I took my letter to Caroline Adams from the jacket pocket, read it through with a grim satisfaction and then consigned it to the flames.

Then I had a look in the notebook. There were a few addresses, mostly female names, which I thought most likely to be those of old school friends. There were several drafts of letters to Shepherd, all violently crossed out and unfinished. I would have liked to read them, but there was no time now. The following pages were blank and I was in the act of throwing the book into the fire when a couple of pieces of paper fell out. I picked them up. A used rail ticket from Columbus bearing yesterday's date. She had evidently travelled overnight. There was a ticket for the left-luggage office at the city railroad depot, which brought a smile to my face. It almost certainly meant she had only arrived this morning, checked her baggage and come straight out to the island. She had not booked into a lodging house or hotel, where she might have confided her plans to someone, or where she would be missed when she didn't return that evening.

The other item was a small square of folded paper which, when I opened it out, proved to be the front page of a newspaper. The headline read: 'CONVICTED KILLER AMONG DEAD IN RAIL DISASTER'. Underneath, the subheading said: 'Accident Saves State Executioner A Job'. And below that there was the police photograph of me, taken soon after my arrest, with my hair sticking up wildly and my eyes staring madly out at the camera. I understood now why Caroline Adams had thought she'd seen me before. The photograph was simply not a good enough likeness for her to remember why. There was also a picture of me as Othello, in blackface, so no possibility of recognition there. As well as the lurid headline and opening story about me, the article contained details of the possible causes of the accident and a list of those identified as dead or injured. It was dated a few days after the accident. It struck me that the late Miss Adams had been more interested in this list than in the sensational headlines and, having reassured herself that Shepherd was not among the dead, had probably not looked at it again since, hence her failure to work out why I seemed familiar. Besides, why would she connect me with a dead man? It wasn't something you would naturally do.

I ripped the notebook to pieces and threw them into the fire. The left-luggage ticket I kept. When I finally left the island and made my run for it, I might find something of use to me there. If I were ever in a position where it might incriminate me by connecting me with the murdered woman, I could swallow it in a moment. I was about to throw the newspaper cutting into the flames too, but something stayed my hand, some unaccustomed foolish sentimentality, if you will; I realised it was all I had of the old me, that picture as the Moor and that horrid police photograph. Of course I had a new identity now, as John Shepherd, and soon, before the winter was over and the snow had melted and revealed my latest misdeed to the world, I would have to have another still. But for now, I discovered I wasn't quite ready to relinquish my past completely; I could not bring myself to say goodbye to my former self just yet.

Even as I did so, I told myself I was being a fool. This little piece of paper could have me hanged. I knew I should listen to this voice, but I didn't. I folded the clipping and looked about for somewhere to hide it. I didn't dare risk a drawer or the pocket of my spare pants. I had a fear of someone poking about in my room and when I now asked myself why, the answer that came was O'Reilly. She and I had become enemies over the matter of Jane Dove and I would not have put it past her to search through my things. Casting about, my eye lighted upon *Moral Treatment* lying on my bedside table. I slipped the cutting between its pages.

I liked the idea of its being in there, with the book right out in the open. It was the last place anyone would look.

I looked out the window. It was dark now, but in the light spilling out from the building I could see the snow still fell, the air almost solid with it. The paths that had been cleared earlier were already covered by a fresh layer I reckoned must be several inches deep. The branches of the trees hung heavy with snow. I was reassured that Caroline Adams would sleep soundly in her bed until spring.

I turned to the fire and was watching the final pieces of paper blacken and crumble into ash when the bell for dinner went. My jacket was almost dry now. I put it on and hurried downstairs to the staff dining room, where I found Morgan already seated and sipping a glass of red wine.

'Ah, Shepherd, there you are,' he said with a smile. 'Let me get you a glass of wine.' He poured it and handed it to me as I sat down.

I hardly dared ask about Jane Dove. I knew Morgan well enough by now to understand that his good humour did not mean that I was safe. It would be just like him to play cat and mouse with me before delivering the killer blow.

When he said nothing, I began to convince myself that this was in fact the case and that he was just teasing me, keeping me in suspense to prolong the torture. In the end I could stand it no longer. I cleared my throat nervously. 'How did it go, the, um, the reading with Jane Dove?'

'Oh that,' he said, as he picked up his knife and fork and began sawing at a piece of meat on his plate. 'I have to hand it to you. She reads extremely well.' He paused in his dissection of the meat and looked up at me. 'I enjoyed it immensely. Especially the pieces from *Hamlet*.'

My hand shook so violently wine spilled from my glass and dripped onto the white tablecloth. I had never taught Jane Dove anything from *Hamlet*; it was not something she had learned.

21

I lay awake half the night; when I did sleep I *restlessed*,
tossing and turning, troubled by a succession of dreams in
which the face of Caroline Adams loomed before me, the
skin purple, the eyes popping out. Another time I awoke
bathed in sweat after I felt my hands upon the clammy,
pimpled neck of a plucked chicken which, when I looked
at it, turned into the face of my Aunt Martha, who surely
merited such a fate since she never intervened to prevent
the violent excesses of my uncle and his vicious belt. But
curiously, when morning finally came, with the sun shining
bright, the thing that concerned me was neither the unfortunate Miss Adams, nor anything like that, but Jane Dove.
The fact that she had read *Hamlet* to Morgan meant she
had been fooling us – well, me, really – all along, simply
pretending she could not read. I wondered what else she
might be simulating and why she should want to do so.
There was some mystery here and I meant to get to the
bottom of it. I liked this girl immensely. I was attracted by
her gangly good looks, her dark haunting eyes, her graceful
neck; but none of that mattered. I would not be made a
fool of; I would not be used.

* * *

As soon as I could escape my duties I went to her room. She was sitting at the window, staring out at the wintry landscape. *Great Expectations* was near to hand and I wondered if she had been reading it and had hurriedly put it down when she heard my knock. She smiled brightly at me. 'Look at the snow!' she said. 'Is it not wonderful?'

I gave a cursory nod and she suddenly looked anxious. 'Oh, sir, did I not pass the test?'

'Oh yes, you passed all right. You passed a little too well.'

She was puzzled now. 'I don't understand. How could I do *too* well?'

'You and I must have a serious conversation. I have tried my level best to help you. I have lifted you out of the tedious indignities of this place and you in return have taken advantage of me and deceived me.'

Her face fell. 'What do you mean? What is it you accuse me of?'

'Dr Morgan tells me you read *Hamlet* to him. How is that possible when you have not learned it?'

She began to laugh.

'What . . . ?'

'I did learn it, from you, when you read it to me and acted it out. I could not help but remember some of it. "To be or not to be that is the question." It just stuck in my mind.'

'Dr Morgan said you read it to him. How did you know which piece was the soliloquy if you could not read the words?'

'That is not the way it happened. When I had finished Great Expectationing, Dr Morgan asked me to read something else. I desperated, as you can well imagine, for I had no other pieces prepared and thought I was redhanded.

The only other book in the room was the Shakespeare and he picked it up and handed it to me and told me to read something from it. My heart was beating as if it was going to burst, I can tell you, as I expected to be found out, but then I saw a chance, a small glimmer of hope. I opened it at random, because, as you say, I could not tell one page from another, but he had sat down opposite me. I lifted the book so all he could see was the cover. I gave him some speeches from *Hamlet* and a bit of *Macbeth*. I am sure I didn't get them quite right, because I was only remembering what I'd heard and had not learned them as we did the Dickens. But he didn't seem to notice. To tell you true, sir, I do not think Dr Morgan familiars much with Shakespeare.'

I shook my head in admiration at the resourcefulness of her improvisation and also at the sheer audacity of it. To think Morgan had considered this girl an imbecile. She had run rings around him, the silly old fool. I smiled. 'That was very quick-thinking of you. I'm sorry I doubted you.'

She ignored that and looked out the window again, avoiding my eyes. 'Sir, I have a request to make of you.'

'A request? What is it?'

'I should like to go skating.'

'Skating!'

She turned to me, eyes gleaming. 'It possibles, sir, really it does. Eva has skates she will lend me the use of and although it is true there is no lake, there is a pond at the back of the house and a couple of the garden boys have cleared the snow from it for Eva and she has been skating there. Please, sir, please let me.'

I was about to say no automatically, because I could

imagine what Morgan would think of the idea, but then I thought, Why not? Where's the harm in it? Besides, I didn't need to ask Morgan's permission. He'd given me a free hand with my experiment, more or less. 'All right,' I said, 'I will get up an hour early tomorrow morning and you can have your skate before breakfast.'

I was beginning to think ahead now, to ready myself for my departure, which would have to be before the snow melted and revealed Caroline Adams's body. On counting the money I'd taken from her purse, I found it to amount to sixty dollars. With what I could pry out of Morgan by way of salary I would have a pretty good stake to finance my flight west. I looked more and more to the future and the new life I envisaged for myself because my existence in the hospital now was underscored by a vague feeling of dread. I worried that Miss Adams might be missed and that she might have told someone where she was going. Every time I was near a window with a view of the river, I could not help looking anxiously out across the black water expecting any moment to see a boat full of police heading toward the island. Of course I had lived for years with that kind of fear, but this time was somehow different. It was having had the noose practically around my neck that had done it. Before, I had convinced myself I was invincible; now I knew it wasn't so. I was not fool enough to think the train wreck had been the work of providence protecting me, or even of the devil, looking after his own. I knew it was pure blind luck, a royal flush in the first deal, such an extraordinary piece of good fortune that I could not help feeling I must have used up all my reservoir of that substance and was now due no more.

The following morning it stopped snowing and the sun shone brightly in a clear frosty sky. Jane and I set off together for the pond, with her animated and chatting away in her strange language and giggling like a schoolgirl. Today we seemed more like child and favourite uncle than doctor and patient, or the lover and his lass we had sometimes felt close to being.

Eva's boys must have been out early, since the pond had been cleared of snow. I shivered when I saw how close it was to where I had dumped the unfortunate Miss Adams, who lay only twenty or thirty yards away from the edge of the ice. But when I saw there was no sign of the body and how effectively it was concealed, I began to enjoy the idea of its proximity. While Jane sat by the edge of the frozen water putting on the skates Eva had lent her, I strolled casually round the pond until I came to the spot where I reckoned Miss Adams lay. I crunched through the snow and then stood watching my charge, and could not prevent a little smile at the idea I was standing on my victim and that I was the only one who knew.

Jane Dove had evidently skated a great deal before; she was certainly no novice. She glided effortlessly across the ice, graceful as a swan, head held high by that deliciously long neck. She criss-crossed the surface, going perilously close to the edges – which was unavoidable because the pond was so small, not at all like the lake she had told me about – but always seeming to know where she was. She swept around the little circle of the pond's perimeter with a confidence that belied her normal shy self. And then, all at once, she stopped skating and let herself slow to a halt, coming to rest at more or less the dead centre of the ice. She stood there on her skates, staring ahead of her, hair blowing in the breeze, looking wild and completely crazy. I did not know what had happened but I had a hollow feeling in my chest. Something from deep inside her seemed to have tipped her over the edge.

I stumbled through the snow to the edge of the pond and called out, 'Jane! Jane! What's the matter?'

Her features were as immobile as her body; she showed no sign of having heard me. Then I had a sudden inspiration, 'Florence!' I shouted. 'Florence!'

Immediately her head swung round and she looked straight at me and, as she did so, began to wobble. Her feet slid in opposite directions and she collapsed in a heap.

It was difficult for me to reach her quickly. My shoes slipped and slid on the ice and a couple of times I nearly fell flat on my back. She remained sitting on the ice, staring at me as if at a stranger. 'It's all right, Florence, I'm coming,' I yelled. She didn't seem to care.

Eventually I was with her. I got behind her, put my hands under her arms and hauled her to her feet. There was a moment when her skates began to slide away beneath her and I thought we were both going to go over, but I managed to stay steady and got her safely upright.

'What's the matter? What happened?' I said.

She regarded me as though she had no idea who I was, then said a single word: 'Theo.'

I waited a moment but nothing else came, so I said, 'Who is Theo? Is he someone you used to skate with?'

Her eyes were staring at me but I felt they were seeing nothing. It was as though the mechanism inside them was focused inwards, looking at something long buried there. She nodded slowly. 'Yes. He was tall.'

Again she offered nothing more and so I tried another prompt. 'Is he perhaps the brother you mentioned before? Is Theo your brother?'

Her brow furrowed, as though she was thinking hard. At last she said, 'My brother? Yes, I think he might have been. He was tall like me. Yes, he must have been my brother.'

It struck me as odd that while I had spoken of this Theo in the present tense, she had used the past. Was this because something had happened to him or was it that she was looking at her former life as something long gone? I could not tell.

With my arm around her shoulders I began to walk her slowly toward the edge of the ice. She made no attempt to skate but clip-clopped clumsily along on her blades. When we made the shore and she was sitting taking off the skates I said, 'All right then, tell me more about Theo.'

Again she stared into some far distant past for what seemed like an age and then at last she looked at me and gave a second take, as though she had just realised I was there. 'I – I can't. I had a picture of a boy skating on a lake, but now it's gone. He's not there any more.'

'Try,' I urged her. 'Come, Florence, you must try.'

She stood up and looked me in the eye, fully engaged now, and said, 'You must not call me that, sir. I am not that person any more. Here I am Jane Dove.' And with that she stalked off back toward the building. I staggered through the snow after her and caught her up, but despite all my fractured attempts at conversation she said nothing further all the way.

It was when we were approaching the building that a sudden movement in an upper window caught my eye. I saw what I thought was the figure of a woman dressed in

195

black looking down at us, but at that moment I caught my foot against something, a branch buried beneath the snow perhaps, and stumbled, and when I had righted myself and looked up again, the woman, if she had ever existed, was gone.

22

It might have been my fevered imagination, of course, all my dark anxieties, the constant fear of discovery and exposure that someone like me has to live with, but this occurrence of the woman in the window began to play upon my mind, because it seemed to confirm a feeling I had had lately of being watched. At odd times I sensed the weight of another's eyes upon me, although whenever I looked about me there was never anybody there.

The only person it might be was O'Reilly. Whenever I was in her presence, perhaps in the day room or else in the patients' dining hall, and I happened to glance at her, I would find her watching me intently, which suggested to me that it was she who was spying on me at other times, when she was concealed from my view.

I had made an enemy of her, of that much I was sure. I could think of no justification for her dislike, except for the business with Jane Dove, which she seemed to take as a challenge to her authority, as indeed it was, for if successful it would threaten the continuance of the harsh discipline she exercised upon the hospital and which I knew she enjoyed. Moreover, I feared she had found my draft letter to Caroline Adams and suspected that I was not who I claimed to be. If that were true, I wondered what kind of game she was playing and why she did not expose me immediately. Perhaps she thought I might be useful to her in some way, and even though she might not have worked out yet what that might be, it was worth having me in her pocket. Or maybe she simply liked having another being within her power. This was less logical, perhaps, but I had seen the savage pleasure she took in her cruelty to the patients. Although I have never been sadistic, I, of all people, understood well enough the Godlike thrill of dictating the fate of another person.

I decided I must not let myself be discouraged by the incident of being imprisoned in the storeroom; I must renew my campaign to gain some advantage over her and so neutralise the hold she had over me. She presented a serious risk to my hopes of getting clean away. I could not manage that if I were under constant surveillance. I made up my mind to find out what lay behind the business of her sneaking off to the third floor.

Following her had gotten me nowhere – or rather it had led to me being locked in a room – she was much too sharp. I would have to explore the third floor some time when she was out of the way. Therein lay the difficulty, for the woman did not appear to take a moment off. Whenever you looked around she seemed to be there, often materialising as if from nowhere like a malign ghost. Or I would go to some room in the building, perhaps an unplanned and unannounced visit, and lo and behold, when I arrived, she would already be there, as if waiting for me.

But there was one situation when she was absent from the island altogether for a whole night at a time. This was when an unmanageable inmate had to be sent back to the asylum on the mainland, where they had better facilities for the restraint of violent patients. O'Reilly was the one entrusted with the duty of escorting such women there. She would take another attendant with her and they would convey the patient, who was usually straitjacketed or sedated or both, to the shore on the morning boat that brought us new patients and supplies. Because there was no boat back to the island the same day, they would spend the night ashore and return on the next morning's boat.

At such times O'Reilly would be gone for almost twenty-four hours. The trouble was these instances were few and far between and I might have a long wait until the next one. It had happened only once in all the time I had been there.

I had been mulling this over when, as luck would have it, an incident occurred that necessitated the removal of a patient. It was on account of the weather. Snow had been falling heavily for a whole day and night and it was impossible for the gardeners to keep the footpaths outside clear for the patients to exercise. Without their daily walk the inmates grew restless and increasingly fractious. There were numerous aggravations at mealtimes especially, with women fighting more fiercely than usual over food, and tin plates had been thrown or used as weapons. The attendants were kept busy, rushing this way and that, trying to quell each little outburst before it transformed itself into something more serious. But they were truly up against it, because the more disturbance there was, the greater the agitation of the whole population. And at the evening meal one night things boiled over and one patient, a grossly built woman who could only have maintained such a weight on the deprived diet offered in the hospital by regularly robbing her fellows of their food, stole a piece of bread from the woman next to her, who retaliated by picking up her fork and stabbing the bully in the eye. All hell was let loose, with the half-blinded woman roaring like a wounded lion, scattering those around her in fear. She seized her enemy and threw her across the table, sending plates and food flying everywhere, and then tried to strangle her, although not very effectively, for she had not the knack.

It took half an hour to subdue her and get everyone else calmed down, with O'Reilly marching up and down the room dispensing blows upon the backs of the rioting patients with a stick. Of course, this only exacerbated the tension and things went from bad to worse.

As it was my duty in the dining hall that day, I decided to take charge. I went up behind O'Reilly and caught hold of the stick as she lifted up her arm to strike another patient. Before she knew what was happening, I pulled it from her grasp and broke it across my knee. She turned and glared at me, eyes burning with hatred. I ignored her and said to one of the other attendants, 'Quickly, go to the kitchen and tell them to bring more food – everything they can lay their hands on, and fast.'

Moments later cooks and kitchen maids came hurrying in with baskets of bread, plates of cold meat and even a great basket of apples, a rare sight in the hospital. They began distributing it at random, throwing it onto the tables. Straight away the half-starved women stopped fighting and began scrabbling around for food. Naturally this occasioned more scraps between them, but there was so much food they soon realised they had no need to fight for it and indeed were actually losing out by doing so. The place quieted down as they mostly became too busy eating to cause trouble. As the mayhem subsided, the attendants gradually guided them back to their seats and a semblance of order was restored. After a momentous struggle with four attendants, the big woman who had started it all was straitjacketed. The woman who had stabbed her was now sitting on the floor sobbing, evidently horrified by what she had begun, but nevertheless she was pulled to her feet and taken off to the violent patients' ward on the third floor. Her abject demeanour made this seem utterly unnecessary now, but the rationale in the hospital was, quite reasonably perhaps, that once a patient had shown herself capable of extreme violence, she could not be trusted not to repeat the action.

The other woman's injured eye was in such a state that after Morgan had examined it he said he could do nothing for her and that she would have to go to the hospital on the mainland, which meant O'Reilly would have to take her.

The following morning, I stood at the window of my room and watched as the trio of O'Reilly, her assistant and the wounded woman, still in a straitjacket with a patch over her injured eye, set off for the landing stage. Just as they reached the front entrance to the hospital grounds, O'Reilly paused and turned her head and looked straight up at me, as if she felt my eyes upon her. It sent a chill through me, the fact she knew I was there, but I made no attempt to hide and stared resolutely back at her. I imagined she was regretting leaving me free to roam her domain at will.

I would need a safe amount of time to explore the third floor, a good hour when I was sure Morgan would not catch me there, and I spent much of the night working in my room to achieve this. After our morning therapies had been completed and several hapless women half frozen in icy water or bound screaming to chairs, I handed him a huge pile of patient reports to check. Normally I gave him a few at a time, as and when I'd got round to them, and in this I was more or less up to date. Overnight, though, I had filled out dozens of them, many of my entries completely fictitious because I hadn't re-examined the patients concerned since my last reports, but Morgan had no way of knowing that, especially with O'Reilly out of the way. Moreover, in many of the reports I made observations and asked questions which I knew would be more time-consuming to answer than the queries themselves had been to frame. I reckoned a couple of hours was the minimum it would take him. Lastly, after my time at the hospital I was beginning to know something of psychology, at least so far as this one person, Morgan, was concerned. I figured the doctor, with his passion for punctuality and his obsession with efficiency, would not be able to leave the pile of reports alone until he had worked through them all.

It was inevitable – *it inevitabled* – that he questioned the quantity of work I handed him in one go and I apologised and said I'd got behind with the reports and had made a great effort to get back up to date, emphasising how I understood the paramount importance of that. Morgan castigated me for my dilatoriness, as I had known he would, and said he would set to work on them after supper that evening, which was exactly as I'd hoped; the patients would be settled down and few of the attendants would be about. The corridors would most likely be empty and I would be able to move around without arousing suspicion or encountering any hindrance.

23

Everything was as quiet as death when I slipped from my room that evening. I had that wonderful feeling that surges through the blood sometimes, the sense that I was all-powerful and that nothing and no one would be able to withstand me. O'Reilly was out of the way, exiled across the water, and Morgan weighed down by all the paperwork I had visited upon him. Everything was on my side. Not once did I put my foot upon a creaky floorboard, not once did I collide with a piece of furniture or trip or stumble in the shadows. I had only a candle to light my way, and its flickering flame threw dancing shadows upon the walls, but neither these nor anything else unnerved me.

I went downstairs, and paused outside Morgan's office with my ear to the door. The satisfying scratch of pen upon paper told me he was hard at work. I made my way to the back staircase and stood at the foot of it for a good minute, listening. I did not want to run into someone coming down it on my way up; it would be tricky trying to explain what business I had to be there.

There was no noise, only the soft sound of my own breath and, from somewhere outside, the lonely cry of an owl, that ghostly predator of the night. Funny, though, how it made me shiver. I had a sudden vision of poor Caroline Adams, lying out there in her icy shroud. I shuddered at the thought of it and made a silent wish that she sleep soundly. I swore, as I had when luck freed me from the train, that I would bury the part of my nature that drove me to do such things. I reassured myself that I had not broken that vow. The removal of Miss Adams had been an absolute necessity for my safety, and not the result of any evil impulse. Satisfied now that no one was about, I climbed the stairs to the third floor.

I found myself in a long corridor with doors either side. In the distance I could hear muttered voices and I followed the sound. I came to a door that was slightly ajar. I was bold as brass now and not ready to retreat. I put my eye to the crack between door and doorjamb and saw inside two attendants sitting in chairs either side of a table. The table was against the wall, which both were leaning against, looking relaxed. There was a bottle of whiskey on the table between them and each had a glass. They were conversing quietly. I retreated, soft as a rat, and tried the doors in the corridor and found them locked. Listening at them, I could hear the sounds of breathing, snoring and people tossing and turning in bed, and the occasional woman muttering in her sleep. These then were the rooms where the difficult patients slept, many of them in isolation because of their unpredictable and possibly violent natures. There was no way of knowing if my madwoman was in one of these rooms, or any way of getting into it if she was. I crept back along the corridor toward the stairs, about to descend, my mission a dismal failure and the mystery of the missing woman still unsolved, when I heard the creak of a floorboard above my head. Looking carefully to the other side of the staircase, I realised another flight continued up, rather more steeply, and it dawned upon me that it must lead to an attic above.

I was standing there contemplating whether to climb up and investigate further, or get out of there fast while my luck still held, when there came the most hellish sound I had ever heard, a manic laughter, twisted from the merriment and jocularity we associate with that sound into something so awful, so redolent of perversion and murderous intent, that I nearly dropped the candle. Behind me the murmurs of the attendants' voices ceased. I heard a chair being pushed back and a voice say, 'It sounds as if she's getting restless up there. It gets on my nerves, so it does. I've a good mind to go up there and give her what for, and indeed I would, but I don't have the key.'

'Yes, and if you did, that would be you out of a job and no mistake if O'Reilly was to catch you,' came the reply of the other woman. 'We're not even supposed to know there's anyone up there at all.'

'O'Reilly's on shore for the night,' said the first woman.

'No matter if she is, it's the same difference,' said the other. 'See no evil, touch no evil and just put up with having to hear a bit of evil, that's what I say,' and she let out a guffaw at her own good humour.

'Well, that's true enough,' said the first. 'I ain't never seen her and I ain't never touched her, but I damned well heard her sure enough.'

'Perhaps another glass will help block out the noise,' said the other.

There was the sound of glasses clinking and then their quiet muttering resumed. I ducked up the narrow flight of stairs to the attic, not an easy climb, for there was a turn in them that took them under the sloping eaves of the building and meant I had to bend low to mount them, difficult for someone of my height, especially when carrying a candle. I reached the top, where there was a single central corridor with doors either side. Opening the first, I found a large room piled with lumber, folded wooden chairs, boxes, the disassembled frame of a bed and the like. Everything was layered deep with dust. My nose began to tickle and I had the devil of a job to prevent myself sneezing and giving myself away. I closed the door and explored the other rooms on this side of the corridor; all were unlocked and were either empty or contained the same sort of unwanted lumber as the first. I made my way back along the corridor, switching my attention to the rooms on the other side, which again were unlocked and put to the same purpose as before. But when I reached the last door, the one nearest the staircase, and turned the handle, the door refused to yield. I pushed my shoulder against it in case it was merely stuck, but it didn't budge; it was definitely locked. I put my ear to it and held my breath to listen. There was perfect quiet and then, before I could move, a sudden rush of footsteps on the other side and the door almost exploded into me, crashing against my ear, as some-thing – someone – cannoned into it on the other side. I fell back in shock and my candle went out.

'Let me out, you devil, let me out!' It was a woman's voice, although you could only just tell, for it sounded like no human I had ever heard, a banshee straight out of Hell. My blood ran cold. Everything was dark and I could almost feel the madwoman's fingers reaching out and taking hold of my throat. She began wailing and sobbing, and banging on the door. I was by no means safe here. It seemed entirely possible to me that the monster on the other side of this flimsy piece of wood – who I was sure was the madwoman I'd come in search of – might smash her way through it.

In my shock at the prisoner's frenzy, I had all but forgotten the precariousness of my situation, that she was not the only thing I had to worry about, when the darkness began to recede. There was a glow of a light from the staircase, growing brighter by the second. Someone was coming up it.

I was in a desperate plight. In a moment the person on the stairs would reach the top, light would flood the corridor and reveal me where I had no right to be. I fumbled around in the dark, seeking the handle of the door opposite the prisoner's, but met only the wall. Just then the person ascending the stairs must have reached the turn, because the intensity of the light doubled. It was bright enough for me to see the door handle. I grabbed it, opened the door and ducked inside, closing it as quietly as I could, although the little noise it made would have been inaudible over the racket the fiend opposite was creating.

I put my ear to the door and listened. Footsteps stopped at the door across the way. And then, the most surprising thing of all, the thing I least would have guessed would happen, a voice, speaking quietly and patiently, evidently through the door to the woman inside. It was a voice I knew only too well.

'There, there, my dear, calm yourself,' whispered Morgan. 'Come on, quiet down. If you're a very good girl, I have a present for you, something very nice indeed.'

He paused and the rattling of the door opposite ceased. The woman's fierce cries subsided into a kind of moan. 'That's better,' said Morgan. 'Now, my dear, you must get back into bed. I'm not coming in unless you do. And if I don't come in, I can't give you any chocolate, can I?'

There was a long silence and then I heard the sound of a key in a lock, the opening of the door and its closing and the sound of the key being turned once more. I held my breath, thinking what to do. Had Morgan gone inside the room, or was he still waiting in the corridor? Perhaps he had just opened the door a fraction, tossed the chocolate through the gap and then closed and locked it again. He might be in the corridor still. I bent down and looked through the keyhole of my door and everything outside was black, from which I deduced Morgan, with his candle, was inside the woman's room. I opened my door and was out in a trice. I stepped softly across the passage, put my ear to the door and listened.

I heard the strangest sound: Morgan's voice, there was no doubt about that, but humming. It was an old tune, one of those popular songs you get in vaudeville shows, although I could not place it, a ballad of some sort. Beneath it I could hear a low accompaniment, a sort of murmuring which put me in mind for some reason of the purring of a cat. It suggested the wild woman within was humming along while nibbling contentedly upon the chocolate.

Here was strangeness indeed! Morgan, the brusque little martinet, the man who happily half drowned helpless women, or chained them to chairs for hour after hour, sitting and lullabying this mad monster.

I longed to stay and listen more, in case Morgan said something that might give me a clue about what was going on, but the risk was too great. He might emerge at any time and I would be caught out – *redhanded* – with no excuse. I had to get away fast while it was still possible. I didn't dare light my candle. There was a faint sliver of light seeping out from under the woman's door, barely anything, but just enough to show me the way to the top of the stairs. I crept to them and began to inch my way carefully down, terrified that all the noise might have drawn the attendants below from their room. I had no idea what I would say if confronted by them. I just prayed it wouldn't happen.

At last, after what seemed an age, I came to the bottom of the stairs and peeped around the corner. The passage was empty and there was enough light from the attendants' open door for me to start my way down the next flight of stairs. Once I reached the turn I paused, took out my matches and lit my candle. It took a moment for my eyes to get used to the sudden brightness but once they had, I hurried the rest of the way down and a couple of minutes later reached the part of the hospital where it was legitimate for me to be. If I was caught now, I could always plead a trip to the library as my excuse for being abroad.

In the security of my room I tried to make sense of all that had passed. It was clear the attendants knew of the woman's existence – how could they not with the noise she made, which seemed to be a regular occurrence – but also evident that they were expected to turn a blind eye and had scarcely any more knowledge about her than I did. I had at least seen her – and touched her, or rather felt her hands touching me. The woman was O'Reilly's special charge. It was she who took her her meals, as I had seen. And what I'd witnessed suggested that, on the rare occasions when she was away, Morgan took over. But a different Morgan from the one I knew in our daily work together. He had calmed this special patient by talking to her softly and soothingly, not by threatening her or tying her up. Why, when I thought about it, his behaviour toward this woman was like nothing so much as Moral

Treatment. Morgan, in this particular case it seemed, practised what I preached.

But why? What was so special about this woman that she merited a different regime from all the other patients? Why was she kept such a secret? Why had both Morgan and O'Reilly lied to me, pretending that the person who attacked me in his office was just one of the women from the third floor?

I went to sleep feeling that I had got almost nowhere in solving the puzzle. I had confirmed the existence of the woman, but for the mystery surrounding her, I had no explanation.

24

We were now moving toward the end of November and the weather had worsened. There were more heavy falls of snow and, looking from a window at the back of the second floor, I noted how pleasingly the snow had drifted so that a great bank of it lay over the remains of the late Miss Adams. She might have been in a pharaoh's tomb for all the likelihood of anyone finding her, although her mausoleum was not permanent and I knew I must solidify my plans for departure. I had hit upon the end of January as the time to go. I would be able to count upon a good month's start before there was any possibility of a thaw and the discovery of the body, and probably as much again after that before any police investigation was on my trail. I knew it was likely they would connect her with Shepherd pretty quickly. Eva, for one, and perhaps others too, had seen Miss Adams and knew she had visited my alter ego.

But after that I reckoned they would lose track of me. They would be looking for Shepherd, after all, not Jack Wells, who was certified as dead and gone. If they traced back and managed to find a photograph of Shepherd, the only people who might spot that it was not the man of that name who had worked at the hospital would be Morgan and the rest of the staff. But even that was uncertain. Shepherd and I looked reasonably alike. We were the same type, and a photograph of him might look sufficiently like me to fool them into thinking the 'doctor' they knew was who he'd said he was. They had no reason to suspect otherwise. The natural conclusion would be that he had killed his fiancée in the heat of some lovers' quarrel and then fled.

At breakfast next morning Morgan said to me, 'I had a long night going over your reports, Shepherd, but everything was in order. You seem to be getting the hang of things here.'

'Thank you, sir,' I replied. 'I thought perhaps you wouldn't have had time.'

'Why would you think that? Didn't I tell you I would go through them?'

'Oh, yes, sir, it's just that I called into your office last evening and you weren't there.'

He coloured and took a sip of coffee. 'Well, I must have popped out for a moment. Nature's demands, you know.'

I could not help teasing him further. 'I went back twice and you still weren't there. The reports were hardly started on.'

He stared at me, with that familiar look of barely controlled anger boiling up inside him. Then he looked away and began buttering a piece of toast as though it demanded his full concentration. 'Ah yes, I remember now. I was tired and needed to clear my head to prepare myself for the long haul ahead of me. I went out for a stroll.'

'What, in the snow, sir? For over an hour?'

He looked me straight in the eye. *He challenged me one.* 'Yes. I find the cold air very bracing.'

I shrugged. 'Rather you than me.'

We concentrated on our food, neither of us looking at

the other. Finally he cleared his throat noisily. 'Anyway, what was it you wanted to see me about?'

'See you about?'

'Yes. Confound it, man. Your visit to my office must have been important for you to return twice. What was it for?'

My questioning had put him at a disadvantage. I reckoned he would be agreeable to my suggestion now, to repair the rift between us and smooth away the suspicions my tone had suggested.

'Jane Dove. I was thinking about how it is good for her to be segregated from the other patients, not surrounded by madness as it were, and to be able to pursue other things, sewing and knitting and –' I was trying to think of something else.

'Reading,' he said. 'Don't forget her reading. She's going great guns at that.'

'No, of course.' A nervous laugh trickled from me. 'Indeed, how could I forget that?'

'You may be right, you may not. I concede there have been some beneficial developments, but overall I couldn't begin to count it any kind of cure.'

'You're perfectly correct, sir. I am not at all satisfied yet. That's why I've been thinking that perhaps keeping her away from the others has accidentally disadvantaged her too.'

'How so?'

'Well, apart from the limited time I can spend with her and those occasional visits from one of the attendants who has been instructing her in her needlework, she is in effect in solitary confinement.'

'Well, hardly, man. She has a nice comfortable room, armchairs, books – not exactly the prison cell that phrase "solitary confinement" suggests.'

'You're perfectly correct, sir. What I meant was that she's effectively shut up alone for long periods of the day. I was wondering if we mightn't let her out a little.'

'Let her out? Let her out?'

'Yes. If you remember the idea behind Moral Treatment.'

'Pshaw! Moral Treatment!' I had forgotten how like a red rag to a bull the phrase was to him.

I tried again. 'The idea of the experiment is that she should be treated as much as possible like a normal person in order to help her become one. Well, it's not normal to spend most of the day sitting looking at the same four walls on your own. In order for the experiment to have a chance to succeed, she must be given a certain amount of freedom, allowed to wander about a bit.'

He took a swig of coffee and tilted his head from side to side, mulling this over. At last he swallowed and said, 'I'm not sure we can have a patient roaming all over the building unsupervised.'

'I agree, sir,' I said, concentrating on cutting up my fried ham. 'It wouldn't do for her to be venturing upstairs, for example.' I paused and could feel his eyes boring into me. I had to resist a smile. He was wondering whether this last remark had any significance, connecting it in his mind with my visit to his office last night. 'Or into your office. We would have to define at exactly what times she was allowed to leave her room and where she was permitted to go. For one thing, it would be no use to my trial if I couldn't find her when I wanted to talk with her.'

He picked up his napkin and wiped his lips, then pushed his chair back and stood up. 'Very well. Work out the details and report back to me.'

'Thank you, sir. I realise it's a big step and I really

appreciate your willingness to give me every opportunity to make my experiment work, even though you don't agree with it at all.'

'Nothing of the sort, man,' he said, pulling out his watch and frowning at it. 'I'm just giving you enough rope to hang yourself, that's all.'

As I hurriedly took a final mouthful of coffee and stood up, I could not help shivering at that most unfortunate turn of phrase.

Over the next few days I thought about how Jane Dove's increased liberty might be made possible and, when I had arrived at a plan, negotiated it with Morgan. She had exercise already in the afternoon, and it was the mornings that were extremely long for her. The patients had breakfast at 6.30 and after that I was at my busiest, supervising treatments, examining any newly arrived patients and writing reports. Before lunch I rarely managed more than a few brief minutes with her, and sometimes not even that. It made sense, then, that she should be allowed to roam at that time.

Morgan set the limits on where she could go. She was not permitted to be where the other patients were; he thought it would upset some of them to see one of their number at liberty when they were so constrained. She was allowed to wander the corridor on the second floor while the others were down in the day room. She could use the main staircase, although she was on no account to venture up to the third floor; she could go outside, providing she kept to the paths immediately around the house. Any deviations from these rules and the privilege would be rescinded. There would be no excuses allowed and no second chance.

After we had settled this and I was about to leave his office, Morgan said, 'Wait a minute, what fools we both are. We've forgotten the most obvious place for her to go.'

I must have looked puzzled.

'Why, man, the library, of course.'

My mouth was half open to protest that it would be of no use to her because she couldn't read when, just in time, I recollected myself.

'She can look at the books and choose them for herself. Such a proficient reader will find a whole new world there.'

I smiled. 'Of course, I cannot imagine why I didn't think of it.' At least Jane would be able to amuse herself there and while away a few otherwise dull hours by looking through any illustrated books she could find.

In fact, once she had her freedom, the library turned out to be where she passed most of her time. Whenever I couldn't find her in her room or walking the grounds, I knew where to look. She spent the long morning hours leafing through the neglected volumes and, coming upon her there one day, going through an illustrated book, I remarked that it was of little use setting her free, because she had made herself as much a prisoner here among the dusty books as she had been when immured in her room.

'Oh, but I like it here,' she replied. 'I feel at home with all these books around me. It's like being among friends. There are so many stories I can construct from the pictures I find. If you have imagination, sir, you are never in jail.'

Well, I could have argued with that, but instead I took the book she'd been looking at from her. It was a fine edition of *Robinson Crusoe*, with beautiful colour plates of the castaway's adventures. 'What story have you made from this?' I asked, handing it back to her.

'I have only just begun to look at it, sir,' she said. 'Do you know the book?'

'Oh yes, it's very famous.' I told her the title.

She opened the book at an illustration. 'Is that the man in this picture?'

'Yes. He's a sailor who is shipwrecked upon an uninhabited island and has to build his own civilisation from scratch. He's stuck there. There's no way to escape.'

'Then he is like us, isn't he?'

I did not reply.

'I mean, we are on an island and neither of us can leave.'

I nodded at the parallel. 'Well, I guess that's true for you, but I'm at liberty to go any time I want, if I chuck in my post.'

She made no reply, but looked up at me. Her eyes were troubled.

'What is it, Jane?'

'I would do anything to escape from here. I dream about it every day. To be out of this wretched place, to no longer be considered mad. And one day, I shall.'

'I'm sure that day will come, Jane. It's what we're working for, your release.'

She returned to inspecting the picture and sighed. 'Sir, we both know that will never happen. No one ever gets out of this place, except to be sent somewhere even worse. Dr Morgan will never let me go. I must find some other way.'

I wondered what she was thinking. I thought how I had made a difficulty for myself over this stupid experiment. If Jane Dove should ever make an attempt to escape, I would be in real trouble with Morgan. There would be repercussions that could endanger my life. I cursed myself for letting my boredom and the strange pull I felt for this girl tempt me into putting myself at risk. Her potential for recklessness was something I hadn't considered. Gradually, though, I calmed myself as I thought how impossible it was for her to get off the island. The river had strong currents and could not be swum, even supposing she knew how, and the only means to shore was the daily boat that brought new supplies and new patients, and the one on Sundays that brought the visitors. No one ever travelled on the former, except when patients were taken by O'Reilly to the city asylum. All required passes signed by Morgan. And Sunday visitors bought a return ticket for the boat and were not permitted to go back on it without one to prevent any patient using it as a means of escape. In my heart of hearts, I knew the poor girl was probably right, that she was buried here for life. But I had to pretend otherwise to her, so I replied, 'That may be true in the normal course of things, but then you are not in a normal situation. If we can make our trial a success and convince Dr Morgan you're cured, I've every reason to believe he will let you go.'

She turned to another picture in her book. I saw it was Crusoe discovering the footprints in the sand and said nothing. I did not for a single moment think I had fooled her.

One morning I went upstairs to fetch a notebook I had left in my room that contained some observations I'd made about a patient I was seeing that day. I had just turned into the corridor when I saw Jane Dove come out of my room. She looked furtive and startled as she closed the door and looked up and saw me watching her. She put her hand to her mouth and said, 'Oh!'

I strode along the corridor and said, quite harshly, 'What

were you doing in my room, Jane? You know you're not supposed to go there. If you break your agreement, Morgan will shut you up again.'

'But, sir, I wasn't in your room,' she said. 'I was looking for you. I knocked and when there was no reply I opened the door to see if you were there.' She stood biting her lip and moving nervously from foot to foot.

'Very well,' I said, after letting her stew for half a minute, for I knew it to be a lie; she had definitely been coming out of the room, not merely looking in. 'But see that it doesn't happen again.'

'Oh, I will, sir, I will.' And she went off quickly along the corridor toward the stairs.

'Oh, Jane!' I called after her.

She stopped and turned. 'Yes, sir?'

'What was it you wanted?'

'Wanted?'

'Yes, what did you want to see me about?'

'Oh!' She was evidently taken aback by this. She shook her head and said, 'Oh, it doesn't matter, sir. It unimportants. It can wait till later.' And before I could question her further, she skipped off down the stairs.

I went into my room and looked around. There was no obvious sign of disturbance. I examined my chest of drawers, opening them one by one. Nothing seemed to have been touched. I shrugged. After all, what was there for her to pry into here anyway? As I picked up the notebook I'd come to fetch from the table beside my bed, my eye caught *Moral Treatment*, which sat next to it. Was it my imagination or had it been moved? I have a habit of always placing a book precisely upon a table, adjusting it carefully so that its edges are parallel to the edges of the surface it is on. It's just a little foible, something I have always done. *Moral Treatment* was ever so slightly out of true, or so I thought. If it had been shifted, it was by the merest fraction, but it wasn't quite right. I could not be absolutely certain, though, that I hadn't been careless in arranging it and that Jane Dove wasn't entirely innocent. Had she even been in my room? Maybe I'd been mistaken in my impression that she had. It was completely possible she'd been telling the truth. She had an openness of expression, a naïveté about her, that made it hard to imagine her lying. I felt reassured. Then I remembered how she had fooled Morgan over the reading, improvising *Hamlet* and taking him in completely.

I picked up the book. If she had been in here, then likely as not she would have examined it, looking for pictures. I flicked through the pages as though that would offer a clue and a piece of paper dropped out and fluttered to the floor. I picked it up. The newspaper clipping. I saw now how risky it was to keep it there or anywhere else. It wouldn't matter if Jane Dove had seen it, because even though she'd probably have recognised the photograph of me, she would not have been able to read the accompanying report and would have had not the faintest idea what it was about. But suppose someone else, O'Reilly perhaps, came in and poked around? I'd been arrogant in thinking them all too ignorant to look at a book. If anyone who could read – and O'Reilly could – had done what I suspected of Jane Dove, I would be caught bang to rights. I put the clipping in my pocket, and later, as I walked through the day room while the patients were at their exercise and I was quite alone, put it into one of the stoves there and watched it burn until I was satisfied it had been reduced to ash. There was no evidence against me now. I smiled at the irony that if Jane Dove had indeed found the clipping, she had done me a favour by alerting me to the foolhardy risk I had run; inadvertently she had helped me keep myself safe.

As was to be expected, O'Reilly was not best pleased with the new arrangement concerning Jane Dove. She even went so far as to complain to Morgan, as I found out when I went to his office a couple of days later and was just about to knock when I heard her angry voice from inside. 'I cannot guess what you were thinking of,' she said. 'Did you think it sensible to give her the run of the place? Did you not think of the risk that she might go where she's not supposed to and give everything away?' It was obvious what she was talking about, the madwoman in the attic.

I heard a murmur from the doctor, but I couldn't make out what he said.

'"Exaggerate"! I "exaggerate"!' exploded O'Reilly's voice. 'On your own head be it. Don't blame me if the whole thing blows up in your face.'

At that, her footsteps came toward the door and I backed off hurriedly so that when it was flung open I was able to give the impression I was just approaching and had heard nothing. She scowled at me and pushed insolently past. I knocked on the open door and put my head round the edge.

'Is something the matter, sir?' I asked, when Morgan acknowledged me. He looked old and tired, I thought, not his usual self.

'Oh, just Mrs O'Reilly,' he muttered. 'She is not enthusiastic about your Moral Treatment. If she had her way, she would have Jane Dove locked up with the other patients.'

'I trust you won't give in to her on that,' I ventured.

'Give in? Give in, sir? Of course not. It's I who run this

hospital, not Mrs O'Reilly. She sometimes tends to forget that, I'm afraid.'

Nevertheless I was uneasy about O'Reilly's fury over Jane Dove. It would be a mistake to antagonise her too much when she had it in her power to expose me. If I was right and she had found the discarded draft letter I had written to Caroline Adams, how would I explain it? How would I justify to Morgan that I had pretended to have a broken hand? Perhaps I could claim I had told a white lie to avoid having to write endearments to her when I was no longer sure of my feelings? Well, it was stretching things to the breaking point of credulity, and although in a confrontation it was possible Morgan might swallow this, even if he did it would show me in a poor light, as both ungentlemanly and devious. It might start the cogs of suspicion whirring in his brain.

I considered my other choices. I could confront O'Reilly with what I knew about the mysterious hidden patient, but would that get me anywhere? Morgan was involved in the concealment of the woman too and, considering the way O'Reilly had just spoken to him about the situation, somewhat in her power over it, so an appeal to him seemed useless.

When I thought of O'Reilly's insolent expression, the way she looked at me and spoke to me, I considered simply eliminating her, stamping upon her the way you would a poisonous spider. My fingers were itching to get around her throat and dispatch her the way of Caroline Adams – but I knew anything in that line was out of the question. It would bring the police down on the place like a hawk upon a rabbit and I would be done for. The only other solution was to try to get my hands on that draft letter.

The very thought of this was too much a reminder of the night I had risked everything in the attempt to find Shepherd's letter of application in Morgan's office. I had no appetite to go sneaking around in O'Reilly's room and running the chance of her pouncing on me there. I cursed myself for not thinking of it while she was away on the mainland, but then it was plausible that she would have taken the letter with her. No, there was no prospect of anything in that direction at all.

And anyway, I could not be sure O'Reilly had the letter. I had only a loaded remark to suggest that she did. I might be reading too much into it; perhaps it was just paranoia on my part. The best thing to do for now was to try not to antagonise the woman further, since if she had the letter, she was content not to act on it for the moment. I was not yet willing to sacrifice Jane Dove to appease her, but I resigned myself to the idea that if push came to shove and there was no other way to protect myself, I might have to do so.

25

By now I had firmed up my plan of escape. In December I would receive my first quarter's salary, which, with the money bequeathed me by Caroline Adams, would be more than enough to carry me to the far west. In January, when I was ready, I would tell Morgan that I wanted to quit. In my mind I often rehearsed this conversation, in which I told him in no uncertain terms what I thought of the harshness and ineffectiveness of his regime and how I could stand to be part of it no longer. I would tell him I was leaving immediately. As this would be without the notice period of a month my employment agreement demanded, I didn't expect him to pay me any more salary anyway, so I had nothing to lose by my frankness. I would do this on a Sunday and take the visitors' boat to shore that afternoon and then head for the nearest railroad depot and a train to freedom.

As far as this plan went, the one fly in the ointment was O'Reilly, if she had the draft letter. After I was gone and the thaw came and the body of Caroline Adams was discovered, O'Reilly would produce the letter and it would soon be obvious to the police that 'Dr Shepherd' had been a fake. I didn't imagine it would take them long to find out that Shepherd had been in the train crash with Jack Wells. Given the manner of Miss Adams's death, it was a small step to figuring out the identity swap and then the hunt would be on for me, with my old police picture on every front page.

Once again, I cursed my carelessness in not destroying that draft note; it was the only mistake I had made, yet that one little error could cost me all. Without it there would be a single murder possibly – but not definitely – committed by a doctor of previous good character, a crime of passion. Even that was a worse case. There was a possibility that when they found Miss Adams no one would connect the corpse with the woman who had called upon me and who, so far as anyone knew, had returned on the boat that had brought her. And if Shepherd were hunted, any photographs of him the police traced and published would be of the wrong man.

As part of my preparations for my flight, I began to grow a beard, which I figured would make me even harder to recognise as Jack Wells. It afforded Morgan no little amusement. 'Ah, you think you will look older and wiser if you hide half your face behind hair,' he said.

'You have divined my motive,' I confessed with a smile.

'Well, perhaps it will add some gravitas. Although, speaking personally, I never saw any need for a beard. In my opinion a perfectly good and manageable moustache is as far in that direction as anyone should go.' He stroked his own, that hacked-off caterpillar on his upper lip, as he said this.

'You may well be right, sir. I'm not set on it. I shall wear it a month and then if I decide it doesn't suit, off it will come.'

Jane Dove was also intrigued by my burgeoning whiskers. 'Why, sir,' she mocked one day, for she was growing ever bolder in the familiarity with which she spoke to me, and was almost flirtatious it seemed to me, 'I swear I did not recognise you. If that forest upon your face grows much thicker, even your friends will not know you.'

'Do you think not?' I asked. 'Am I to gather from the amusement it affords you that you do not approve of beards, even though so many men choose to wear them?'

She was thoughtful a moment, then said, 'I seem to recall someone I knew once – do not ask me who or when or where, for I do not know – but someone said to me that a man who covers his face with hair is trying to hide.' She said this with a smile, meaning it as a throwaway remark, but I found I could not reply in kind; what she had said was a little too near the mark for that.

I picked up the book I'd brought with me from the library to read to her. It had no illustrations but I thought she might like it.

'What is it called, sir?' she asked as I opened it.

'*Jane Eyre.*'

'Jane, sir, just like me.'

'Yes,' I said, 'just like you.'

26

Although Jane Dove spent the vast majority of her liberty in one place, the library, when the day was bright and sunny she loved to get outside for a while as well, and one morning, about a week later, I caught sight of her through the window of the restraining room, where I was supervising the torture of another poor lunatic. She was building a snowman. So intent was she upon what she was doing, she seemed completely lost to the world. She was picking up great handfuls of snow and thrusting them onto the base she'd constructed, laughing and chatting away as if to another person. At that moment she seemed like a child playing a child's game, girlish and carefree. I felt a pang in my chest as I watched, a stab in the heart as it came back to me, a scene from long ago, myself as a small child, making a snowman, together with a woman whose face I could not picture but who I knew must have been my mother, and I realised this was a buried memory of a happy time before she died and I was condemned to the horrors of the chicken farm. Tears sprang into my eyes as I watched, at the thought of all that my life might have been. 'Some good I mean to do, despite of mine own nature.' The words leapt into my brain as lines I've learned often will. Edmund in *King Lear*.

my defining role, in many ways. The words could not have been more apt for all I felt now and I resolved that if I could manage it without hazard to myself, I would somehow get this lost child out of here and give her the chance of a life that I had never had.

Next day, I paused in my reading of *Jane Eyre* and said to her, 'I have been thinking how we might obtain your release.'

She sighed. 'It impossibles, sir. I am as much a prisoner as Jane and Helen Burns at Lowood. There is no way out.'

'But there could be. If we can convince Morgan you are cured, I may be able to persuade him to let you go.'

'I wish you luck with that, sir.'

'No, listen. I've been thinking. What are your symptoms of madness? Do you attack people? Do you rant and rave? Do you mutter to yourself? Or foul yourself? Or take off your clothes in public?'

She blushed.

'I'm sorry,' I said. 'I didn't mean to embarrass you. My point is that you exhibit none of the typical signs of insanity. The thing that brought you here – the main thing, that is – is your amnesia. You cannot remember anything about yourself. That is the principal reason. Losing your memory is not the same as being mad, even though in your case the two have been conflated. So what we must do is get your memory back.'

She recoiled, an animal at bay. 'I have told you, sir, I unremember anything at all.'

'All right, all right, calm yourself. I know that. You cannot recall your past life, so we will have to provide you with one.'

'I don't understand.'

'We make one up! If we can persuade Morgan that your memory has returned as a result of your treatment here, then he will have no justification for keeping you any longer. In fact, I'd go so far as to say he might well want to get rid of you, because your obvious sanity would represent a challenge to his methods. I think under those circumstances he would have to let you go.'

Her eyes lit up. 'You really think it would take no more than that?'

'Well, I can't guarantee anything but it's certainly well worth a try. It's better than doing nothing, surely you can see that?'

'And what if I unconvince him? What then? Will he not say your treatment of me, your "Moral Treatment", has failed and send me back to dwell among the living dead?'

'Don't you see, sooner or later that will happen anyway? He will not permit this trial to go on for ever. Once he feels he can reasonably say it has failed, you will be back in the day room for good.'

Her lip trembled, her eyes filled and a tear rolled down one of her cheeks. 'I do not want to think of that,' she said, the last word almost lost in a great sob that shook her whole thin frame.

'Jane, it has to be thought of. We must act now before it is too late.'

'Very well,' she said. 'What must I do?'

'You must invent a past for yourself. Start thinking about it; imagine the life you would like to have now, if you weren't here. Think of the house you might have lived in, picture the rooms there, think of little details of furnishings and so on. Make up a family for yourself, the people who lived there with you.'

Her eyes sparkled with excitement. 'I will do it, sir! I will try to imagine a life I might have had. I will lie in my bed tonight with my eyes tight shut and picture how it might have been and then I will tell you tomorrow.'

'We only need an outline to begin with, a kind of frame upon which we can hang more and more details. Then we will have to come up with a story of what happened to lead you to be wandering the streets of the city alone and a reason for why your family no longer exists. The aim will be to construct a realistic former life we can offer to Morgan.'

She was smiling now. 'Oh, sir, it's a brilliant plan! I shall love the making up. By tomorrow, I promise you, I will have a past.'

The following day was one of those gifts from nature that make you grateful to be alive, especially if you have no right to be. The sky was clear blue and the sun shone bright – a winter sun with little warmth, it was true, but a bauble of cheer and hope nonetheless. Everything stood out sharp the way it does in good light: the skeletal branches of the trees, the very brick of the building. I looked out my window at the snowman Jane Dove had made the day before. She had fashioned his beady eyes and wide mouth from stones and he seemed to be smiling up at me. I had a great surge of optimism as I returned his smile. It was all working out well. On such a day I could even believe my stratagem to free poor Jane would do the trick. I was safe and prospering here for the time being. I had the plan for my escape in place. And then, just as I was thinking this, my eye caught a movement – a shadow of something passing overhead, a moving speck upon the virgin snow – and looking up, I saw a solitary rook flying toward the river. A shiver ran through me and suddenly the day seemed bleak and cold. O'Reilly, she was the rook. I had to have a ruse to deal with her but

I could think of nothing. I knew only that I could not leave a hostage to fortune. Everything must be perfect.

The rook disappeared over the horizon and with it went the momentary fear I'd suffered. I would take care of O'Reilly, I felt sure. Something would occur; it always did. What could be more hopeless than being on a train en route to the death house? Who could have foreseen that a train wreck would save me, and yet it had happened. I could not believe I'd been spared only to perish because of an interfering busybody.

I was whistling as I entered Jane Dove's room and she seemed as cheerful as I.

'Well, Jane, how goes it? Are you a woman with a past now?'

She did not seem to get the joke but replied innocently, 'I am becoming so, sir. I have been awake half the night thinking of it. It was very strange. When I made up one thing, another would jump into my mind and then another. At first they seemed unconnected, but then they began to fit together, like the pieces of a jigsaw, although there are still some holes that I can't seem to fill.'

'Don't worry about that for now. It's best not to rush this but to let it form gradually, otherwise your story will seem too artificial, too contrived, and in that case it won't convince. Tell me what you have so far.'

'My name is Florence.'

'Yes, you have told me so already. Florence what?'

She looked at me suspiciously. *She suspicioned me one.* 'Just Florence at present, sir. And I lived in a large house.'

'How large? The sort of house you see on a street in town?'

She laughed. 'Oh no, sir, much, much bigger. As big as this hospital. Why, even the library is one hundred and four of my shoed feet long and thirty-seven wide. The house has many rooms, and yet nobody lives there but my brother and me.'

'You have a brother?'

'Yes, he is called Giles and is three years younger than me.'

'And how old are you?'

She hesitated and looked away. 'I – I unremember, sir.'

'You must be sixteen.'

'You think so, sir?'

'No, I have no idea how old you are. I mean you must *say* you're sixteen. I don't think anyone will believe you're older. But you have to say you're sixteen.'

'Why? What does it matter?'

'Because at sixteen you're reckoned to be able to fend for yourself. If you say you're younger, even if Morgan agrees to let you go, he will simply hand you over to the authorities. You'll be shut up in an orphanage. If you're sixteen, you can be set free.'

'All right, I am sixteen.'

'What else have you "remembered"? What of your parents?'

'My parents are both dead, sir. I am under the protection of my uncle, whom I never see because the house is in the country in a remote place and he lives a long way off in New York City. It has a long drive rooked by an avenue of fine oaks. There is a man who looks after the horses and the grounds, and there is a housekeeper.'

'Names?'

'He is called John and she is called Mrs Grouse. There is a maid named Mary and a cook named Meg who bakes delicious cakes.'

It all came out very pat; the way she answered my questions was so slick, I thought, this girl should be a writer – except she can't even read, let alone write – because making up a story comes so natural to her. She relates everything as though she is looking at it with her mind's eye and believes it to be true.

'Is there no one else in this great house? No one to look after you?'

'I told you, sir, we have Mrs Grouse and the servants.'

'What about your education?'

She bridled. 'You know very well I have none.'

'But why don't you have one? Morgan will want to know.'

'I have told you it is unallowed. My uncle loved a woman who got herself all booked and cultured up and surpassed him in both and then someone-elsed.'

'I see.' I thought, I will have to do something about the way she talks. If she carries on like this to Morgan, he will still think her mad. 'So he wouldn't allow you and your brother –'

'Giles, sir.'

'On account of too much learning having spoiled, as he saw it, his love affair, your uncle wouldn't provide an education for you and Giles.'

'Oh no, sir, just me. Because my uncle thought the fault was in letting *women* be educated. It unapplied to Giles.'

'So Giles was, what, at a school?'

'For a little, after the first governess died.'

'You had a governess who –'

'Not me, sir, Giles –'

'Giles had a governess who died?'

'Tragicked on the lake.'

'This would be the lake on which you went ice skating.'

'The very same, sir. What a memory you have!' She had a mocking smile as she said this.

'And how did she, um, tragick?'

'A boating accident, sir. She fell in the water and drowned, poor thing.'

I confess I was sitting there stunned with admiration at how she had thought the whole thing through in just one night and constructed an odd – and yet precisely because of its singularity – convincing narrative.

'And that was the end of Giles's education, I presume?'

'Oh, no, sir. There was another governess. Or it may have been the same one . . .'

She bit her lip and looked up at me anxiously, *anxioused me one.*

'What do you mean? How could it have been the same one when the woman was dead?'

She looked at me earnestly. 'Tell me, sir, do you believe in ghosts?'

'Do I – ?' I held up my hand. 'Jane, Jane, stop now. This is all getting a bit crazy.'

Her whole body bridled at this.

'I'm sorry,' I said, 'wrong word. What I mean is if you start talking about ghosts, Morgan will think it's a sign of madness. You need to rein in your imagination a little. You're getting too carried away. This isn't some penny dreadful, some sensational novel you're inventing. It has to sound like a real life. In many ways, the duller the better.'

Her eyes were on the floor. I could not tell what she was thinking. She looked up and said, 'It was just how it came to me, sir, like a story I was being told.'

'I can see that and I think you've come up with something wonderful, but the main thing is to make it credible, not to entertain. Now, there is one thing in your "life" that *is* very unusual, and even perhaps, slightly fantastic, and that's the business of your uncle forbidding you to learn to read and write, although on the other hand, even in this day and age there are plenty of people who believe things not too dissimilar, that a woman's place is in the kitchen and so on. But that is enough oddness for one person's life. We need to keep everything else normal. For instance, was it necessary to drown the governess?'

'Oh yes, sir!' It came out straight away and she put a hand over her mouth immediately it was said, shutting the stable door. 'I mean, that was the way it happened in my imagination. You are right. For our purposes she does not need to die.'

'Good. She can stay and teach Giles, then.'

'Very well.'

'Is that everything? Have you thought of an explanation of how you came to be here?'

'No, sir. This was as far as I got. The thinkery of it tired me out. I'm sorry.'

I raised my hands in protest. 'Don't apologise. You've done amazingly well. In just one night you've created an identity for yourself, a believable one.'

'You think it will do, sir?'

'As far as it goes, yes. But at some point we will have to move the story forward. We will have to explain how you got from your life in that big old house to being found wandering around in a city. We need a story for that.'

'I will try again tonight.'

'No, don't,' I said. 'There's no rush. It's important to do the thing properly. If we go off half-cocked, Morgan will smell a rat. What I would like you to do now is to concentrate on that life you have invented. I want you to walk around that great house in your mind, to see every detail of the furnishings, to invent conversations with the governess and the cook, to imagine what you did every day. It's what actors do when they take on a role. They try to imagine what it is like to be the person they are playing. They invent a story for the character's past and so almost come to *be* the person.'

'Goodness, sir, you know a lot of things. One would begin to think you were an actor yourself, to hear you talk of it.' Her eyes were wide-eyed with innocent admiration, hero worship even, as she looked at me.

I shrugged. I did not want her thinking too much along that line. It was a little too close for comfort. 'Oh, not really. It's common knowledge, and I've heard actors talk about such things. Anyway, I must be going. Now remember what I've said. Don't try to force things. Just close your eyes and wander round that house and become the Florence who lived there. When you can live and breathe her, we'll work on the next bit of the plot together.'

And so began a new phase of our existence. Every afternoon when I accompanied Jane on her exercise walk I would say, 'And what has Florence been doing today?' and she would recount the activities of her alter ego as if they had really happened and were part of her own history. She had a knack of invention and her peculiar use of words had a way of painting pictures for the listener, so it felt you were seeing the things she described before your very eyes.

She invented this character named Theo, a neighbour's son, about her own age, whom she described as a great gangling heron of a boy who could not be trusted in a drawing room because of a congenital clumsiness, and yet – and here's what made him so much more real – he was transformed the moment he put on skates and stepped onto ice. It was he who taught her to skate one day after she insisted they must meet outside in order to protect the furnishings of her house, to which she now had given a name, Blithe. They skated around the lake behind the house together and this ungainly boy Theo 'gracefulled like a swan' and earned her admiration.

As the days passed Theo came more and more into the narrative. He fell madly in love with her and, fancying himself a great poet, bombarded her with romantic verse, which was actually the most awful doggerel, of which she sometimes made up examples, such as one snatch that went 'what boy on earth could be so dense as not to madly love Florence?'.

This poor boy 'poetried' her in pursuit of a kiss, she said, which she never granted, not so much because she found him unattractive but because she could not find it within herself to reward bad verse. It was only later, when I was alone, some time after I had parted from her on the day she told me this, that I wondered at her natural instinct, that she knew bad verse when she heard it. Then I thought, but when might she have heard good verse?

And at that point I slapped my forehead and broke into a laugh. Why now she had fooled me! I had been so drawn in by the narrative she had built – helped in places by me, it's true – that I found myself taking it for fact and imagined it as her actual history. But it wasn't, it was all a fiction. Who knew what had happened in her real past, the one she couldn't remember? It was perfectly possible that in that other unremembered life she had had real verse read to her all the time, by a relative perhaps, and had developed a discerning ear, able to distinguish good from bad.

This incident convinced me, as November gave way to December, that her account of her life was now so solid that there were no chinks in it and that it would fool even Morgan. It was not ready to take to him, however, for one bit was missing. We had no plausible explanation of how Florence had got from her life at Blithe to where she was now. What had led to her leaving that earlier, seemingly idyllic life and going mad? How had she left the house in its remote rural location and ended up wandering the streets of the city?

There were other questions that needed addressing too. Where was her uncle? Couldn't he be traced and contacted and summoned to take her back? Obviously not, because there was no uncle, there was the rub. So something must have happened to him. The most likely story would be that he'd died. But how? And if he had, why had Florence been left alone? Either she must have had other relatives who would have – and would now – take her in, or else she had none, in which case wouldn't she have been heiress to the fine house and the fortune that likely went with it? And where was little Giles, her brother? I suggested to Jane this last difficulty could be easily overcome; we would simply *uninvent* the boy, remove him from the account altogether because he wasn't necessary to it. At this, though, she became extremely agitated and kept saying, 'No, no, no, we cannot do that. It impossibles to have everything else without Giles.' No matter how I conveyed the avoidable problem this created, she could not be persuaded and so the boy was allowed to live on, an additional encumbrance.

Try as we might, we were not able to produce a scenario to explain what had happened to overturn Florence's life so dramatically. More and more we felt ourselves defeated by it and gradually, as the days wore on toward Christmas, we began to spend less and less time on it and retreat again into the book I was reading her.

27

The hospital now was transformed from its everyday drab and dreary appearance. The attendants had been busy putting up paper chains and tinsel, which produced a sad kind of cheerfulness; it was so strange, so at odds with the place the rest of the year round. In the day room, one of the patients who could play the piano had begun practising carols ready for an entertainment that was granted the inmates every year on Christmas Day, and when she struck up a tune many of them would accompany her by singing the words – or in some cases alternative words of their own – with varying musical success. Mostly they mumbled or croaked and were dreadfully out of tune, but some could sing beautifully and on one occasion as I walked through the room I was stopped dead in my tracks when a lone voice rang out the words of 'Hark! The Herald Angels Sing', clear as a bell on a bright, frosty morning. It caught you like a fist plunged into your chest and throttling your heart. It choked off your breath and made tears spring to your eyes. I was helpless while it continued. It seemed to sum up every hope in the world, and in that lay the pity of it, that someone could give pour forth such optimism while imprisoned there.

Christmas Day dawned bright and clear, which further lifted the mood in the hospital. There was an undercurrent of expectation, as though some atavistic memory had been stirred in the inmates of Christmases past, an excitement at what the festive season would bring, although in truth there was precious little for them to look forward to. Lunch was a stingy treat. There was lentil and bacon soup, followed by roast chicken in parsimonious portions, enough to tease the appetite but not to satisfy it. There were extra potatoes and even boiled vegetables, things never normally seen here, and jugs of gravy, the latter regarded as such a delicacy that the attendants had their work cut out preventing some of the diners from picking up the jugs and quaffing them as if they were beer.

When lunch was over, the inmates repaired to the day room, where the pianist began to work her way through her repertoire of carols, which were sung by a small choir made up of a selection of patients who could sing well and some of the attendants, although the performance was naturally accompanied by some of the audience who joined in, often with cacophonous results. Still, the atmosphere was jolly and, after contributing to the singing ourselves a little, Morgan and I retired to the staff dining room for a late lunch.

It was a sumptuous affair of roast goose, the first such meal I'd had in a year or more, and I tucked into it with relish. We drank a fine red wine and Morgan grew so relaxed that he called for a second bottle, which we began to work our way through steadily. Under the influence of the alcohol, all my anxieties, all the nervous tension of my scheming, melted away and I felt myself caught up in the warm feeling of the season as I looked at Morgan, who sat rosy-cheeked opposite me, regaling me with anecdotes from his distant college days, and beyond him at the greetings-card scene outside and Jane Dove's snowman standing sentry in the radiant sunlight in the place he'd occupied for weeks now.

As I stared at him, I had the sense of something being different, something about him that was not right. He did not seem to be the same person he had been before. At first I could not put my finger upon it. Then I saw there was something odd about his nose – that is, the stick Jane had put there to represent it. It was no longer pert as it had been but was drooping onto the line of stones that were his mouth. His eyes were strange, too. The two pieces of coal that formed them had slid down, giving him the look of a mournful clown. My chest was tight and I could not breathe. My stomach was an empty pit in spite of all the food I'd just eaten. I felt a terror I did not understand. And then, all at once, I did.

I realised Morgan had stopped talking. I tried to gather my wits together. He was staring at me. 'Good God, man, what is it? You look as if you've seen a ghost.'

I almost laughed when he said that, except I seemed to have lost the power of uttering a sound. I pushed my chair back from the table and scrambled to my feet, only to find my legs would not support me and I had to hang on to the edge of the table.

'What is it?' Morgan said again. 'Are you feeling ill? Have you had too much wine?'

I ignored him and stumbled toward the door and somehow staggered through it. I hurried along the corridor and out the main door and nearly fell over. The surface of the snow was slick and slippery now. It had not been before. I slid and tottered along the front of the building and reached the snowman. Behind me I could hear Morgan calling me to stop. I looked the snowman in the face and he seemed to be mocking me. I put the palm of my hand on his cheek and let out a sob. I watched as a teardrop of water ran down the length of his nose and dripped to the floor. It was true. He was melting.

Morgan was beside me now. 'What's the matter with you, Shepherd? You're behaving most strangely.'

'It can't be! It can't! It's not meant to be happening for weeks yet. It simply can't be true.'

But it was. The thaw had come.

Morgan put his arm around my shoulders, in a surprisingly tender way, and turned me about face so I was no longer looking at the snowman, then steered me back toward the building. It was growing dark. In the dead silence I could hear the drip drip of water from the branches of the pine trees we passed. As we reached the open front door I turned to Morgan and said, 'The freeze is supposed to last until February, isn't it? You told me so; you said it always lasted.'

He gave me a bland smile, appeasing me in my sudden madness. 'Well, I was going on past experience. I'm not an expert on weather. The freeze usually does last until then, but it's not unknown for the temperature to rise before. It's very rare, I grant you. The weather is unseasonably warm today, but whether this thaw will continue or not is anybody's guess. Let's hope it does, eh?'

I stared at him as though he was mad.

Inside, I gradually came to my senses, enough to worry about what I might have said. I went over everything carefully in my mind. I could not be entirely sure but I was fairly certain I'd not given anything away. Back in the staff dining room, Morgan sat me down and poured a glass of brandy, which he offered to me. I was about to take it, as I was shaking and in dire need of something to quiet my nerves and restore my spirits, but had the sudden good sense to wave it away. 'Thank you, sir, but no. I think I may have taken too much in that way already. I'm not used to it, you know. My family were hot on temperance.'

I don't know what made that jump into my mind but it was fortuitous; it gained Morgan's sympathy. 'I'm sorry, I didn't know. And here I was, plying you with drink all through lunch. Should have known better with your Quaker leanings.'

'It's not your fault, sir. I should have known better myself and gone more easy. I cannot apologise enough for my behaviour. I don't know what came over me.'

He waved this away. 'No need for sackcloth and ashes, old man. We've all taken a bit too much at one time or another. No harm done.' He studied me for a moment and then glanced out the window. 'Something about that snowman, was it? Something that upset you?'

'I – I think it reminded me of a clown,' I said. 'I could never abide them as a child. They terrified me. Even today you couldn't get me to a circus to save my life.'

'Really?' He raised an eyebrow. 'Most strange. Wonder what could have caused that.' He peered at me with a forensic interest.

I was in a state of terror. I managed to put on some appearance of normality for Morgan but it wasn't easy. All the while the steady dripping of water from the eaves was a torture that

245

made it difficult to concentrate on anything else. Every so often there would be the soft sound of a heap of snow sliding from the roof and hitting the ground.

Eventually I pleaded a headache on account of the wine and slipped away from him. I needed to be alone to try to think of a way out of the fix I was in, to devise some means of escape before the snow all turned to water and revealed the late Caroline Adams to the world.

After dark, I went outside and surveyed the grounds as far as I could see by starlight. Now that the sun had gone down, it had turned colder. Was it wishful thinking or could I detect an easing-off in the frequency of the dripping? I walked around the building and stared in the direction in which Miss Adams lay awaiting her resurrection. The light was too feeble to see that far, but I was relieved that the deeper drifts of snow seemed hardly to have diminished at all. I reckoned Miss Adams had a good three feet on top of her and I figured it would take quite some time to melt. I guessed I had a day or two at least, even if the temperature remained this high.

As I went back inside, it occurred to me that in my distress I had neglected to look in on Jane Dove, who had had a lonely day of it. I had suggested she might put on her old patient's uniform and join the rest of the inmates in their celebrations of the day, but she had been horrified at the idea. 'I never want to return to that, sir,' she said fiercely, 'not even for a day. Not for an hour, or a minute or a single second. I am not one of them.' And so she had spent Christmas Day on her own, the only seasonal note for her being Dickens's Christmas Books, which I had found in the library and left with her, that she might look through the illustrations. It was what I found her doing now, sitting by her window.

'My snowman is melting.' It was the first thing she said to me and it made me wince.

'Well, he was never going to last for ever,' I said, putting a brave face on it. 'Though I confess I had hoped to have him with us a bit longer than this.' I stood beside her and we both gazed out the window at the diminished figure outside. It was a grim sight.

She lifted up her book. 'Have you time to read me some of this? I cannot make out the story, try as I might, although I can see it ends with a Christmas meal.' I saw it was *A Christmas Carol*.

'Not now, Jane. Something more important has come up. We need to lay plans.'

'Is it a bad thing? Your face seems to tell me so.'

'Yes, I'm afraid so. I had a discussion with Dr Morgan about the recovery of your memory and I'm afraid he did not react in the way we had hoped.'

The book slipped from her grasp and fell to the floor. Neither of us attempted to pick it up. 'But surely he must agree that my loss of memory is the chief reason I have been put here?'

I took a turn around the room, in part to help my thinking but also to hide my face from her. 'You would think so, but that is not the way he sees it. He insists it was merely one factor amongst many that made him judge you insane. He says it would not have been sufficient on its own to make you a patient here.'

'B-but how can that be?'

As I made the turn in my walk and looked up at her, I found her eyes boring straight into me. It was like being cross-examined in court. I could only look down again. I continued pacing.

'But, sir, it's not just my memory that has improved. I can read now. Has he forgot that?'

I stopped and faced her. 'I put that to him, but he refused to be moved. He said most people can read, including most madmen. It is not an indication of mental health.'

She took a moment to absorb this and then said, 'But doesn't it show I could take my place again in the world? That I can manage myself and be managed well enough to learn to do it? That I have made such great progress shows I am cured.'

I stepped to her side, went down on one knee and grabbed her hand. 'That's just it, Jane, that's just what I hadn't reckoned with when we pulled the trick of pretending you could read and spent so many weeks inventing your past. Morgan doesn't ever allow anybody to be cured. It's against his creed. Managed sometimes, yes, but cured, no. No one ever gets out of this place. It is a life sentence without parole.'

She flushed with anger now and pulled herself forward on the arms of her chair. 'What has all this been for, then, this experiment with your Moral Treatment? Why did he let us waste so much time and . . . and . . . hope on that, when he never meant me to be cured?'

'It was partly an indulgence toward me but mainly so he could prove me wrong and bring me to his views in order to make me more enthusiastic for his barbarous methods.'

She sank back and tears rolled down her cheeks. She buried her face in her hands and let out a great sob.

I watched with satisfaction. It was exactly what I had hoped for. Eventually she dropped her hands, and looked at me. 'So the experiment is over? I am to go back amongst the others?'

I nodded slowly. She bit her lip, fighting to hold back another fit of crying, unable to speak for what seemed an age, until at last she whispered hoarsely, 'When?'

'As soon as the holiday season is over and all the staff are back from leave. A few days.'

She broke down again. 'Oh, sir, I cannot stand it! I cannot bear a single day of it, I know.'

'You won't have to.' I released her hand and stood up. 'I am going to get you out.'

Her head jerked up. 'Get me out? But how?'

'Escape. I will help you escape. We will leave together.'

She stared at me. 'But what about you? Won't you get into trouble with Morgan? Might it not cost you your post?'

'I will explain everything to you and you must do exactly as I say and play your part well to the very last detail. As for me losing my post, I intend to escape with you. I am never coming back.'

'You would do that for me? But why? I do not understand why you would give up everything to help me.'

I laughed. 'I came here to help people because that's what I thought the job of a doctor was, but now I find I am useless. No, worse than that, I'm only here to assist in the oppression of the poor unfortunates incarcerated here. I have no interest in remaining if I'm not doing any good. I'd be bound to quit sooner or later, and this news about you makes it, well, just a little sooner than I intended. At least this way I will save one patient; that will be something to be proud of in my whole shameful sojourn here.'

She looked at me with something like adoration. It was

the equivalent of a standing ovation. 'Oh sir,' she said, tears again streaming down her cheeks, 'I thank you from the bottom of my heart.'

I grabbed a chair, pulled it up close to her and said in a whisper, 'Now, here's what you must do . . .'

28

By the time I had finished explaining my plan to Jane, it was well after the hour for the patients' evening meal to start and it was my turn to supervise tonight. I went first to my own room, where I picked up the heavy iron poker from the grate. I took a pair of socks from their drawer and wrapped one around the ash-covered end of the poker that went into the fire and secured it by tying the other sock around it. Then I slipped the poker into the back of the waistband of my pants and pulled my jacket over it so it could not be seen. I made my way to the patients' dining room, hoping the stiffness in my back the poker caused was not too apparent to anyone else. I paused before I went in, composing myself for what was to come. I needed to be poker-faced as well as poker-backed.

I was met with an impudent glare from O'Reilly. 'You're late,' she snapped.

'I'm so sorry, Mrs O'Reilly. I can promise you on anything you care to name that it will never, ever happen again.' And I gave her my most winning smile. I was pleased to see how this puzzled her and how throughout the meal she continued every now and then to glance at me, trying to figure out what I was at. I maintained an easy smile, although my heart was a steam engine pounding away in my chest and the blood was singing in my temples. It was a desperate plan I had dreamed up on the spur of the moment and there were so many ways in which it could go wrong. My mind was feverishly working it through, trying to spot the inevitable flaws. There were none I could think of, but from past history I knew only too well that that didn't mean they weren't there.

Eventually the meal came to an end. Because of the holiday, the patients were not to be put straight to bed but were to have an hour's singing in the day room. While the attendants got them in line and shepherded them out, I watched as in the background O'Reilly slipped away into the back corridor. I waited until the patients had gone and the room was empty, then I went through the back door to look for O'Reilly. I could hear her in the kitchen along the corridor, evidently loading the tray of food she would be taking upstairs.

I stepped again into the disused stockroom and shut the door behind me. I was counting on O'Reilly not thinking I'd be fool enough to try the same trick twice and lock me in again, in which case all would be lost and I would swing.

I heard her steps in the corridor and then starting up the first flight of stairs. I tiptoed from the room to the foot of the staircase, where I listened until I heard her begin to ascend to the third floor, and then, quiet as I could, I crept up to the second. There I stopped and listened again until O'Reilly's footsteps sounded in the corridor above, about to mount the stairs to the attic. Then I abandoned all caution and took the stairs at a run. I pounded up them so fast O'Reilly had only just rounded the turn to the attic. She stopped, tray in her hands, alarmed at the sound of the oncoming footsteps.

'You!' she said, as I rushed up the bottom flight.

'Yes, me!' I hissed, and as I reached the top step, I put my hand behind me and pulled out the poker.

'What do you think –' She tried to retreat, but fell back-wards against the steps. She dropped the tray, which clattered toward me, soup and water spilling everywhere, tin plates and cup and water jug ringing on the bare wooden steps. When everything had finally come to rest, we both watched spellbound as a solitary apple bounced down from step to step like a child's ball and vanished somewhere below.

'I am come to give you a treatment!' I cried with a flourish of the poker.

She turned and tried to scramble up the stairs, which was just the way I wanted her. I brought the poker down with all my might upon the back of her skull, so hard I could hear the crunch of bone. It was all so sudden she hadn't even time to cry out but slumped onto the stairs with nothing more than a dull groan. I examined the back of her skull and was pleased to see the sock had not only kept it from getting ash-stained but had stopped any cutting, which wouldn't have fitted my story. Instead of a gash there was nothing more than a large depression where the cranium had caved in.

I put a finger to her throat and felt for a pulse. How I would have preferred to squeeze that throat and watch her eyes goggle in amazement while I pressed the life out of her, but alas it would not have answered to my purpose.

I turned her around so she was lying on her back facing the upper flight of stairs as though she had fallen – or been pushed – backwards down them. I collected a couple of things that had been dashed from the tray when she dropped it, a piece of bread and the tin mug. I put them on the uppermost two steps, then placed the tray itself on the landing at the top, right outside the madwoman's door, as though O'Reilly had dropped it there. It was vital it should appear that she had been at the top when she fell.

Just then, as I began to calm down, I became aware of a noise behind me and realised it was the madwoman shrieking on the other side of her door, no doubt agitated by the noise. I ignored her and stood on the top landing and surveyed the tableau I had created until I had satisfied myself that everything appeared correct. Returning to O'Reilly, I raked my fingernails down one of her cheeks, enough to cause a vicious-looking graze.

I took her bunch of keys from the loop on her belt and tried them in the door in front of me until I found one that fitted the lock, although I didn't turn it fully but left it so the door remained locked with the key in it and the rest of the bunch dangling there. Then I put my poker under my jacket again and hurried downstairs.

The dining hall was empty and I slipped through it unseen into the front corridor. In the distance I could hear the sound of singing. I reached the main stairs without encountering anyone and took them at a gallop. I went into my room, removed the socks from the end of the poker, put them back in their drawer and restored the murder weapon to its normal place.

29

Once I'd more or less stopped shaking, I went down to Morgan's office, again not meeting anyone, as by now the patients were preparing for bed and all the skeleton crew of attendants who were not on leave were seeing to them. Outside the office door, I paused and ruffled my hair. I pulled my necktie askew and, taking hold of my shirtfront, ripped it. Then I knocked on the door and opened it even as Morgan's voice was in the middle of telling me to enter. He looked round from his seat at his desk and gasped at the dishevelled figure I must have cut.

'Good God, man! What on earth has happened to you?'

'There has been – there has been –' I stood there panting, as though I had just run there. I had played messengers bringing dramatic news enough times to be convincing in this.

Morgan stared at me open-mouthed, nodding involuntarily, willing me to go on. 'Sorry, I've run all the way here.' I hammed up struggling for breath. 'You must come with me, sir. I fear Mrs O'Reilly is dead.'

'Dead?' He was too stunned – as anyone would be at such dramatic news – to do any more than parrot the word. He got up. 'How? What has happened?'

'Killed, sir, by that madwoman who set fire to your study and attacked me.'

He blanched. He looked like a corpse, all the blood drained from him.

'You must come with me right away, sir, before someone else finds the body.'

I turned and strode from the room and heard the tapping of his little feet behind me as he caught me up. 'How did she die?' he said as we hurried along.

'She was pushed down the stairs, sir. I arrived as it happened but too late to save her.'

By now we were in the back corridor and I started up the back stairs. 'I don't understand,' he said. 'You say you saw it, but what were you doing here? What business had you in this part of the building?'

'I wanted to ask Mrs O'Reilly something about a patient,' I said, making the turn of the first flight of stairs. 'I wanted to do it before I retired for the night. I observed her leave the dining hall by the back door and followed. Unfortunately I was too far behind to prevent what happened. We had best move quietly, sir, in order not to disturb the attendants on watch over the secure ward.' Indeed, we could hear them above us, yelling at the inmates to settle down for the night.

We reached the foot of the final two flights of stairs, the ones that led from the third floor to the attic. The apple lay incongruously on a step halfway up. I went first and picked it up. Morgan looked at it as though he'd never seen one before.

'Mrs O'Reilly had a tray of food she must have been taking to the patient. It went everywhere during the assault.'

'Assault,' muttered Morgan. It didn't seem to be a question; rather that he was registering the word and what it meant.

We rounded the turn of the stairs and came to O'Reilly's lifeless form lying on the bottom steps of the second. Morgan pushed past me and knelt down and took the woman's pulse as I had done, at the throat. Then he put his ear to her chest and listened for what seemed like ages. Finally he looked up at me and shook his head. 'You are quite right. She's dead.'

He struggled to get to his feet and I gave him my arm to help him up. Our faces came close together and he looked me in the eye, like a frightened man. 'How did it happen? What did you see?'

'I was at the bottom of the stairs, round the turn. I heard the sound of keys jangling and then of a key turning in a lock. As I reached the turn in the stairs and looked up I saw the door fling open and the madwoman rush out at O'Reilly. The tray went flying and everything on it came crashing down the stairs. O'Reilly was taken unawares and, with her hands occupied by the tray, unable to resist the fury of the attack. By the time she'd dropped the tray, the woman was raking her nails down her face. The force of her assault sent O'Reilly flying down the stairs. She landed near the bottom and I heard – I heard –'

'Yes?'

I looked him in the eye. 'Oh, sir, it was the most awful sickening sound, the crunch of bone.'

He winced. We both stood looking at the dead woman. O'Reilly was staring glassily up at us. I did not like the look she was giving me, which seemed to contradict my story. I bent and pulled her eyelids closed. I lifted her head and we both peered at the back of the skull. Morgan grimaced. 'Looks like she fractured it on the wood of the stairs,' he said.

Before I could reply, there was a rattling at the door above us. Morgan looked up. 'The patient –'

'Safely locked in her room.' I indicated the state of my clothes. 'I had a bit of a tussle with her – she was a real fury but in the end I managed to manhandle her back inside and lock the door.'

Morgan stared up at the door for a long moment, took a step back and then sat down heavily on the top step of the next flight down. He put his head in his hands. 'What a mess,' he said. 'What a horrible mess.'

'That's true, sir,' I said sympathetically. 'Mrs O'Reilly was, well, not to speak ill of the dead and such, a harsh woman, but she didn't deserve to be killed.'

What a liar! I told myself. If ever a bitch deserved to die, it was this one lying on her back before me now.

'I didn't mean that,' said Dr Morgan. 'You do not know what this is.'

'I know more than you think,' I said quietly. 'I know the woman up there is your wife.'

His head jerked around. 'How do you know that?'

'It was the only explanation for why she was kept hidden.'

He blinked a couple of times and reached up to brush away a tear. 'I have loved her for twenty-three years. She was always high strung. Even when I first knew her, her eyes could look a little wild, although I never saw the madness in them to begin with. I thought it romantic when they flashed with fire. Hah!' He paused again to wipe his eyes. 'The first few years of our marriage were, well, wonderful, I would say. She was a very passionate woman. But she always had a temper and her fits grew more and more extreme and difficult to control. She disgraced me in public more than once with her yelling and use of inappropriate language.'

He paused, biting his lip, as if reliving those painful scenes, too distressed for a moment to carry on. 'Eventually her reason started to go. She often talked nonsense and claimed she was haunted, under assault from ghosts. She saw them everywhere. She became violent during her rages, increasingly so. In the end it reached the point where she was a danger to herself and others, to the extent that she needed to be certified.'

'But you couldn't do it,' I said.

'No, I couldn't do it.' He looked up at me, his eyes appealing. 'I had worked at the city asylum. I knew how they treated them there. I could not condemn the woman I loved to that. It was just then that I was appointed to this post. No one knew me here or that I was married. I brought her here and kept her hidden away. That way I could see her and, instead of the harsh treatment she would have received at the asylum, give her love and kindness. I thought that in that way I could prevent her growing worse, stop her mania progressing.' He stopped, overcome by a sudden sob. I stood silent while I waited for him to continue.

'It didn't work,' I said. 'The kindness didn't work and she grew more and more violently insane.'

'Yes,' he whispered.

'It's why you have no truck with Moral Treatment,' I said. 'Because it didn't work for her.'

'Yes. I turned against it. She had been treated with every degree of gentleness and consideration. She just grew more crazy. Physical restraint was the only way to keep her under control.'

'And O'Reilly became your accomplice in keeping it quiet?'

'I needed someone to look after her, someone I could rely on not to talk. And someone strong who could handle her. I came to an agreement with O'Reilly. I paid her extra to do it and to keep her mouth shut. Oh, no doubt others amongst the staff knew or heard rumours of this mysterious madwoman locked away upstairs, but none of them had any idea who she was or why she was there. O'Reilly was reliable and discreet and she kept Bella under control, although by the end she was practically blackmailing me, demanding more and more money.'

'But why did it have to be such a secret?' I asked. 'Why did she have to be hidden away?'

He seemed amazed by the question. 'Isn't it obvious, man? A psychiatrist who can't even manage the mental illness of his own wife? How would it have looked if I'd had her certified? Where would my reputation be then? And what would anyone have said if she'd been in plain view here? That the head doctor's wife was the craziest patient in the hospital.'

'So you took the risk of shutting her away like this.'

He nodded. 'I took the risk and it has not paid off and now I shall have to take the blame. It's over, my whole career gone; all because I tried to do the right thing by the woman I loved. It has led to O'Reilly's death. I'm finished.'

He pulled himself wearily to his feet and began to stagger down the stairs.

'Wait!' I called. 'There is another way.'

He stopped and turned around, regarding me warily. 'What do you mean?'

'Well, I'm the only person who knows how O'Reilly died. I don't see any need for anybody else to know. After all, what use would it serve? Your wife cannot be called to account by law when she is obviously insane. What is done is done.

260

It would be another tragedy if that should also put an end to the good work you do here.'

'What are you saying?'

'O'Reilly died by falling down stairs. It doesn't have to be these stairs. If we carry her now to the foot of the main staircase, no one will know she didn't meet her death by falling down them. We are both doctors. You can sign the death certificate and I will countersign it.'

'You're suggesting we falsify a death certificate?'

'But that's just it, we wouldn't be. The cause of death was falling downstairs. It's not a lie.'

He said nothing. I felt he must refuse. He was such a proper man, such a martinet and stickler for the rules.

'Think of your work. Of all you've achieved here that will be lost. Forget yourself. You owe it to the hospital, to all your patients here.'

'You think so? That what I do here is more important than the truth?'

'Why, of course! Who could possibly disagree? Besides, what good would the truth do? You would lose your job and your wife would have to go anyway.'

'Anyway?'

'Well, yes, you must see that. You cannot continue to keep her here. We can make this all right this time, if you agree to my plan, but sooner or later she may do something similar again. Even forgetting about that, you would have to find someone else to replace O'Reilly to look after her and rely on that person to keep the secret. That might not prove so easy.'

He considered all this and said nothing.

'Sir, your wife needs to be kept somewhere secure. She must be taken to the city asylum.'

'I'm not sure I can . . .'

'Whatever you do, that is where she will end up. This way she will go without the tag of murderess to her name.'

He put his head in his hands again and sat silent, thinking all this over.

'Sir,' I said at last, 'I have offered to help you conceal the precise sequence of events here. I will only do that if you will agree to your wife leaving immediately, that is on the next boat out, tomorrow morning. We can get her out without anyone knowing. That way if there should be any questions about O'Reilly's death, any kind of investigation, she won't even be on the premises.'

He said nothing. 'Sir,' I said, 'I absolutely insist that she leave tomorrow morning.'

He looked up. 'But it will still reflect on me that my wife is a violent madwoman.'

'No, sir, I have thought of that. We will send her not as your wife, but as a fictitious patient, one we will invent. We can sit up tonight and write out case notes for her. No one will be any the wiser.'

He nodded. 'Yes, yes, that would work.' Then he suddenly choked and let out a sob. 'B-but it would mean I would never see her again.'

I considered this. 'Not necessarily. As her former physician, what would there be to stop you looking in upon her when you visit the city asylum? There could be nothing suspicious in that and anything she said during your visits would be dismissed as the ramblings of a lunatic.'

He blanched at the word.

'Sir, the alternative is the same. If we come clean about what has happened here tonight, she will be taken from you anyway.'

'It's not a bad plan. As you say, the damage is already done to O'Reilly. Nothing can bring the poor woman back. We must look to other things and my work here. I will do it for the good of that.' He paused. 'There's one problem. How can we put her on the boat? O'Reilly is the one who takes people across as a rule.'

'I will take her. You sign the authorisation and I will take her over. She will be off the island before it's common knowledge about O'Reilly.'

He nodded again. 'She will have to be in a straitjacket. You won't manage her on your own otherwise.'

'All right. Now, let's go to your office and construct a history for her and when everyone is asleep we'll come back and carry O'Reilly to the foot of the main stairs and leave her for one of the attendants to find tomorrow morning while we are still in our beds. We will already have Mrs Morgan in a straitjacket. When it's about half an hour before the boat leaves, you will call all the staff together to tell them about the unfortunate accident to Mrs O'Reilly, and while that's going on, I will slip out with your wife and go down to the boat. We will leave the island without anyone knowing we've gone.'

As I finished talking, I realised he was looking at me strangely. 'I'm impressed, Shepherd. I never would have thought you could have come up with such a, well, such a *devious* plan – and so immediately too. It has every chance of being successful. Come, as you say, let's go and work on those notes.'

30

The notes didn't prove too much of a problem, because Morgan had the idea of taking those of a long-deceased patient and simply adapting them. We had only to copy them out and make a few alterations here and there. There was a certain tension in the air because we could not be absolutely sure that someone wouldn't stumble upon O'Reilly's lifeless corpse, although Morgan assured me it was extremely unlikely, as no one but her or he himself ever went up those attic stairs. Still, I was mighty relieved when, around midnight, we crept back up to the scene of the crime and found her just as we had left her.

'We had better clear up all this spilt food while we're here,' I said, indicating the debris strewn over the staircase.

'Good grief!' said Morgan. 'She has not been fed! My – the woman up there.' And just then we heard a low whining from the room above. 'I can't let her starve, no matter what she has done.'

He began to pick up pieces of bread and cheese. I put a hand on his arm.

'No, stop. It's too risky. If you go in to her it may cause a commotion and wake up the attendants below; we can't risk that. Leave her be. It may seem cruel but if she is hungry, she will be more manageable in the morning.'

He looked up reluctantly at the woman's door. 'All right. I don't like to do it but you have a point. It may be possible to bribe her with food in the morning to make her more cooperative.'

We put all the things back on the tray and left them outside the door of the room. We could not risk being seen taking food from the kitchen in the morning, so stale bread and cheese would have to suffice to end the woman's fast; it could not be helped.

We went back down the stairs and picked up O'Reilly, I taking her head and shoulders, Morgan her feet. The body was surprisingly light for one that had seemed to contain such a force of nature when it was living. We had just begun to move when Morgan hissed, 'Wait!' and motioned me to put her back down. Then he ran up the stairs to the mad-woman's door. He was back down a moment later. 'Her keys!' he said, brandishing them. 'It would be odd if they were not on her belt. She never went anywhere without them.' He detached one. 'We shall need this to open my wife's door tomorrow.' He put it in his pocket and attached the remainder to a loop on O'Reilly's belt.

We picked up the corpse again and began our journey to the main staircase. I was in an awful funk, terrified we would run into another member of the staff, even though it was the middle of the night and no one had any reason to be abroad. The silence was ominous and every time it was broken – once by the hoot of an owl, another time by the wind beating the branch of a tree against a window as we passed – I near jumped out of my skin. We encountered nobody on our journey and eventually reached the main staircase and placed O'Reilly on her back at the bottom, making sure the arrangement of the body was consistent with a fall.

When this was done, we stood and looked at each other with that bond of guilty complicity that comes from a shared wrongdoing. It was as well Morgan and I would never work together again. It would have been impossible to carry on after this. It was as I was thinking this that Morgan stuck out his hand, taking me by surprise. 'Thank you, Shepherd,' he said as I took hold of it. 'I won't forget this, I promise you.'

I simply nodded. The strong man. The saviour. The handshake done, we arranged to meet outside his wife's room at five next morning, to put her in the straitjacket, and then we parted.

I had precious little sleep that night. No sooner did I close my eyes than Caroline Adams appeared before me, a hoary ghost, clad head to toe in a shimmering layer of frost, and when she vanished I heard the deathly clinking of O'Reilly's keys. The wind buffeted the house and it seemed that every window in the place rattled in its frame, every door banged to and fro and every floorboard creaked, a nervous symphony that played upon my dread. It was a relief when morning finally came. Until, that is, I looked out the window. The sky was clear blue and the sun a hot golden ball. Half dreading to do so, I looked down at where the snowman should have been. He wasn't there. He had stolen away during the night. The lawns in front of the house were practically clear of snow, with only a few patches here and there stubbornly lingering on. The warmth of the sun through the glass felt like July to me, rather than December. I cursed whatever weather god had fixed his mind against me. I realised that it was entirely possible that Caroline Adams's corpse was already exposed and, if not, soon would be. It was touch and go whether I would get off the island before it was discovered.

I dressed hurriedly and went to meet Morgan. It was still very early and no one was stirring. He was waiting for me outside his wife's room. He had in one hand a glass of water and in the other a small travelling bag. 'I thought you would have no overnight bag, so I brought this for your stay at the city asylum. I have put the patient's papers and your travel permit for the boat inside, together with the straitjacket. You must show the documents to the captain to prove you have my authority to take the patient ashore.'

I thanked him. He held up the glass. 'It's a sedative. It will keep her calm for a short time, I hope until you get her across the river. I can't be certain how long it will take effect for. I have erred on the side of caution because we don't want her so sleepy she can't walk, but in case she becomes too animated during the trip, I've left more in the bag. It's a soluble powder and has hardly any taste, so you can give it to her in water. Just don't use it all at once, or she'll pass out. Here, hold the glass while I open the door.'

I stood well back as he inserted the key in the lock and turned it carefully so as not to make any noise. It was exactly what you might do with a caged wild animal. Slowly, he opened the door. I stood ready for the woman to rush out screaming, a picture I had put into my own mind by my story to Morgan about O'Reilly's death, but there was no movement or sound from within. Morgan stepped through the doorway and I followed cautiously. The madwoman was lying in the foetal position asleep on her cot, as peaceful as a child. She was still fully clothed because it was O'Reilly who normally prepared her for bed each night, and Morgan when O'Reilly was ashore. Last night he had not dared venture in upon her.

He sat down on the side of the bed and gently stroked her arm. 'Bella, time to wake up, my darling. I've brought you a drink.'

Her eyes blinked open. There was something so sudden about it, it made me jump and a little of the liquid in the glass spilled over the rim. Morgan gestured for it and I held it out to him. He got one arm behind the woman's head and lifted it and then took the glass from me. A look of panic sprang into her eyes and I thought for a moment she was going to dash the glass from his hand, but instead she bent her head to it and drank eagerly, gulping it down. Morgan looked at me and silently mouthed the word 'Thirsty'. Of course, the woman hadn't been given any food or drink the night before.

Morgan handed the glass back to me and sat her up fully, exactly as you might an invalid, and seeing him so gentle with her in contrast to the way he was with the patients in the treatment rooms, I understood that this was how he saw her, as someone sick, not as a dangerous lunatic. 'Fetch the food,' he said.

I went and got the tray from where we'd left it the night before and placed it on the bed. Immediately the woman grabbed the hunk of bread and started tearing it with her teeth. She devoured it and the cheese in a few brief minutes and then looked around wildly as if for more.

Morgan had his hands around her shoulders and was making comforting cooing noises to her. She smiled and seemed quite at ease. I could see the drug was already taking effect. 'Look in the bag,' Morgan said to me, his voice calm and even. I went outside to the landing and opened the bag. There was the straitjacket, with the travel permit and patient dossier on top, and a paper packet that I presumed was the sedative powder. I lifted them up and took out the jacket, then replaced the other stuff and closed the bag. I had sense enough to put the straitjacket behind my back when I went back into the room.

Morgan was talking softly to his wife and she was looking at him and paid me no attention. 'Now!' Morgan suddenly cried and I held out the jacket in front of her. He grasped the top of her right arm, the one next to him, and held it out toward me. The woman tried to struggle but I took her wrist and thrust the sleeve of the jacket over it. She was obviously a little drowsy and hadn't the strength to resist and when she lifted her left arm to ward me off, I slipped the sleeve over it and within a few seconds Morgan was securing the buckles and she was held fast before she knew what was happening. She began kicking out with her legs and wailing.

'Leave us a moment,' said Morgan.

I must have looked puzzled. His face crumpled. 'Please, my good man. I would like to say goodbye.'

I went out and gently closed the door upon them. Between the woman's cries I could hear Morgan murmuring to her and eventually her noises calmed. After a few minutes the door opened and Morgan beckoned me inside. The woman was sitting in a chair beside the bed. Morgan went to a cupboard in the corner of the room, opened it and took out a woman's travelling cloak.

'Put it on her when the time comes to leave,' he said. 'And make sure the hood is over her head.'

We left her there, sitting in her chair, dozing under the influence of the sleeping draught. Morgan consulted his watch as we hurried down the stairs, for once not out of habit but of necessity. 'We must get back to our rooms before the discovery of O'Reilly's body,' he said. 'When we two have made an examination of her, I will call the staff meeting in the day room, and the start of it will be your cue to slip back up here and take Bella down to the boat.'

31

I had not been back in my room above a quarter of an hour and had only just had enough time to pack some clothes in the overnight bag when I heard a great deal of yelling from downstairs and hurried footsteps and the banging of doors. I sat tight, as Morgan had told me to do, until there was a knock at the door. I quickly shoved the bag inside my closet and opened the door, to find Eva standing there.

'Come quick, sir. There's been an accident. It's Mrs O'Reilly, sir. I think it's serious.'

I followed her along the corridor and down the stairs, at the bottom of which a small crowd of attendants had gathered. 'Make room, make room, give her air!' I heard Morgan's voice call from within the throng. I stopped dead in my tracks and my heart froze within me. Was O'Reilly still alive? If so, then I was finished. I looked this way and that, thinking to flee, but just in time caught hold of myself. Of course! Morgan was only acting his part, which was sensible, for why would he assume the woman was dead if he did not already know? I pushed my way through the spectators and knelt down by his side. He had his stethoscope to O'Reilly's chest, listening for a heartbeat. The crowd about us were all whispering and murmuring and he suddenly looked up, face red with anger, and snapped, 'Be quiet! How do you expect me to hear anything with that racket going on?' Instantly the hubbub subsided, leaving a dreadful silence in which you could sense everyone holding their breath.

After what seemed an unconscionable age – which I thought was playing to the gallery a little too much for safety – Morgan slowly stood up, shaking his head. 'No, she's gone, I'm afraid.' He looked at me. 'Shepherd, help me carry her to the sickbay, would you; we need to examine her together to determine the cause of death, though I'd say it seems pretty obvious. She took a tumble down the stairs and smashed her skull.'

As I bent to lift her, I had the inspiration to improvise so that I seemed almost to drop her and thereafter carried her awkwardly, giving the impression I had never carried a corpse before and certainly not this one. Morgan was quick on the uptake and took his cue from me, so that we made quite a difficulty of the whole procedure. The funny part was, I suddenly thought, that instinctively we'd each taken the same end of the body as we had before. I saw O'Reilly's face was a strange purple colour, as though in death she was as choleric as she had been in life. I could not feel sorry for what I'd done.

As the crowd parted to let us through, Morgan said, 'All right, all right, there's nothing more to see now. Please go about your duties as normal. The senior attendant in each department should cover for any tasks Mrs O'Reilly might have performed. I will address the entire staff later.' He lowered his voice and said to one of the senior attendants who was nearby, 'Please have the patients locked in their bedrooms after breakfast, would you? I shall want all the staff assembled in the day room later, when I will speak to them.'

In the sickbay we placed the body on a bed. Morgan turned to me and held out his hand. 'Good luck, Shepherd. I can't tell you how grateful I am. Assuming everything goes to plan, I look forward to seeing you tomorrow morning.'

We shook hands and I sneaked back up to my room while the patients were at breakfast. According to Morgan's time-table, I was to wait there until the staff meeting began and, while everyone was occupied there, go and fetch his wife and head down to the boat dock. The thing was, though, I was no longer on Morgan's timetable; from now on I was on my own.

I took the bag from the closet and finished my packing. Then I waited while the patients were taken from the dining hall back to their rooms. I could hear some of them protesting because of this break in routine. I couldn't help thinking how odd institutional rigidity is. They were arguing because it was not what was normally done, when in fact the day room was so deathly dull they would almost certainly have preferred to spend the morning dozing on their beds.

When the noise on the stairs finally stopped, I made my way to the attic. I opened the door carefully, still appre-hensive the incumbent might come at me like a hurricane, but she didn't. I found her as we'd left her, sitting in her chair, drugged and empty-eyed. I took her under one arm and pulled her to her feet. She was a heavy woman and it wasn't easy because she was too sleepy to assist me. When

I had her upright, I arranged the cloak around her shoulders, laced the front collars together and pulled the hood over her head so her face was in shadow. I said gently, 'Come on, my dear, we're going for a little walk.' She was docile and allowed me to lead her out. I took her down the stairs, a pretty hazardous journey because in her somnambulant state she stumbled a couple of times and nearly fell, but I managed to buttress her against the wall and steady her. It seemed an age before we reached the ground floor.

There was no one in the main corridor. The staff and patients were all out of the way, busy upstairs now, but I couldn't be sure what Morgan was up to. If he saw me, he would wonder what I was doing heading away from the front door, and why I didn't have the bag. I hurried the woman along, practically dragging her because she was so dozy, and in this fashion we reached the safety of the treatment rooms. I opened the door of the restraining room, tugged her inside and closed the door behind us.

She was now showing signs of awareness and I realised Morgan had not given her nearly enough sedative to keep her quiet for the journey across the river, although on the other hand, given that I didn't intend to do that, it was for the best; if he'd given her any more, she might easily have passed out before I could have gotten her downstairs. She looked around the restraining room, as anxious as a cornered animal. I was tempted to put my hands around her throat and squeeze the life out of her, which would definitely have made the next few minutes easier, although it would have been dangerous in the long run, as it would have given the game away about John Shepherd much sooner than otherwise, if indeed it was given away at all. As things stood, even when Caroline Adams was found, her death would not be connected with Shepherd for at least a day and maybe even longer. If anyone found my draft letter to the unfortunate Miss Adams in O'Reilly's belongings, without her testimony to where she found it, there was nothing in its contents to connect it to the dead woman or to Shepherd and it would most likely be disregarded. It was even more unlikely that the death of Miss Adams would be connected with a dead convicted killer. But two strangled women at the hospital might have sounded an alarm in the memory of a homicide detective.

I spoke kindly to the woman as I backed her toward the restraining chair and positioned her just in front of it. I undid the ties of the cloak and let it fall from her shoulders to the floor. Then I unfastened the straitjacket buckles and pulled it off her. She began giggling sleepily, pleased to be freed. I put my hand on her chest and pushed her firmly into the seat of the chair and thrust myself forcefully onto her, pinning her down. She began twisting and turning but I thumped her head against the back of the chair and held it there with one hand while with the other I fastened the strap around her neck. All the while she was snarling like a rabid dog and trying to bite me, so the moment I was finished, I leapt free of her.

I was in a cold sweat now watching her writhe about. She kept trying to stand, but of course she couldn't, with the strap tight round her throat. I was terrified she would scream and attract attention, but it didn't seem to occur to her. That choker must have meant every little move she made was a torture and she began gagging for breath, and finally her struggling subsided. I went round behind her, got down on the floor, crawled along the side of the chair and grabbed her left leg. She attempted to kick out but I had it tight and got the strap round it, which was not easy as I had to lie on the floor to avoid her hand, which was flailing about and trying to seize my hair.

Once the leg was strapped down, her movements were much more restricted. I crawled away, walked round behind her, forced her right arm down onto the arm of the chair and strapped it to it. After that the remaining straps were relatively easy. Once she was fully restrained, I took one of the gags from the cupboard and, after another tussle, managed to get it between her teeth. She was trussed up like a chicken ready for the oven.

I wrapped the cloak around the straitjacket to make a bundle that nobody would be able to identify. I walked over to the door and listened at it. I couldn't hear anything. I inched the door open and listened again. Nothing. I stuck my head out. The corridor was deserted. I went out and shut the door behind me. With no treatments scheduled for today anyway on account of the holiday – and, with myself and O'Reilly both absent, none likely for some time after that – it was possible the woman would remain there a good couple of days. I reflected with no little satisfaction that it was not much more than Morgan had imposed upon some of his patients. He had tried Moral Treatment on his wife without success; perhaps now it was time to give his normal methods a chance to work.

I ran up the main stairs, heart in mouth at the prospect of meeting someone, although as long as it wasn't Morgan, who believed that I was with his wife and preparing to leave once the staff meeting started, it wouldn't really have mattered. A member of the staff might have had a momentary curiosity as to what it was I was carrying, but it wouldn't have signified much to her.

I achieved my room safely, retrieved the bag and hurried to Jane Dove's room. She was in her chair and leapt up when she saw it was me.

'Do as I say, there isn't a moment to lose,' I told her. I pulled the cloak off the straitjacket and held it up. 'You must put this on.'

She was transfixed by the evil garment, not moving an inch. Her eyes flashed with defiance. 'I – I uncertain I can do that,' she stuttered as I took it toward her.

'You must,' I said. 'It's your only chance. If you don't, you'll be lost here for ever. Don't worry; I will tie the straps loosely so it won't be too uncomfortable. I'll take it off as soon as we are on the other side and out of sight of the boat.'

She slowly lifted up her arms and I slipped them into the sleeves. Then I fastened the straps, but very loosely as I had promised.

'There,' I said, when it was done. 'It's as comfortable as I can make it. You could probably wriggle out of it if you wanted to.'

She moved her arms about and twisted her body this way and that, until finally she seemed satisfied that this was so.

I put the cloak around her and fastened it at the collar and pulled the hood over her head.

'All right,' I said. 'Just follow my lead and don't attempt to speak. Keep your head bent so no one can see your face.'

I opened the door and peered into the corridor. It was still empty. I signalled to her and she followed me out. I closed the door behind us. I walked briskly to the top of the stairs with Jane behind me, moving awkwardly, finding it difficult to walk without swinging her arms. I was worried she might fall on the way down. I could not afford another tragedy of that sort, and put my arm around her and helped her down every step, cautioning her not to hurry but to concentrate on treading safely. Once at the bottom, I pulled her toward the front door. I had it open and we were just about through it when I heard footsteps. Morgan was coming out of his office. He was only some twenty feet away. I was pushing the girl out when Morgan looked up and saw us. I froze, unable to move until I saw what he would do. I was sure he would not be able to resist approaching us for a last word with his wife. If he did that, everything would be over for me, my plans would be shattered. Once he discovered the woman in the cloak was Jane Dove and not his wife, he would go looking for her. When he found her trussed up in the restraining room, it would naturally trigger him to suspect I'd lied about O'Reilly's death. Any time soon, Caroline Adams would be found and my duplicity would naturally make me the prime suspect.

I swear my heart stopped beating. He looked uncertain as he took half a step toward us. It brought me back to life. There was only one thing I could do. I shoved Jane through the door, gave Morgan a conspiratorial wave and stepped outside, tugging the door shut behind me. I could feel his eyes boring into my back as I seized Jane's arm and marched her off. All the way down the drive, every crunch of the gravel under our feet, I was waiting for the sound of his footsteps coming after us. I was counting on his not wanting to ruin the plan we'd devised to overcome his desire for a last look at his wife.

The story would be that I was unwell and confined to my bed, so that nobody would be aware I had ever left the island. His wife would be smuggled ashore without anyone knowing of her existence and no explanation necessary to the staff concerning the identity of the patient taken away. It would have been impossible to correlate that with no patient being missing from the roll call.

It was a long walk to the boat dock. I told Jane that now she must run. I tugged her along by her arm, all the while terrified I might pull too hard and make her fall. The whole thing had taken an inordinate amount of time. The boat had not been warned to expect any passengers and I was worried it might already have left without us. When we arrived at the small dock I saw smoke belching from the boat's funnel and a sailor on the dock in the very act of loosening the mooring ropes.

'Wait!' I shouted.

He didn't hear and stepped aboard.

'Wait!' I yelled, louder this time. 'For God's sake wait!'

This time he heard and when he saw us running toward him, leapt back onto the dock and began tugging on the rope to bring the boat alongside again. He shouted at another crewman on the boat and this second man grabbed another rope, jumped ashore and began assisting his fellow. The captain, for such I took him to be, leaned out the doorway of the boat's cabin and, seeing us, evidently shut down the engine, for the boat stopped straining at the ropes and the two sailors eventually had her firmly up against the dock again. The captain left the cabin and came over to us.

He was an old man, a real sea dog, with a captain's peaked cap and a white beard. He stretched a hand out and between us we helped Jane Dove aboard.

'I was not told anyone would be coming ashore today,' he said, as soon as we were both safely on deck. 'Where is Mrs O'Reilly?'

I opened the bag and took out Morgan's authorisation and handed it to him. Something warned me not to tell him the chief attendant was dead. I didn't want to alarm the man with anything out of the ordinary, but mainly I realised Jane Dove didn't know of O'Reilly's death. I didn't want her thinking of the coincidence that the woman should have met with a violent accident at the very time we were making our escape. It might start her wondering unpleasant things about me.

'She is indisposed,' I muttered. 'I am Dr Shepherd. I'm taking this patient to the asylum.'

He seemed satisfied and began studying the authorisation. It took him an extraordinary length of time. I glanced at the jetty, trying to appear casual to hide my anxiety. I expected any moment to see we were pursued. I looked back at the captain, who was still concentrating hard on his reading. I couldn't work out if this was because he wasn't literate and was trying to make out he was, or if, as his appearance suggested, he'd formerly held important nautical positions and, having come down to commanding this humble vessel that ferried supplies to lunatics, wished to claim as much importance for himself as possible.

If he was genuinely reading, he must have read every word of the document ten times over, moving his lips as he did so. It took so long I almost resigned myself to being caught. Eventually, though, the old boy looked up from the papers and said, 'You're taking her on your own? With no escort?'

'We're short of staff, on account of the holiday and Mrs O'Reilly's indisposition. And this one's pretty docile.'

He looked at Jane, who bent her head lower so her face was concealed in shadow by her hood. 'Docile, eh?' he said. Then he shot a suspicious look at me. 'So why are you taking her to the asylum, if she's so easy to manage?'

Why had I said that? I could have kicked myself. I had no answer to the logic of what he'd said. I stood there floundering, unable to think of a word. How stupid of me, after all my planning, to set such a trap for myself!

Just then Jane came to my rescue. She let out a low moan and began to mutter something, slurring her words and swaying. The captain stared at her.

'I can't understand a word of that, my love,' he said. He looked at me. 'Sounds drunk.'

I took my cue from this, realising what Jane was up to. 'Drugged,' I said. 'I mean, heavily sedated. Believe me, you would not wish to have her on your boat if she was not. In fact, I'd be grateful if we could make haste as she'll be the deuce of a handful to manage once the sedative wears off and I need to have her safe in the asylum by then.'

He smiled and said, 'Don't you worry about that, sir. We'll have you on the other side in a jiffy.'

He nodded to his men and they cast off once more and leapt aboard. He returned to his little cabin. There wasn't one for passengers and I took Jane to one of the seats in the centre of the deck and sat her down. The water was choppy and the little boat rocked as it clove through it. The noise of the engine made it difficult to have any conversation. Instead, we both sat and watched over the stern as the island began to retreat further and further behind us. We had done it. We had got safe away.

The river was wide at that point and the small boat took its time making the shore. All the time I scanned the two shores and the river itself. I didn't know what I was looking for; I just felt an undertow of dread. For while we were on the boat we were in another kind of prison, from which we could not flee. Unreasonable though it was, I was convinced that a boat manned by a dozen policemen would intercept us. I would not feel secure until I had both feet on dry land and at least the chance to run away.

But the crossing passed without incident and eventually we were docking on the shore. As soon as the gangway went down, I had Jane upon it and was about to step on it myself when I saw the captain approaching.

'My word, doctor, you are anxious about that drug wearing off, aren't you?'

I managed a grim smile. 'Well, I wouldn't want to bear the consequences. They don't pay me enough for that.'

At this he let out a great belly laugh, as if it were the funniest thing imaginable. 'Well, you hurry along then, sir. I'll see you tomorrow.'

I turned to him in surprise. 'Tomorrow?' I had no idea what the man was talking about. I didn't anticipate seeing him ever again in my life.

'Yes, tomorrow,' he said, looking a bit puzzled now. 'In the morning, when you go back.'

'Oh, yes, of course. I wasn't thinking. I'll see you tomorrow.' Stupid fool! I was causing the man to be suspicious. I managed to rally myself and said cheerfully, 'And you may depend that I won't be in so much of a hurry to get off your boat then, captain!'

He let out another belly laugh and I turned away and bundled Jane Dove down the gangway and moments later we were on the wharf, and I thought to myself, Now we have thousands of miles we can run into.

32

We found ourselves pitched ashore on a wharf used by all kind of commercial craft. There was no passenger terminal nor any facility for travellers. The island boat was for deliveries, not people. I had to hold on to Jane because she was unsteady on her feet without the use of her arms and the boards of the wharf were wet and slippery. Once on dry land we stood looking about, utterly lost on the fringe of the city. Seeing our helplessness, a passing sailor stopped and said, 'If you take that street there you will find cabs passing to and fro, sir.' I thanked him and we followed his advice. A cold wind blew off the river and the street itself was grey with slush. Sure enough, we saw a cab almost straight away. I made sure Jane's cloak was wrapped tight around her so the straitjacket wasn't visible and then hailed it and asked the driver to take us to the railroad depot.

Inside the cab I reached under Jane's cloak and unfastened the straps of the straitjacket and she slipped it off. I rolled it up tight and opened the travelling bag and squeezed it inside with my own clothes. 'We cannot risk leaving it in the cab,' I whispered to her. 'It would be noticed immediately by the next passenger and put us in the cab driver's mind.

We must take care not to leave a trail behind us that would be easy to follow.'

We reached the depot safely and made our way to the main concourse, where there was a large departure board with all the destinations displayed upon it together with the times of the morning's trains.

'We will head for St Louis,' I said to Jane. 'That should be far enough west to be beyond reach of anyone here.'

'You would take me with you, sir?' she said. 'But why? You have helped me escape from that place and given up your post to do so. If you take me any further, you risk more trouble for assisting me.'

I knew she was right. Once the hue and cry was raised, they would be hunting for the two of us together and it would be harder to avoid notice. But the truth was I could not bear to give her up just yet. I had grown fond of her company after being alone inside my head for so long. And yet, even as I thought this, a shadow passed across me, that old familiar feeling that I had resolved to bury for good. There had been a quickening of the pulse and a sudden hunger in the pit of my stomach when I had my hands beneath her cloak undoing the straitjacket. I could almost have fainted at the touch of her long and slender neck. Was I quite sure I had not allowed my fingers to linger a moment longer than necessary there?

'I will get you to St Louis, where you will be out of danger, and we will decide there what you can do afterwards. Now, let's see when the next train is.'

We both looked up at the departure board.

'Oh, it's not for another hour,' she said.

I looked at her and then back at the board. She was right. It was another hour. For a moment I did not know what to say. My head was in a spin and I could not think. I could feel the pulse racing in my brow. I looked around the concourse to see if there were any cops. I looked back at Jane Dove. She smiled back at me, innocence personified.

What a conceited fool I had been! All this time, all these long weeks, I had been in the presence of a great actress; she had upstaged me quite. I had not appreciated her artfulness until now, when she made her first, and only, mistake.

I tried not to appear flustered. I handed her the bag and said, 'Look after this a moment, while I go and buy the tickets, and then we'll take some refreshment.'

It was with a heavy heart that I walked over to the ticket booth. The words stuck in my throat when the clerk asked me what I wanted and I tried to speak and he had to ask me again. 'A single ticket to St Louis,' I said at last.

I pocketed the ticket and returned to Jane. 'Let's get something to drink,' I said, and led her to a bar next to the depot. We found a table and she sat down at it. I asked her what she wanted and she said tea. I fetched it from the bar, along with a large glass of beer for myself. I had a sudden terrible thirst and also I needed Dutch courage for what I had to do.

Jane Dove sat and prattled happily, about what I hardly knew. I was only half listening, looking at her and thinking what a great shame it was and yet, at the same time, glad that I could give in to the old feeling with a clear conscience. She could not be left to tell everyone who I was and where I was going. Jack Wells had to remain dead. All this was whizzing through my mind when I realised she was asking me something.

'What?' I said.

'Why, sir, I don't believe you've heard a word I've said,'

she said, laughing. 'I asked if you would fetch me some sugar, please.'

I went to the counter and asked the assistant, who gave me a small dish and a spoon. I returned to Jane and she stirred some into her tea. She took a sip.

'That's better. They gave us tea with no sugar at the hospital,' she said.

I took a swig of beer. Her whole face glowed. The dark hollows in her cheeks were gone.

We finished our drinks in silence, each occupied with our own thoughts. I looked out at the station clock. There were still forty-five minutes to the train. Just then a train guard in his uniform sat down at the next table.

I indicated him with a nod of the head. 'That man is a railroad detective,' I whispered to Jane. 'I don't like the way he's looking at us. I think we should go.' Without giving her the chance to disagree, I picked up the bag, stood up and walked out, with her following.

Outside I said, 'We should avoid the concourse, just in case. It's best not to be visible until it's time to board the train. We don't want people noticing us and remembering where we went. Let's find somewhere quiet.'

My heart was beating fast now and I could feel the sweat break on my brow. My head was swimming and I had to tell myself to get a grip. I had done this kind of thing so many times before; I must not let myself weaken now. I must not allow my demeanour to give me away.

I led her to the end of the row of tracks. The last one proved to be a siding. At the end of it stood a train shed. Its roof sagged and the windows in the side were broken. It looked derelict and unused. My legs were wobbly and I could hear the catch in my throat as I said, 'Let's stroll down there, where we'll be out of sight. We can head back just before the train leaves.'

There was nobody about. The platform came to a dead end, but we were still too much in the open. 'Down here,' I said, indicating a length of rusted track that was obviously no longer in use. At its end stood the derelict shed. 'We can hide in there.'

She looked at me warily. 'I'm not sure we should, sir. Something about it scares me. It looks so abandoned and bleak.'

I stepped onto the track and began to walk along the middle. I felt unsteady and there was a tremor in my voice, try as I might to sound confident. 'Nonsense. You'll be perfectly safe. You're with me.'

I had the bag in one hand and took hold of her hand with the other. She made no attempt to move and I had to pull her along so that she stumbled after me. Inside the shed there was the smell of rotten wood. The light through the cracked and dusty windows was dim. There was an old locomotive, bronzed with rust, and bits of abandoned rolling stock. I felt suddenly faint.

I let go Jane's hand and took out my handkerchief and wiped the sweat off my brow. Jane stood watching me, her eyes full of suspicion. I took a step toward her. She backed off.

'Come now, Jane, don't be silly. It's only me. I thought we were friends.' I took another step forward.

She took another back. 'Sir, please, you are frightening me.'

I looked at her long white neck. I remembered Caroline Adams's neck, the crunch of the bones; I remembered all those other pale necks, all those dead chickens. And then, unaccountably, there were suddenly two Jane Doves before me, no three, no more, whirling around me, my head spinning like a top.

'I have to admit you had me, Jane. You suckered me completely, right up until today. Then you made your only mistake.'

The silence was broken by the distant sound of a train whistle.

She nodded. 'You mean the departure board?'

I smiled.

'Sir, it wasn't a mistake.'

I took another step toward her, but this time she stood her ground. All at once the earth beneath seemed to tip and I thought it was an earthquake, but it wasn't the earth that was moving, it was me.

I doubled over and was sick. I sank to my knees.

'I wanted to see what you would do. To see if you would show yourself as your newspaper self. Oh, sir, what an evil man you are.'

'You should not have tried to outmanoeuvre me, Jane. You are about to find out just how evil. This damned fever will not stop me.'

'Sir, it's not a fever. It is all the sleeping powder I found in the bag while you were fetching the sugar. I put it in your beer, sir. Do you think I would follow you to such a lonely place as this otherwise?'

I stared at her. She was looking at me as you might a dying dog. I fell face down at her feet. She stepped over me and picked up the bag. I heard her undoing the clasp. She began tugging at me and turned me over on my back. I could not move a muscle.

'Now, sir, in which pocket did you put the ticket? It was

only one ticket, wasn't it? You were not going to waste money on a ticket you would not use.'

I tried to speak, but no sound would come. My eyes were growing heavy and I struggled to keep them open. I watched as she tucked the ticket inside the top of her dress. She bent over the bag but my eyes were blurred and I could only just make out her shape. I felt her hands on me, pulling at me, and then nothing, everything was black.

I had one of those dreams where you know all along you are in a dream and yet you cannot leave. I was in the henhouse at my uncle's farm. I was sitting on the floor with my back against a post, unable to move. I was watching Jane Dove. She was walking among the birds and every so often she would pick one up and twist its neck. She had such wonderful technique that I was full of admiration and I wanted to applaud. Except I could not move my hands. My arms were completely numb. And then I heard a man's voice and felt a hand upon my shoulder, shaking me. It was a great struggle to open my eyes, so heavily lidded were they. In the end I got them open and saw two policemen standing over me. I tried to scramble to my feet, but my arms were pinned. I looked down at myself and saw the straitjacket.

'It's exactly as the note said,' I heard one of the policemen say, 'lying here in a straitjacket.'

'I'm not sure it's him, though, the Wells fella,' said his colleague. 'I remember the posters of him.'

'Ah, don't you be so certain of that. Take away the beard and he'd look different.'

'I am ... I am John Shepherd,' I said, 'Doctor John Shepherd. 'I – I've been tied up like this by a patient. Now, take this thing off me, would you?'

The first policeman shook his head. 'Oh, no, sir, I don't think we can do that. I think we need to take you down to the precinct house and see what the captain has to say about all this.'

They bent down and grabbed me by the shoulders and pulled me to my feet. 'I'll willingly come with you,' I said, 'if you'll only take this thing off me. I'm not a lunatic.'

'That's as maybe, sir, but if you don't mind, I think we'll leave things as they are for the time being. It will save getting the handcuffs out.'

They began to drag me off. My head seemed to explode with the sudden scream of a train whistle, although then again, maybe it wasn't that at all, maybe it was me.

ACKNOWLEDGEMENTS

I would like to thank Patrick Janson-Smith and Laura Deacon, Charlotte Humphrey and Tara Hiatt at HarperCollins Foreign Rights; copy-editor Tim Waller for such a fantastic job on this book and its predecessor, *Florence & Giles*; and, as always, my agent Sam Copeland at Rogers, Coleridge and White.

Thanks too to all those people who have given me such strong support over the last few years, especially Nicola Morgan, Gabrielle Kim, Ben Hatch, James Smythe, Claire King, Josh Alliston, Kate Mayfield, Kim Curran, Andrew James, Lorna Fergusson, Barry Walsh, Mike Jarman, Sarah Callejo, Rhian Davies and Scott Pack.

BIBLIOGRAPHY

Ten Days in a Mad-House by Nellie Bly (Elizabeth Jane Cochrane) (Ian L. Munro, New York, 1887)

Mad in America: Bad Science, Bad Medicine, and the Enduring Mistreatment of the Mentally Ill by Robert Whitaker (Perseus Publishing, New York, 2002)

Mania: A Short History of Bipolar Disorder (Johns Hopkins Biographies of Disease) by David Healy (Johns Hopkins University Press, Baltimore, 2008)

Diary Written in the Provincial Lunatic Asylum by Mary Huestis Pengilly (Author, 1885)

Women of the Asylum: Voices from Behind the Walls, 1840–1945 by Jeffrey L. Geller and Maxine Harris (Anchor Books, New York, 1994)

The Psychopath Test: A Journey Through the Madness Industry by Jon Ronson (Picador, London, 2011)